Redesigning Rose

Lydia Laceby

www.lydialaceby.com

Cover Design: Jane Speed – Carte Blanche Creative
http://carteblanchecreative.com/

Formatting: Polgarus Studio
http://www.polgarusstudio.com/

To my Mom, Granny and Granny
The three strongest women I've known.

CHAPTER ONE

I didn't want to betray my husband's trust. But this was my mother, not his.

"Mom, is everything okay financially?" I asked, running my thumb along the rim of my mug. I couldn't hold back any longer. I'd sat for a week on the fact that my mother didn't approach me, but chose to go directly to my husband with her financial issues. Although disappointed, I was even more devastated that she had to ask him for money. And disturbed.

"Of course, dear. Why wouldn't it be? I told you I've always been conservative with my investments, so the market dips haven't affected me as much as others."

"But Frank said..." I paused, my gaze traveling around the house I grew up in, the one I worried all week my mother might lose. Thoughts clicked and slotted into place like I was completing a Rubik's Cube. Mom's house had been paid off since she received the insurance settlement for Dad's car accident. Click. She had only recently retired from her administrative position at the bank after almost twenty years. Click. And then there was the inheritance Gram left her. Click.

"You've never had to borrow money?" I asked, carefully selecting my words.

"Of course not," she said, sounding offended.

I searched her face, lightly lined with life's stresses, and could only conclude she was telling the truth. My husband had lied to me. And not just your run of the mill "Dinner was delicious" when it was horrible kind of lie, either.

"Is his business finally rubbing off on you?" Mom asked with an amused smile. "Are you worried about the markets now too?"

I didn't respond. I couldn't even move. My world had teetered and then tipped. I suddenly knew how disoriented people were in the Middle Ages when they discovered the Americas. My world had shifted and went against everything I knew.

"Are you okay, Rose?" she asked when I didn't respond.

"I need to get home," I said, forcing myself out of the chair.

Once down the hall, I focused on shoving my feet into flip-flops, desperate to flee.

"Are you sure everything is all right?"

"Everything's fine, Mom," I said, bobbing my head and attempting to exude sunny cheerfulness while kicking at my uncooperative footwear. I was lying. But how could I explain how devastating the few sentences we'd just exchanged were when I wasn't sure I understood them myself? I avoided looking at her. I'd never been a good liar, never been able to hide anything. *Unlike my husband.*

My thoughts reproduced faster than fruit flies. Frank had already lied to me about where the money went, but what if his deceit spanned more than the large withdrawals from our bank account? Could he be involved in some kind of Ponzi scheme? He did work in the finance industry. But then wouldn't the bank account be padded, not plundered?

I slapped my palm against the wall to protect against the ceramic tiles which suddenly buckled and shifted like a fun house floor.

"Has Frank ever asked you for money?" I asked, my heart revving in my chest like an Indy 500 car.

Mom shook her head, her eyes wide. "Heavens no. What's going on, Rose?"

My breath whooshed out like a punctured tire. I curled my hand against the wall before pressing it flat and shoving off to kiss her cheek. "I just wanted to make sure you and Frank don't ever leave me out of the loop if something's wrong. I saw a talk show the other day. You wouldn't believe what some families forget to tell each other," I babbled while waving my hand around.

Mom's fingers clutched the pearl necklace she had worn for decades and dragged it back and forth on her neck. I ignored her tell-tale worry sign, knowing I couldn't dispel it. Not now. I needed to figure this out on my own.

I snatched my purse off the floor and yanked open the door. It took every effort not to bolt down the street, but I didn't dare run. Instead, I kept up appearances by turning back and waving like I always did. Mom raised her hand above her shoulder and wiggled her fingers. I resumed my forced walk, knowing she would stand guard, watching and waiting. The habit that began during my grade school days continued when I moved into a new home with Frank only a few blocks away. She would wander back inside only once I rounded the corner. Rain or shine, snow or sleet, she always saw me off. The only exceptions were illness and vacations when I checked her house.

I stopped.

What if the missing money was for the trip to Paris I'd always wanted? Or something equally benign? But wouldn't Frank have put a trip on his credit card to accumulate points? And why lie about my mother asking him for money? How could he think I wouldn't ask her? It was the most absurd excuse–although it definitely worked to distract me from considering a vacation.

I nibbled my lower lip. Was I just grasping for excuses, eager to avoid taking a hard look at my husband?

I heard a grunt and turned to the noise.

"Mrs. Thompson," I said, striding over to where she stood on the sidewalk, barely visible behind the over-sized garbage bin. Both blue-veined hands clutched the handle.

"Here, let me help you," I said.

"Thank you, dear," she said, releasing her grip and padding up the driveway in her slippers.

"You really should exchange this bin for the smaller size."

"And let the city charge me for extra garbage when my daughters and their families visit? Forget it. I'll just keep manhandling this one."

"You get a few free tags to use every year," I said, hoping I could convince her. Without anyone to help her each week, lugging the various bins in and out must be difficult. "You've never put out much more than a small bag each week ever since I can remember."

"Recycling may be a new concept to you young folks, but my generation never wasted a thing. You can't live through a war and rationing without learning to conserve, to re-purpose things."

"Well, at least consider it," I said. "You really shouldn't be dragging this thing to the curb every other week."

"Maybe one day. Your mother is lucky you live so close to help her out," she said, patting her fluffy white hair, which had reminded me of cotton candy for the last decade. "How is that handsome husband of yours?"

"Oh, he's fine. Busy with work. You know how it is."

"They certainly get that way, don't they. Don't let him be too busy to give you a wee one. Your mother can't wait to get her hands on a grand-baby."

I nodded and turned away to wrestle the bin over to the side of the garage. I blinked rapidly to stop the tears. The reminder of Frank's stubborn refusal to start a family was like dousing the wound his lies had created with rubbing alcohol. An entire bottle of it.

"Would you like some lemon cake, dear? I made it fresh this morning."

"Thank you, but I need to get home. Dinner won't cook itself."

"That's a good wife. You don't see that too often these days."

I forced a smile as I waved and walked down to the street. I trampled down thoughts of a baby and focused on figuring out why Frank lied. My wide stride covered the six large blocks home in what felt like seconds. I slammed the front door closed and leaned against it, breathing heavily.

Would a good wife do what I was about to?

I flung my purse on the floor and flew upstairs. I had never snooped on my husband before. I never had any reason to. But now it would be unreasonable not to.

I strode into Frank's office and yanked up the venetian blinds with a violence that surprised me. I squeezed my eyes shut and inhaled slowly to a count of five. On my exhale, I counted backwards before opening my eyes.

Dust danced and swirled in the stream of sunlight. I waved my hand around to disperse it. How did Frank work in this disgusting mess? Cobwebs had claimed the sports memorabilia and framed degrees that adorned the walls. The massive mahogany desk and fully stacked shelves were littered with piles of paper. Only the laptop and leather chair were spared. Frank's office was the one room in the house I didn't clean. He never expected me to and I had never given it a second thought, figuring it was his man haven.

I grabbed the closest stack of papers.

"Stupid, stupid, stupid," I muttered, flipping through last month's bills, random receipts, and junk mail. They were things I hadn't paid attention to in years until I randomly opened a bank statement last week and discovered a depleted account.

I thought the missing money was perplexing, but when I confronted Frank about the large withdrawals and he told me where it went...

"The money went to your mother," Frank had said without even taking a breath.

If jaws hitting the floor was an Olympic sport, I would have won gold.

"Mom needs money?" I said, dropping into the chair beside me, completely stumped.

He sighed and tapped his fingers on the granite counter top. "I wanted to tell you, but she begged me not to."

"But when? Why?"

"Apparently she's the one keeping things from you, baby. Not me."

"But you didn't tell me you were lending her money. Technically, a lie of omission."

"That's on her. She refused to let me to tell you."

"Mom needs money?"

"She was mortified asking, especially since you offered to have me help her years ago with her finances. She had such a hard time. You know how proud she is, how stubborn. It must have been hell for her to ask," he said, shaking his head and frowning. "Don't make this more difficult for her, Rose. She's old. She may not be able to take any more stress. I'll handle it. I am sorry, though. I should have told you," he said, reaching out and trailing his hand down my hair.

I inspected his handsome face before settling on his hazel eyes. He was right, as usual. I didn't want to make everything worse by marching over there and confronting her for not confiding in me. There was one thing he was wrong about, though. "No secrets, Frank," I had said. "Don't ever lie to me again."

He held my gaze. "I'm so sorry, baby. I didn't mean to hurt you."

A lawn mower buzzed and I jumped, almost decorating the office with paper.

How could Frank lie about my mother like that? And so easily. Was it the first thing that popped into his head after I confronted him last week? He was so quick to say it, and it had sounded so plausible.

And I was so quick to believe him.

I slapped both hands over my mouth and bolted down the hall. Breakfast, lunch, and all the cups of tea I'd consumed that morning flew into the toilet, as undigested as my thoughts were.

I scoured my teeth and gargled with half a bottle of mouthwash before marching back into the office on a demented autopilot mission to uncover the truth. I suspected that not only had shock settled in for a visit, but that if I didn't uncover the truth now, I never would.

The plush leather chair groaned when I dropped down and flipped open Frank's laptop. I unclenched my curled fists and stabbed the glowing blue power button.

"I promise to love, cherish, and honor," echoed through my head while the laptop whirred to life.

A log-in screen popped up.

"What the hell?" My fingers gravitated to my bottom lip where they pinched and pulled.

The cursor taunted me with its flickering. Why was Frank's personal computer password-protected? Was it always? Or did he just add the security feature the other day after I read through the statements and demanded answers? What was going on?

I wiped my clammy hands on my jeans and began typing.

*****

Some time later, I found myself in the kitchen. I drifted over to the stove, set the kettle down, and flicked the burner on. According to the stove clock, I was right on schedule for my mid-afternoon cup of tea, sugary delight, and *General Hospital* break.

I examined the paper cuts on my hands. I moved to the sink and filled a glass with water. I set the glass down after gulping from it. Haze shrouded every movement I made, yet my brain buzzed with activity.

Nothing about Paris had surfaced. Nor had any other vacation possibility. And even more questionable items had appeared along with numerous withdrawals in previous months, each for thousands of dollars. Frank's lies piled up and I forced myself not to flee, not to run and break down in bed. I continued, typing in potential passwords and various word combinations while flipping through papers in between attempts, desperate to uncover the truth. I refused to confront Frank until I had something solid, some tangible proof, particularly knowing how easily he had lied the last time. I needed something he couldn't cover up.

I avoided considering what else he might be hiding.

"A watched kettle never boils," I muttered like Gram used to, my fingers drumming the counter top. I moved away in a superstitious attempt to rush the water to a boil. I should have paid more attention. I should have demanded to be a part of our financial life. I should have watched my husband more closely. I should have... What? Spied on my husband all the time?

What kind of a life was that?

Tea abandoned, I floated back upstairs and dropped into his chair, not certain I could be bothered to continue. Even if confronted, I was more certain than ever that Frank would never tell me the truth.

I swallowed down the doubts Frank's pile of lies had created and resumed typing every last thing I knew about Frank, from "Rocky," the cat he had when he was ten–which took me forever to remember–to the word "money." Nothing I knew about him cracked his code. That his laptop was even password-protected in the first place gnawed at me, chewing away at the trust I had in my husband.

I tried my name. Of course not.

I rolled my aching shoulders back in circles and rubbed my forehead. I looked around the office for clues. What was Frank's favorite thing? What could he have used? *Please don't let it be some combination of numbers I would never crack, like his first cell phone number or his childhood phone number,* I thought.

Frank's favorite things. What did he love the most?

What did Frank love the most?

I whipped my head up and punched in "Frank." The laptop beeped and shuddered to life beneath my wrists.

The deep throaty cackle that flew from my lips stopped abruptly and my heart dropped down to my toes. Birds twittered outside while I stared at Frank's computer. The internet browser remained open where he had left off. This morning? He was up here before he left. He spent a lot of time up here. Alone.

Breasts that defied both gravity and imagination took up half the screen. I glanced down at my B cup. Did it mean he didn't like mine?

What were those tassels covering the nipples? Wait, were those even tassels? Was that a chain? And...clamps?

I reached for the mouse and clicked.

I blinked.

I pressed down again. And again. And again.

I didn't know much about porn, but even I knew this wasn't what the average Joe searched for. One image and I might have been able to excuse it as an email joke, but thirteen of them strung across open browser tabs and I couldn't come to any other conclusion.

"In for a penny, in for a pound," I said, repeating the phrase I'd heard all my life as I threw myself down the rabbit hole and opened Frank's browser history.

I scrolled down the list of links. There were hundreds. I forced myself to breathe and began clicking. It was like a car wreck I couldn't help but gawk at. Except I was scanning through the deepest fantasies of a man I apparently knew nothing about.

A porn addiction wasn't the worst thing I could have found, I thought, my mind drifting over an affair and moving on as another image appeared.

It's just fantasy, it's just fantasy, I repeated to myself, the mouse growing hot in my hand. Our sex life was decent. Frank had never asked me for anything kinky in bed–and this stuff definitely qualified as kinky. That meant it was only fantasy. Right? Frank had never requested I wear leather, chains, or clamps. He'd never produced handcuffs or whips. He'd never even tied me to the bedpost with a silk scarf. Or vice versa. We were pretty vanilla when it came to sex. There was no spicy chai in our repertoire.

I opened another link. Why was this classifieds page in with all the others? We had no need for used items, job searches, or garage sales. I scanned the page further, my second glance revealing something even more sinister. I rubbed my arms, suddenly chilly.

I clicked the one highlighted link on the page, following Frank's trail.

Personal ads flooded the page. Over half were marked as viewed, further cementing Frank's unusual interests and illuminating the fact that he was searching.

Frank was searching.

I blinked to clear the blurry screen and scanned the page. Frank's name appeared in the top right hand corner. He had an account. And he hadn't logged off. My hand felt like it had been dipped in molasses when I forced my finger to press down.

I landed in Frank's fantasy inbox. Messages crowded the screen.

A rushing sound filled my ears.

I read one after another, unable to stop. Names. Dates. Times. Places.

It wasn't just fantasy. *It wasn't just fantasy.*

I rocked back and forth in the chair, staring at the screen. My breath slowed into a steady rhythm. Everything slowed, including my heart. I thought it would stop.

I found myself wishing it was an affair. One person. Messages from Mistress Marlena, Dominatrix Debbie, and Queen Kiki tied up my mind. Probably like they tied up my husband.

I stumbled away from the computer, out of Frank's office, and began circling the house. I tried to place the dates, to see if any were familiar, and attempted to determine whether his demeanor was different. I couldn't grasp how this had happened. How could I have been so stupid?

I stopped at the patio doors, fists clenched. The mailbox clanged, signaling the day's delivery. The missing money vaulted to center stage in my mind and how easily distracted I was dominated my thoughts. I stood rooted to the floor, looking out over my newly planted gardens, when events slid together in a kaleidoscope of understanding.

The abrupt change of topic whenever Frank didn't want to discuss something. The other times he blurted out random things, or subtly changed the subject when it didn't suit him. He deflected attention away so I would forget whatever I was irritated or upset about. It had to be something important to me or my attention wouldn't have been as easily diverted. Distractions like my mother requiring money. Or an unprompted baby discussion he had once initiated in the middle of an argument about the new sports car he'd purchased. I hadn't been able to muster the energy at the time to argue that you don't buy a sports car when you want to start a family, you buy a mini-van. But thoughts of a baby had blazed through my brain and diminished the sports car infraction.

I leaned my forehead on the cool glass. Tears splashed onto my toes.

In my mind I scrolled through Frank's generous, thoughtful gifts and began making matches. A spontaneous European vacation last year–after a difficult baby discussion. One-carat diamond stud earrings–shortly after a tearful Mother's Day. A pair of Manolo Blahnik's early in our relationship during my *Sex and the City* phase–after he ignored me during a business trip to New York City. I was being continuously bought off. I was like a mobster's wife, accepting all the generosity the lifestyle provided while overlooking why it was given or how it was obtained.

Frank's gifts weren't always lavish, and the small surprises frightened me even more. I couldn't pair them with offenses and feared what they all meant. I tried to match them with the new dates swimming in my mind. A new spade after mine grew splinters, two enormous flower urns, random bouquets, my favorite chocolate bar, an underground sprinkler system after I had complained one drought-filled summer about having to water every day, even though I hadn't minded much and protested the expense.

And then, last week, just two days after the statement suspicion, Frank had presented me with the Holy Grail of gifts. Not even my engagement ring came close. After a candlelight dinner, a dozen long stem roses, and a sincere apology about not mentioning my mother's finances, he surprised me even further with a small rectangular box. Nestled inside lay a diamond-studded pendant in the shape of a rose, an exact replica of the one Gram used to wear on a chain under her strand of pearls. The necklace she had given to me for my thirtieth birthday, the one that had disappeared in the sand or surf during a Caribbean vacation the year after she passed, the one I could never bring myself to research replacing because I knew it would reopen the gaping wound her absence left.

I had softened, becoming as pliable as rubber. I capitulated and forgave, and tickling thoughts at the back of my mind considered a baby as we moved back and forth in our familiar rhythm. I even wondered whether to initiate the baby conversation again.

I shuddered with revulsion at how easily distracted I was, how easily I forgot, and how easily I forgave.

Was it possible to have the pendant made that quickly? Or did he already have it tucked away, waiting to distract me from some massive misconduct? Or had he stolen it from around my neck while I slept for just such an occasion?

I resumed walking, looping around the house in circles. Nothing looked familiar. The years we spent together evaporated in a haze of wonder. I questioned every memory while wandering from room to room. Would I ever believe anything again?

At some point a distant ding returned me to the present and vaulted me into the future. I opened my eyes. I was in the bedroom, in our bed. I dragged my sleeve across my face and glanced at the clock. Frank would be home in three hours and the text message ding was probably him confirming our plans. We were supposed to be going out for dinner.

I unfurled myself from the fetal position, slapped two feet onto the floor and pushed myself off the bed.

I knew exactly what I needed to do.

*****

Three hours later, I collapsed onto the bed I had shared with a man I thought I knew, a man that had been lying to me for months, years, probably since the day we met. It was the first time I had sat down or even paused. My limbs were heavy with fatigue; yet adrenaline charged over me in waves like the sea battering the shore during a hurricane. Keep moving, it urged with each rush.

A framed photo of our wedding day glared, accusing, from my bedside table. I reached over and tipped it face down before it could change my mind, before I lost my nerve. I stood and walked to the two bulging suitcases standing guard by the bedroom door.

I had no idea if I was making the right decision, whether I was right to run. But I knew I couldn't stay here. I couldn't wait for Frank to spin more lies to cover the ones he'd already concocted. I couldn't look at his face while he continued lying, breaching every one of our marital vows. I wasn't sure I would be able to look him in the eyes again. I needed time to sift through the rubble of my collapsed marriage, or what I thought was a marriage. I couldn't fathom how we might rebuild it.

I tugged one suitcase down the hall before bouncing it off each stair with a thud. It almost toppled me twice. I returned for the second one and dropped it on the marble tile in the foyer, where I waited to catch my breath before beginning the long trek to the car.

I probably could have just packed a suitcase and come back, but the thought of Frank's grand gestures kept me going. There was only one left he could ply me with and if he finally consented to a baby, I didn't know what I would do. And he knew it.

I squeezed my eyes shut and wiped the tears which hadn't stopped leaking the entire time I packed.

I yanked open the front door and lurched out to begin the mad dashes back and forth. Superhuman strength hoisted the suitcases, but not without bouncing one off my thigh as I rushed, wary of one particularly nosy neighbor and Frank's potential early arrival. I wasted valuable time glancing over my shoulder.

Since Frank's text sent me scrambling out of bed, I had scurried, lifted, crawled and run around the house like a disorganized burglar. I yanked, grabbed, gathered, and dumped clothes, toiletries, and jewelry into piles. I raced in and out of Frank's office where I shoved stacks of paper from his desk into the photocopier and then dropped the copies into an empty paper box I found in the bottom of his office closet. I threw, tossed, shoved, and crammed my belongings into bags, boxes, and anything else I could use for transport and lined them up at the front door.

Dread at the thought of Frank coming home curdled my stomach; yet I did nothing to hide my exodus. Cupboard and closet doors remained ajar, drawers left askew or abandoned on the floor, and Frank's office left in disarray. I'd even kept his laptop open on the "What to take with you when you leave your husband" page and its handy checklist, which I used to gather essentials like my passport, birth certificate, and marriage certificate. Most useful was the information about obtaining your spouse's social insurance number, apparently the number one forgotten item and most missed if you had an uncooperative spouse.

The key that had opened the door to my home for seven years bounced off the bottom of the mailbox with a hollow clank. I fished it back out and dropped it back into my purse. What if I'd forgotten something important? *What if I was making a mistake?*

Shoving the last thought away, I turned away from my home, away from my life, and climbed into my SUV. I cranked the ignition and meandered down the street. It wasn't the deluge of tears that slowed me.

I had no idea where to go.

CHAPTER TWO

The North Toronto neighborhood that had been etched into my brain since childhood blurred as I drove around in circles. My foot still light on the accelerator while rounding another block, I struggled to comprehend how my life went from definitive to decomposed in less than a handful of hours. I swiped at the tears and discovered I had landed on my mother's tree-lined street.

I tallied the pros and cons of a hotel over my mother's. Splurging on a fancy hotel with sumptuous sheets and nothing but the television for company, or cramming into the single bed from my childhood with only my Sweet Valley High and V.C. Andrews novels for distraction. A king-size pillow-top mattress without a warm body beside me or a minuscule bed I would probably roll out of. The droning of mindless television or endless questions and chatter. Both options seemed equally horrific; both would magnify my solitude.

I crept along and sailed straight past her house. I couldn't do it. I couldn't admit to her my marriage was probably over. I could barely admit it to myself.

I pulled over in front of a row of houses, put the car in park, and closed my eyes. A hotel downtown was definitely out of the question. I shouldn't be driving that far. I probably shouldn't be driving at all. My brain was more muddled than if I'd ingested a double dose of medication with a "do not operate heavy machinery" warning label. How many people are driving around at any given moment under extreme emotional duress? There's no warning label or breathalyzer for that.

I should find my phone. It would help me find the closest hotel. I pried one eye open and slammed it shut again against the glare, against the situation, against the world. Maybe if I just rested them for a little longer before subjecting them to the blinding late afternoon sunlight. And the truth.

Tap. Tap. Tap.

My eyes flew open and then slammed shut at the offending glare. I attempted to angle my head toward the noise, but my neck had more kinks than an old rubber hose. I lifted a lethargic arm and dug my fingers into the flesh to massage the knots and opened my eyes in a painful squint. I discovered a steering wheel.

Tap. Tap. Tap.

My eyes adjusted to the sunshine beaming through my windshield and my neck gave way, turning toward the noise. A face peered in at me. I screamed.

A muffled "Sorry," accompanied waving hands outside my window. When they dropped, I blinked a few times and looked closer.

"Becky?" Emerald eyes beamed at me beneath black bangs. The same emerald eyes that had twinkled while she quipped "there had better be wine" last week when the gardening class turned into a club and we headed to my house for the "lesson." And prior to that when I first met her looking clueless in the garden center. She had just bought her own townhouse and was determined to buy every shade of pink impatiens because her ex-husband hated the color.

She motioned to roll down the window.

"Taking a nap?" Becky asked, gathering her sleek black hair behind her before leaning down. "What's going on?" She glanced past me and her eyebrows furrowed.

I followed her gaze. Why was my pillow in the passenger seat? I continued rubbing my neck before turning to see what she was gawking at in the back seat. Boxes. Bags. Suitcases.

The fog of sleep lifted.

I crumpled into the steering wheel, emitting a high-pitched howl that was sure to have all the wolves in the country running. Tears gushed like a broken water main.

"Oh shit. What happened?"

I could only give her a snot-filled snort, gagging myself in the process.

Becky reached in, opened the door, and dragged me out. My brain somehow connected with my body and locked my knees so I didn't tumble us both into the street.

"I live right there," she said, nodding her head at the townhouses. "Think you can make it?"

I gasped for air. Could one suddenly become asthmatic?

When I didn't answer, Becky led me to the curb where she nudged me to sit. She curled up beside me with her arm draped around my shoulders. I sobbed into my lap until the heaving returned to streaming tears.

Becky squeezed my knee. "Think you can make it over there now?"

I nodded. She left me on the curb and climbed into the SUV, her perfect butt on full display in black spandex yoga pants. She started the car, rolled up the window, and returned with my purse weighing down her shoulder. Double-checking to ensure the keys were tucked safely inside, she grabbed my hand. A new wave of tears threatened. Frank had brought the purse home as a surprise after I'd admired it on a shopping trip. It must have followed a disagreement about something. I couldn't remember what, but there had to be one. Or it was a guilt gift. At the time I thought it charming and romantic that he had remembered exactly the right one. How could I have been so stupid?

I bit my bottom lip. The metallic taste of blood filled my mouth. I swallowed the sobs, determined not to embarrass Becky further in front of her neighbors while she hustled me down the sidewalk to her home.

*****

I held up a hand to shield my tear-scorched eyes from the drooping sun as Becky dragged me into her townhouse complex. The sun's blinding glare bounced off the sea of white brick buildings, offset only by black asphalt and a handful of tiny green shrubs.

She tugged me to the right. I stopped moving. Becky had led me to the only spot of color in the complex.

"Yours?" I asked.

She nodded with a huge grin, her eyes lighting up.

"Your neighbors must have been pissed." It was the most I'd spoken since she'd found me.

"Whatever," she said, guiding me up the path to her front door. "It's a freehold townhouse anyway so I can paint it whatever color I like."

It was fire-engine red.

Becky kicked aside shoes while mumbling apologies about not expecting visitors. She dumped my purse on the stairs and pushed me down the hall. Exhaustion prevented any apology of my own about intruding. It didn't stop me from wondering how many pairs of shoes Becky owned, though. There were at least eight pairs littering the hallway. Unless I was seeing double. It was a strong possibility.

In the kitchen, she pushed me down into a chair at a table squashed into the tiny kitchen space. My knees didn't need convincing and buckled when she placed her hand on my shoulder.

Becky stared down at me, both hands planted on her hips. "Tea or something stronger?"

"Stronger," I squeaked.

"Wine or whiskey?"

"You have whiskey?" My voice was hoarse. I couldn't picture this petite girl slugging back a couple of fingers of Jack.

"For special or stressful occasions," she said, procuring a bottle of Canadian Club Reserve out of thin air.

"Wine?" I croaked.

"I didn't think you looked like a hard alcohol kind of girl. You never know, though, in extreme circumstances."

She called me a girl. I felt like an old lady that had trudged through a war and lived a lifetime.

"This is my brother's. I don't touch the stuff," she said, shoving the Canadian Club out of the way across the table, a bottle of Cabernet suddenly in hand.

Becky poured two glasses before plopping down beside me. She remained silent for a few minutes while I slurped my wine in between chest heaves that had yet to completely subside. "What happened?"

I held out my empty glass while sorting out what to say. I hadn't discussed Frank with anyone.

She tipped the bottle to refill my glass. "Did you have a fight? From your car, I assume you left? Does he know? I left a Dear John note. You never know how it's going to happen. Or if..."

I grabbed a tissue from the box Becky pushed at me and blew my nose.

"Sorry, I'm not known for being subtle. No pressure," she added, throwing up her hands with a grin, but her eyes betrayed her laugh. She was concerned. And it ruffled me.

I continued chugging to avoid responding. I couldn't talk about it. Not yet. Where would I even begin?

Becky's head cocked to the side. "Your phone?"

I strained to listen. Frank's ring tone. I sprinted down the hall and yanked the phone out of my purse.

"Where are you?" Frank barked. "I made reservations for 6:30."

He obviously hadn't been upstairs yet. I walked the ten steps back to Becky's kitchen.

"Exactly how long have you been lying to me, Frank?"

"What are you talking about? Is this about the other day? I thought we…"

"I've had a few hours to consider it now, and I'm fairly certain you've been lying to me since the day we met." My calm demeanor surprised me. Maybe I had drained all the emotion out already. Maybe I was just empty.

"I haven't lied to you."

"You haven't lied to me?" I said, my voice rising. "You haven't lied to me? Didn't you tell me my mother asked you for money?"

"She did," Frank said, his voice low.

"You're going to keep denying it? Seriously, Frank? Do you think I'm a fucking idiot? You must. You really must to keep lying to me and think you'll get away with it. And maybe I have been an idiot, but no more. I'm done."

Becky's eyes widened and her hands flailed before she bolted down the hall. Her ample breasts bounced in the tight fuchsia tank top on her return. I watched her drop a piece of paper on the table and start scribbling with a pen she somehow knew where to find in the mess. The mess I only just noticed.

The kitchen grew bright with evening sunshine, and I observed the room with sudden clarity. Remnants of a pizza dinner lay strewn across the counter and coffee mugs were scattered everywhere. I heard the sizzling of a BBQ through the open screen door and the room suddenly filled with the scent of seared meat wafting in with the breeze. I gagged.

"Rose, I…" Frank began, and then stopped.

I glanced down at the note Becky had scribbled. Her penmanship was as messy as her home. I cocked my head at her and she waved mouthing, "Tell him later."

"What, are you out of excuses? You can only spin so many lies before they tie you up and trap you, Frank."

"It's not…"

"There's nothing more to say." I jabbed the disconnect button and dropped the phone in my lap. Even if he had tried to explain, even if he told me the truth, I wouldn't have believed it. I would never believe anything he said again.

"Why was I so polite after the man made a mockery of me?" I asked Becky, who only managed a shrug before my phone rang again. On autopilot I picked it up.

Becky frowned.

"Don't hang up on me again, Rose," Frank threatened. I heard the familiar creak of his leather chair, confirming he'd reached his office. "What the hell did you do in here?"

"Don't bark at me, you bastard," I said, jumping up and stalking down the hall. "I did nothing wrong. Except fall in love with you. And trust you. That was my biggest mistake, you lying sack of shit. How could you do this to me? How?" I thought it was the sobbing I had to worry about with the windows wide open, but it was the world witnessing my obscenities. For the first time in my life, I didn't care.

"It's not what you think."

"Of course it's not what I think. Stupid Rose. How could I not believe my husband? Fine. Explain it," I said, taking in Becky's amused smirk before turning around again, pacing up and down the hall.

Silence. He was probably trying to figure out which secret he should cover first.

"Do you need some help getting started? Using 'Frank' for your password wasn't too smart," I said.

Frank's sharp intake of breath thundered through the phone. Becky snorted into her wineglass.

"You went on my computer?" he said, and from his spluttering tone I knew he had turned his angry shade of tomato. "You had no right."

"Too late to impose rules now. Any right you had to tell me what to do is beyond done." I felt delirious from all the screaming, the crying, and the wine on an empty stomach.

There was no sound on his end except his heavy breathing.

"So. Explain," I demanded and continued when he seemed reluctant to answer. "Internet browser history never lies. We could start with the porn you seem to enjoy. Would that be easier? Is it fantasy or reality? Never mind. I saw your inbox. I know all about Mistress Marlena. What's your preference, Frank? The clamps, cups, and chains, or the other creepy stuff I found?" I asked, dropping my voice to make him squirm. He would never admit to it. But I knew. I spent far too much time reading those messages than I should have for my own sanity.

"It's not..."

I cut him off. "Or would you like to explain the finances to me? I know you think I'm dumb with money, but even I'm smart enough to read bank statements to see how much money you've been withdrawing. I'm assuming it's not cheap, that fantasy of yours. Does Mistress Marlena tie you up, whip you, and trod on your balls with her thigh-high pleather boots? Do you use 'Frank' for your safe word too? Does she shove her boots in your face and whip you until you lick them? Does she squat over you and piss?" I couldn't continue, my own humiliation seeping through. How did I not know? And why the hell did he marry me?

I spun on my heel and paced back to the kitchen where Becky's emerald green eyes protruded so far out of her head I thought she was going to need surgery to reattach them.

"Frank?"

Silence again. I yanked the phone away from my ear to check the connection. He had hung up on me. I silenced and dropped it on the table before stretched my hand out to ease my knuckles, which had turned white from my death grip on the phone.

I looked up and found Becky pouring whiskey into two tumblers. The ice popped and crackled when she handed a glass to me. She pursed her lips and blew out a quick breath, sending her black bangs fluttering.

"Wow," she said.

I snorted.

"Wow," she repeated.

I had rendered the chatty girl with a million shoes and fire-engine red door speechless.

"Cheers," I said, clanking her glass with mine before sending the burning amber liquid down my throat in one shot.

*****

"Clothes, bedding, files I'll need," I said, rattling off everything I had managed to pack. I took another minuscule sip of whiskey. I couldn't handle any more than a sip after the first shot sent me leaping out of my chair and hopping around the kitchen from the forest fire in my throat and chest. My antics had sent Becky into a fit of hysterical laughter. "I tucked all my jewelry in my purse."

"That's why it was so heavy. Okay, I scribbled you that note in case you need to go back."

I whipped my head back and forth in protest.

"You need your things."

"I'll buy whatever else I need. I don't care about the other stuff."

"You will. The shock will wear off eventually and you'll regret not bringing your grandmother's silverware or whatever..."

"Shit. Gram's tea service," I interrupted, smacking my hand down on the table.

"See. There are things you'll regret not having once the dust settles."

My mind zoomed from room to room around my house, realizing all the things I'd forgotten. Maybe I should have planned this better.

"You couldn't have known. It was a shock, and if you'd stayed he would have found some way to convince you," Becky said, reading my mind and adding kernels of wisdom.

I nodded slowly, nibbling the painful bump on my lip where I had drawn blood earlier. It was true. I couldn't have stayed without confronting him and he would have spun more lies to explain or finally given me the thing I wanted most in the world, something every diamond on earth couldn't even match.

"Shit, I have to go back."

"Don't worry, you have me to help," she said, patting my hand. "Make a list of the things you want, things you'd be devastated if he destroyed."

I imagined Frank stomping on the shards of Gram's shattered tea set and tossing all my photos one by one into the fireplace–not only of the years I'd spent with him, but all my childhood pictures. The ones with Dad and Gram. Why didn't I think to take them?

I crossed my arms over on the table and dropped my head down with a thunk.

Eventually, between alcohol, expletives I wasn't even aware I knew how to use, and tears, I told Becky everything.

"Rose, you did right." She waved her glass around in a toast, red wine sloshing over the edges. I couldn't even remember when we'd swapped the whiskey for wine.

"I can't believe the money. He thought I was too dumb to figure it out." Now slurring, I reached for the wine bottle and missed. Becky caught it before we almost had a perilous loss. It was the last bottle.

"I can't believe the porn."

"*You* can't? How do you think I feel? Typical Frank, always wanting the biggest and best of everything. Why couldn't he have just liked feet?"

"There's no way you could have known. I'm all up for exploration, but people hide that weird shit. My friend's friend found her husband's tranny porn hidden above the basement bathroom ceiling tiles. God knows why she was up there, but she was so glad she found it before their boys got old enough to start snooping for daddy's porn... What was my point? Oh... Hiding it. You couldn't have known, honey," she said, poking my arm with her index finger before pouring us each another glass.

"I don't know. Sometimes I wondered if something was wrong with him in bed. He did it, but he never seemed as into it as he should have been. I chalked it up to marriage. You get bored." I slammed my glass down. "I trusted that fucker. I could have a disease and not even know. Remind me to go to the doctor, okay? I'm gonna forget."

She nodded and we sat in silence, digesting the possibility of my disease-infested nether regions.

"I'm not sure if a dominatrix actually has sex with her clients," Becky said eventually.

"Close enough. And those messages... The things he was doing?" I wrapped my arms around me as another shudder ran down the length of my body.

"You didn't print any? As evidence."

"Ugh. Like I need the reminder. They burned onto my eyes." I said, poking at them. I missed and jabbed my temple. "You know what the worst part is? I knew."

Becky's eyes widened.

"Oh no. No! I didn't know all that."

She shrugged. "People do weird things." She trailed the ssss, sounding like a snake. "What about those women or men who stay when they discover their partners want a sex change operation? Or find out their partners are gay and ignore it for whatever stupid reason." She sighed. "I miss Oprah."

"Maybe I'm just not strong enough to stay?"

Becky looked at me like I'd sprouted tentacles. "You're strong. You left. You needed time to think and took it. He obviously hasn't been treating you well."

"I knew something was wrong but I ignored it," I said in a whisper. "I didn't want to believe my marriage was less than perfect."

She nodded solemnly. "I know."

"But I glossed over it. I ignored what was right in front of my face. Like this." I held my hands in front of my eyes, fingers splayed wide and sang out, "I see you."

"Hindsight, Rose. Hindsight. It's the universe's biggest clairvoyant. The things I wish I had known too. Did the same thing. Packed up. He didn't know. We fought like crazy. Mean and dirty. We're better off without them." She raised her glass again and clanged it against mine. Red wine splashed onto the grimy white ceramic tiles like blood splatter.

I stood and shook my head to clear it, but only managed to make myself dizzy. I reached out for my chair, missed, and toppled over onto the floor.

"That's it. You're cut off," Becky said, snatching the glass out of my hand, which, like any good wine lover who takes a tumble, I hadn't spilled a drop of. I did however mop up Becky's wine with my jeans.

"Nooo!" I wailed, climbing to my knees and clasping my hands together. "Please, can I have it back? Please?"

"You sure?" she asked, grabbing my shoulders. "Are you sure you can handle it?"

"Yes, ma'am," I slurred and tipped over at her touch.

She handed it back to me and I took a swig from my position on the floor.

"What were we talking about?" Becky asked.

I shrugged.

Becky groped for a small black object on the counter and music blared. She reached for my hand and pulled me up. "C'mon. Let's dance."

I wrapped my arms around her. "My savior," I screamed so she could hear me above the music she was belting out the words along to.

Becky threw her head back and laughed before continuing to shimmy around the room. "You're probably not going to love me in the morning."

*****

I couldn't feel my tongue. Where was my tongue? One eye blinked from the offending sunlight while the other strained to become unglued. Where was I? I bolted upright and sent the

Pepto-Bismol pink room spinning. My bedroom wasn't this bright, and definitely not pink. I looked around with the care of a whiplash patient, unwilling to upset the parade marching through my head. The curtains were hot pink. I was in Barbie hell. I tried to swallow. I found my tongue. It was stuck to the roof of my mouth.

Where was Frank? Had we gone to a hotel? I checked the floor. No shoes, no suitcases, and the pink walls were definitely not standard hotel fare. A bed and breakfast? My hands roved over the bed. Probably not, with this lumpy futon. What a nice duvet cover. It was the same as mine. And that was my pillow. Why the...

"Noooooo!" I wailed as the memories came barreling back. My hands grasped the blanket with an audible crinkle. I unfurled my fists. My favorite cream duvet was littered with leaves and thin strands of grass. Swirls of brown and green stained the length of it. I strained to remember. At some point last night I had become convinced my duvet and pillow were essential to my survival. They were in the truck. I must have dragged them across the parking lot when I thought I was carrying them. Wait, no. I tossed the blanket down and curled up on Becky's minuscule patch of grass. Did she join me?

I moaned from the mental exertion. Before taxing my brain further, I needed drugs. I stood with turtle speed and placed my hand on the pink wall to steady the spinning. Why hadn't anyone invented teleportation yet? I had always hated *Star Trek* in its various revivals, yet strongly supported teleportation. Would it work if you didn't know where you wanted to go, though? The location of my purse remained a mystery.

I focused on the task of moving, hoping Becky stocked Advil in the bathroom cupboard. A deafening creak that could have doubled as a gunshot reverberated in the room. I whipped my head to the source of the noise. Not a good idea.

Becky tiptoed into the room.

"Shit, you scared me. I thought Frank had found me," I said, pressing my fingers to my temples. "Make it stop. Please."

"Me too. Advil's somewhere," Becky said, turning to leave. Her straight raven hair resembled a tangle of fishing line. Several leaves dotted its length.

"Were we going to sleep under the stars?" I asked, wincing with each step.

"I think I remember something about a blanket."

"I wanted my pillow and duvet. I guess I wanted something from home."

"It wasn't until we realized we'd left the wine on the table that we crawled to the front door." Becky giggled. "It's been years since I've had a night like that. At least a decade. Maybe more. Good times."

I followed her down the hall, picking leaves out of her hair like I was grooming a monkey. We found solace in her medicine cabinet with exactly two extra-strength ibuprofen. After two tall glasses of water which we both tried not to gag on while we gulped, Becky wedged herself next to the toilet while I sprawled out in her bathtub and tried not to think about whether she'd scrubbed it since she moved in.

"When did you move in here?" I asked.

"Seven months ago."

I shuddered. The bathtub was a better choice than the toilet though, where mold and mildew were making themselves at home around the rim.

We moaned in tandem, the alcohol fumes synchronizing our groans like pheromones would our menstrual cycles, and didn't budge until the painkillers kicked in and we were able to speak without cringing or moaning. Then we discussed the day's mission: coffee, orange juice, McDonald's, a nap, and more Advil. Not necessarily in that order.

When we could finally stand up, we both averted our gaze from the mirror.

CHAPTER THREE

I froze at the entrance to the kitchen.

Becky bumped into me, hip-checked me out of the way, and made a beeline for the coffee maker.

"What the hell happened last night?" I asked, stepping around red stains on the floor. Mugs, wine glasses, and high ball tumblers littered the table along with bags of munchies and several empty bottles of booze we had apparently somehow managed to consume.

"One hell of a good time," Becky said, in between counting out scoops of coffee.

I righted toppled wine glasses and collected the bottles together. The counter was so cluttered with dishes, take-out containers, and enough mugs and Tim Horton's cups to start a coffee shop, I couldn't even decipher its color. I moved a pizza box to the floor and shoved a few mugs together to make some room before transferring the contents of the table to the counter so I could clean it.

I swept my palm across the table to gather crumbs into my hand, but it kept sticking to the surface like my socks were sticking to the floor. "Did we even end up drinking much of it?"

"Judging by the thumping in my head, I'd say we did."

LYDIA LACEBY

"God, what a mess. I'm so sorry," I said, unearthing the bottle of whiskey from under the table.

"Don't be ridiculous. I had a fabulous time. Don't tell me you didn't?"

"No, I did too." The alcohol had both dampened and magnified my emotions the previous night and now my hangover dulled the enormity of Frank's transgressions. My body was in survival mode. It couldn't handle anything such as emotion taking away from the need to recover from what must have been near alcohol poisoning.

"Don't let me fall for any of his shit, okay?" I said, my voice quiet but firm.

"Will do," she said, kicking her heels and saluting.

"Thank you," I said, pulling her into a hug before turning back to tackle the counters.

"Stop cleaning," Becky commanded.

"Uh…"

"Seriously. Stop. You don't have to. You're my guest."

"Becky? Do you even have clean mugs for coffee?" I asked with as much tact as I could.

Becky jumped out of the chair she had slumped into. "Sorry. I'm a bit of a slob."

"Go, sit down. I'll wash a couple of mugs. It's the least I can do to repay you for putting me up for the night," I said, snatching two large mugs and rinsing them.

"You should stay with me until you figure everything out. If you can live with the mess," she added, looking sheepish.

Although we had only met a handful of times before, I felt honored Becky would open her home to me and wondered if I would have done the same if the situation had been reversed. Definitely not with Frank in the picture, I surmised.

At least if I stayed with Becky, Frank wouldn't know where to find me. And there were no memories of him here like there would be at Mom's–primping for our first date, the joyous looks on my mother and grandmother's faces when I showed them my

34

engagement ring, and then ten months later after I had stepped into my wedding dress and turned around.

"I'm proud of you. It takes a lot of guts to leave a marriage. In fact, I think it's easier to stay. It's the known versus the unknown. You've got the hardest part out of the way. So stay with me until you know what you want to do. I won't let you do anything stupid."

I felt tears prickle, but nothing fell. Dehydration, maybe. "Thank you. I might take you up on that."

"Fabulous. Now my brother won't think I'm a complete lunatic for getting him to put the futon upstairs instead of in the living room when he brought it over the other day," she said, noticing my confusion and waving her hand in the direction of the living room. "The camping chair situation. I'm close to saving enough for a couch now anyway, but don't tell him that." A mischievous grin enveloped her face. "We like to torture each other."

The memory of Becky's story came barreling back. "This is the first place of my own," she had said sometime after we swapped the whiskey for wine. "I crashed on my brother's lumpy futon for months before finally getting it together. Now I watch a fourteen-inch TV without cable from a camping chair. I was so distraught when my marriage fell apart I ended up fixating on my wrought-iron wine rack. I insisted my ex give it to me instead of important things, like the couch. Now I have to replace everything myself and can barely afford it. But at least I get to choose what I want. I always used let him have his way. He was a bit of a bully. I didn't see it until after I had wasted five years of my life with him."

"Coffee," Becky said, slapping her hand down on the table and startling me back to the present.

"Last night is a bit fuzzy. How long have you been separated again? If you don't mind me asking," I added quickly, not wanting to pry or make her feel uncomfortable, even though I sensed Becky wouldn't have a problem talking about anything.

"Nine months yesterday."

I gaped at her like she said she'd given birth while climbing Mount Everest. "It's only been nine months?"

"It gets easier."

"I can't believe it's only been nine months."

"And one day. It really does get easier, Rose. Honestly. Sorry the futon is so lumpy though. And about the dog hair. There's enough to make a wig, but I've got sheets. Shit, I forgot to do it up last night. Not much of a hostess, am I? No Martha Stewart here. God, what would she say about those atrocious pink walls?"

I snorted into my mug and looked up, horrified, but found Becky's eyes twinkling before she broke out into a grin. We both collapsed into giggles. I loved that she didn't take herself so seriously. I wasn't used to it.

"What kind of dog does your brother have?" I asked once we stopped laughing.

"A beagle. Cute, but crazy and sheds worse than a cat."

"I hope he doesn't miss the bed he gave up for this homeless bag lady," I said, smiling. I filled a glass with water and stood staring out the window above the sink at Becky's tiny yard.

"What are you thinking about?" Becky asked, her voice enveloping me like a soft cashmere sweater. I wanted to curl up in the comfort. I had been subjected to hard edges for so long.

"A dog. I've always wanted one…" I hesitated. "I guess I can get one now."

"Now that's what I want to hear," Becky squealed. "What else have you always wanted, but couldn't do or have with Frank?"

"Gardening. A horticultural or landscaping degree maybe," I replied so quickly I didn't even know the thoughts were there, hidden dreams lurking.

I paused, considering the question further, and realized just how much I'd compromised. "Maybe a cat and a dog. A smaller house. I always hated the monster house he convinced me we'd fill with children. Oh, babies. I want a baby." My inhale caught in my chest and I sank to the floor, shoved my head between my knees, and tried to breathe. Seconds later Becky was beside me on the cool tiles, her warm hand rubbing circles on my back.

"You don't need a man to have a baby anymore, honey. But you're young. You'll meet a wonderful man and have lots of babies."

"Is this as much of a pep talk for you as it is for me?"

"Yep. In the meantime, I'm happy to be on my own, doing things my way, and getting to know myself again."

"But I'm almost forty," I said. My whine would have given any two-year-old some serious competition.

"Forty is the new thirty. Besides, you have a few years until forty," Becky said, nudging me with her shoulder.

"I have to tell my mother," I whispered, remembering Mom's recent hints of grandchildren. She might never get to be a grandmother now.

Becky snorted. "It took me weeks to tell my mother."

"She didn't call you?"

"I told her we had canceled our home phone to save money and to call me on my cell."

"Interesting." I rolled the idea around for a moment but decided I had to tell Mom soon. Frank might go there to try and find me.

"I felt bad for deceiving her, but I knew she'd freak. I felt like such a failure. Not to mention stupid."

"You felt like a failure too?" I said, my voice squeaking.

"Of course I did. I don't think you can help it. If you tried anything and it didn't succeed you'd feel some grade of failure. For some reason, the institution of marriage seems to carry more weight. It's more personal than if you couldn't grasp something like knitting. This is our lives. And it sucks. But you know what? No one cares. They don't look at you and go, 'She failed at marriage.' They think what a shame or that it's sad or too bad it didn't work out. Then they get bored and move on. Some probably look at us with respect; envy even. So don't let that overwhelm you. No one else sees it that way but you..." She paused. "And my mother."

I nodded, trying to take it in, but wondered more about Becky's mother and how accepting my own would be.

When I figured out how to tell her.

*****

"Good morning, Sunshine."

I bolted upright, startled by the bright sunlight and the unfamiliar perky voice uttering morning pleasantries.

Brain cells, hazy with sleep, caught up. Memories flooded. I moaned and hauled the covers back over my head, instantly missing my quiet mornings with Frank. Our routine had consisted of ruffled newspapers, slurping coffee, and a quick peck on the cheek as he left. Who was this crazy person so chipper early in the morning? Didn't she know I spent the night weeping?

"Sorry to wake you, but try not to spend your days in bed. You'll regret it. Trust me. Go sit outside, dig in the garden, or go for a walk. Here's the spare key."

Becky's morning appeared to involve animated gestures and talking. Way too much talking.

I dropped the key on the make-shift night table, an outdoor plastic table Becky had lugged upstairs from the backyard. I made a mental note to scrub it today and eyed the digital clock. 7:15 a.m. When was she leaving?

"I called Martha and moved Garden Club to her place tonight." Becky eyed me over what must be her third or fourth coffee. It was the only reasonable explanation for her chirpy attitude so early in the morning.

"Oh no, no, no. Not going to do it. Not ready to face anyone," I said into my pillow.

"Calm down. It'll be all right. I'll tell them for you. We don't have to talk about it."

I shook my head in protest. "Definitely not ready to tell anyone yet."

"Then we don't have to say anything. I think you should go, Rose. It would be good for you." Her stern voice reminded me of my mother.

"Do I have any choice?" I asked, flinging back the covers and stalking past her to the washroom, hoping she would wander off to work and leave me alone. She nipped at my heels and I closed the door in her face.

"Are you sure you're going to be all right on your own today?" Becky said, her muffled concern penetrating the door. "Is there anyone I can call? Should I stay home sick?"

"No. No. I'll be fine. Go to work," I said, ducking around the mirror and attempting to exude confidence I didn't feel. My voice echoed in the small bathroom, home to a single sink, regular bathtub, and toilet. It was a significant downsize from my lavish master bathroom with bay windows overflowing with plants, perched above a jetted corner tub deep enough only my head would surface. The toilet, bidet, and double sink dotted the remaining area with plenty of room for both Frank and I to circle each other without irritation.

I slid down the wall opposite the toilet and shoved my fist in my mouth to stifle the threatening sobs. I wasn't sure I would ever be fine again.

*****

"Have you been here all day?" Becky demanded. She whipped the curtains open and planted her hands on her hips.

I yanked the duvet over my head to avoid the harsh light, turned away, and faced the wall. How did I end up in *Groundhog Day*?

Could I glue the curtains shut? Maybe staple them?

The lumps shifted beneath me when Becky lowered herself down. She put a hand on my shoulder.

"I know it's hard, honey, but you should get up."

I closed my eyes. Silent tears melted into the cottony patch of pillow against my cheek.

"Come and eat something? I brought home pizza."

I remained silent. Eventually, she shuffled off downstairs.

I moaned and kicked off the covers. I hated being rude and upsetting her when she was being so kind. I sat upright and ran a hand through my tangles of hair before attempting to scrape it back into a ponytail and plodding downstairs.

"I'm sorry," I said. "I know you're trying not to let me mope about."

She grabbed two plates out of the dishwasher. "It's only day two. Maybe you have to. Maybe it's part of the process."

"I don't think I'll make Garden Club tonight. I don't have the energy, the enthusiasm, or the smiling face required. I'll look like a crazy clown if I try to smile with my blotchy face, puffy eyes, and Rudolph nose."

"Concealer? Foundation? It covers almost anything, you know. You're our leader. We need you," Becky said before I could throw out more excuses.

"I don't know, Becky. Maybe if it wasn't so soon after..." I stopped. I bit my wobbling lip to stop the tears. "Will I ever be ready to say it?"

Becky dropped three slices of pizza on her plate and looked at me. I fidgeted under her scrutiny.

"Maybe you're right. Maybe you should stay home."

I sighed with relief and wiped my cheek with my sleeve.

"You'll be able to say it one day. It took me six weeks, three days, and eleven and a half hours."

"How..."

"My mother. That's how long it took me to tell her," she said, taking a hearty bite. Fake bacon dropped off her pizza onto the table.

I gagged and pushed my empty plate away. At least she didn't force me to eat.

"Can you tell them I'm sick? Stomach flu or food poisoning. Something?" I blurted out to avoid thoughts of my telling my own mother.

"I told Martha I was having plumbing problems to wiggle out of having it here and now we'll be giving excuses about you. What little liars we are."

My stomach lurched. Lies. I didn't want to lie. Not after everything. But maybe people lie for different reasons. What if Frank's lies were justified? What if I was tossing away my marriage for nothing? Should I let him explain?

"I'll go," I said, slumping down so far in the chair my ass was hanging off the end.

There was no way I could stay home alone with the tsunami of thoughts Becky's statement had just generated.

CHAPTER FOUR

I had survived Garden Club, only bolting to the bathroom and dry heaving once. I made it through Becky's wake up calls–both morning and evening–for a week and I plowed through more wine than I had consumed in the last year. But I couldn't keep my head buried under my duvet forever.

I shuffled my feet along the sidewalk. With every step, I wished my feet would take root like the hundred-year-old trees draping over the streets I dawdled along.

I stopped on the sidewalk in front of my mother's house. Much of the Tudor-style home my parents had purchased when they discovered they were pregnant with me had remained the same, including the diamond mullioned leaded-glass windows and the two trees that had once dotted photographs of my childhood.

I walked down the side of the house, grabbed a trowel, and dropped to the grass in front of the nearest flower bed. From past experience, I knew she would find me. Gram and Mom had been thrilled when I picked up a trowel as a teen instead of boys, alcohol, or drugs. The garden was where I worked out worry, anger, and frustration. It was where all our difficult conversations took place, so at least I wouldn't shock her with blurting out what I had to tell her. She would already know something was wrong.

The three of us had spent hours together in the garden. As a toddler I mixed coffee grinds into the soil beneath roses with my plastic red shovel alongside my grandmother while she told me stories about her life. I gardened beside both women as I grew older and helped Gram when she became too frail to continue. We must have turned over the flower beds thousands of times together over the years both at Mom's and at Gram's prior to the heart attack that took her from us five years ago.

I faltered. When had gardening become so lonely for me? When had I stopped coming to Mom's house and gardening with her? She lived so close and we didn't have the angst-filled relationship other mothers and daughters have. Did it happen after Gram died? After we transplanted the last perennials from her garden before putting her house up for sale? Were the memories of us gardening together too much? Or was there a shift before, after I got married and had a garden of my own? I struggled to remember, but couldn't. The only thing I knew was gardening had become a solitary pursuit for me, a very lonely one compared to the laughter–and sometimes tears–we used to share while digging in the dirt.

Lost in my thoughts, I didn't know how much time had passed before Mom lowered herself down beside me on her hot pink kneeling pad. We worked side by side in silence. The pesky clover and creeping charlie surrendered easily from the earth, soft after the overnight rain. I didn't even realize I was crying until she gathered me into her arms.

I pulled away, swiped my hand across my face, and blurted it out. "I left Frank."

Her creased eyes widened with a sharp intake of breath, which she released through pursed lips.

I stiffened and looked away at the house behind her, the house that had already seen so many tears.

"Sorry, a bit of a shock. What happened?"

"What didn't?" I said, the G-rated version of Frank's lies tumbling from my lips. I kept the X-rated version to myself other than to mention there had been some online activities.

"Are you okay?" she asked, pushing my bangs out of my eyes when I finished spewing my story.

"I have no idea."

"You said you left because you needed to think, but you seem pretty certain now. Are you sure, Rose?"

"When I packed up and drove off I had no idea what I was doing. That day is so hazy I barely remember it. But after rehashing everything again and again all week, I can't think of one happy memory without wondering what lurked behind it. I'm questioning the good I saw in him, like how wonderful he was with you and Gram. But now I can't help but wonder how much of that was a lie too, an act, especially after he lied so easily about lending you money."

"You never found out anything about where the money went?"

I hesitated, unsure about confiding in her about his sexual deviance. I didn't know how to explain the missing money to her without telling her. "I don't know if I even care anymore. Besides, I doubt I'll believe whatever he tells me now anyway."

"Oh, Rose," Mom said in a sigh.

"It's huge, Mom. How can I ever forgive him for lying about you, about everything? For treating me so horribly? How can I believe anything good he might do ever again without wondering first whether it's a lie or manipulation of some kind? I can't wrap my head around how to get past this. How I can ever trust him again? How can I go back?"

"Only you can know that, but you need to be sure."

"I think I am," I said, my voice a squeak as fresh sobs tightened my throat.

"Tearing the Band-Aid off is easier than tugging it hair by hair. You will get through this though," Mom said, squeezing my hand. "I know it feels like the end of the world right now, but it will get easier."

"You were so strong when Dad died, Mom. I don't…" Tears streaked down my cheeks and she collected me in the strong embrace I remembered receiving after every heartache I had had in my life. How could I have thought she wouldn't understand or would question my decision?

She cupped my face and wiped my tears with her thumbs. "I wasn't always strong. Gram pulled me through, but she also knew grief. She would have been just as proud of you as I am, honey."

My shoulders heaved with fresh sobs. I would have hacked off both arms, never to be able to garden again, for another hug from Gram or to sip a cup of tea together and talk. Her death had sliced through me like a scythe. At least I had Frank at the time to hold me up, like Gram held me up after Dad's car accident.

"I didn't know how to tell you. I feel like such a failure. I think…" I stopped, not realizing the real reason behind my hesitation to tell her until the words were almost out of my mouth.

"What is it?"

I frowned. "I think I felt bad about leaving my husband when yours was taken from you."

"Don't be silly. I wish I'd known how much you were struggling."

"You wish? I wish I'd had a clue. I think I always knew something was a bit off, but would never have been able to tell you what." My voice turned to a whisper. "I wondered over the years if this was all there was."

"Marriages are funny. They're like fortresses. Doors are barred, windows covered, and they're often heavily guarded. You can't hear screams or cries, struggles or fear, ambivalence or questioning, and often can't get a glimpse of the inside. My marriage was far from perfect, so I can understand why you didn't talk about it. I didn't. And everyone struggles, Rose. But I do think you're a very brave woman. Tea?"

"Thanks and yes, please," I said, dragging my hands over my damp face and wondering about marital fortresses. Were marriages really impenetrable? If I hadn't let all my girlfriends slip away would I have talked about it? After spending the last week with Becky I'd come to realize how much I missed having a female presence in my life. Someone other than Mom, and Gram when she was alive.

"Everything will turn out all right," Mom said, tugging open the patio door with both hands.

I need to ask Frank to fix it for her, I thought, following her through the door into the kitchen. My throat constricted when I realized that was no longer an option. How was I going to manage without him?

"Will it?" I said, staring down at the kitchen counter. "I haven't even told him it's over yet. What if I'm not strong? What if I go back? What if he's the only chance for me to have a baby? To start a family?" I bit down hard on my bottom lip to stop from sobbing again as my deepest worry surfaced.

Mom flicked on the kettle and turned to face me.

"For goodness sakes, Rose, you're thirty-six. That's not old."

"But...But..." I stammered. "I have to date. Find a man. Keep him. It could be years. I don't have years."

"You may not have forever anymore, but you have time. So many women have babies into their forties now."

"But I'll be so old. I don't want to be the old mom to my kids, the ancient wrinkly one among all the twenty-something parents. I don't want to be too exhausted to chase them and play with them or go through their teenage years when I'm plagued with hot flashes. And I want you to enjoy being a grandmother." It was the worst of my underutilized womb's cries. It would crush me not to have my children experience the love and joy I had with Gram. And Mom with them. But each month my eggs began their journey, only to be abandoned. I had shoved the thoughts down for so long that they gushed and bubbled to the surface with the speed they warn scuba divers about. There was a reason things should rise slowly to the surface.

I sprawled my palms over my chest. I had no idea a heart could physically ache.

"You need to get over the age thing, dear."

I snorted.

"Rose, you're going be a wonderful mother whenever you have a child. And you don't need a man to have a baby anymore. There are other options these days. And of course I'll enjoy my grandchildren whenever they arrive," she said, placing my mug on the table and settling in the chair beside me. We both ignored her fingers, knobbed with arthritis, when she brought the mug to her lips.

"You're not the first person to tell me that. My friend Becky said the same thing yesterday about not needing a man."

"She sounds like a very smart woman. I like her already."

"She'll love you too," I said, realizing how well the two women would get along. I dabbed at my eyes with the bottom of my T-shirt before getting up to give my mother a hug.

*****

The conversation with Mom bolstered my courage and I ventured out the following day with a three-chore list: Discuss adding more gardening classes with my boss, stop at Starbucks for a coffee, and shop for groceries to make a home-cooked meal as a thank you for Becky.

I covered my red-rimmed eyes with a pair of Becky's over-sized sunglasses, shoved my grocery list in my purse, and double-checked that my cell phone was restored to its proper pocket, a subject I had gently broached with Becky the prior evening.

"I'm ready to have my cell phone back," I had said after forcing myself to eat a few bites of the Thai curry she brought home. During my first night with Becky, a lengthy, drunken debate about an itchy trigger finger occurred and we concluded Becky should hide my phone and only bring it out in her presence. I had scurried around searching for it several times since, with an overwhelming desire to send Frank a text message. It seemed easier than calling, although in both instances I had no idea what I would say or type, but I craved contact. For some reason, I actually missed him.

Becky set her fork down. "Are you sure?"

I plastered on my most confident smile and nodded.

"All right," she said, her voice conveying her doubts. She hopped off her chair.

"You're great at hiding stuff," I called out as she strode down the hall. "You'll find Christmas presents you forgot about in May and a gooey mess of Easter Eggs in July. You'd better draw a map and keep lists or you're screwed."

I heard her bound up the stairs and into her bedroom. There was a pause before her footsteps resumed.

"I have my secrets," Becky said, striding back into the kitchen. "You learn all sorts of tricks when you have a mother like mine. She was an evil snoop. And then there was my brother. Privacy was minimal in my family. You're sure you won't despair dial?"

I shook my head and she held out the phone with great reluctance.

Her concern lingered in my mind as I walked over to the garden center. Haze draped over the city, foreshadowing another sweltering day. Sweat gathered between my breasts and trickled down my back even though it was only nine in the morning. The four days of unseasonal scorching heat had snatched the top story of every newscast, with interviews, weather forecasts, and information about seniors staying indoors, the urgency of hydration, and where to locate cooling centers along with their hours. You couldn't go anywhere without talking about the weather and saying or hearing, "Enjoy it while it lasts, we'll be shoveling snow soon enough," with laughter all around.

Abby waved when she spotted me. She was busy counseling the new cashier, so I wandered over to the herbs. This was one of the days I didn't miss working in the garden center, where sweating occurred just standing around.

"You're sure you don't want to come back for more shifts?" Abby asked, rolling her eyes as she approached. "That's the fifth time I've shown her how to process a coupon."

"I might have to," I said, looking down to discover my fingers rubbing a leaf of basil to oblivion, its sweet scent filling the air. At her puzzled look I pressed my basil covered fingernail into the soft skin on my thumb, hoping the pain would prevent a breakdown from the words I had yet to say.

"I left Frank."

At my voice catching, Abby grabbed my arm and ushered me into the back room. She pushed me onto a stool and plopped down onto the one next to me.

"Oh, Rose. I'm so sorry. What happened?"

"The girl from the classes who loves pink? Becky? She found me. I'm staying with her. Anyway, it's a long story. But I might need the extra income. I came to talk to you about the other classes."

"When?"

"I'd like to start them next week."

"No, when did this happen with Frank?" she asked with a gentle smile.

"Oh, last weekend."

"Are you okay?"

I shrugged. "Becky's keeping me entertained, but I need something else to occupy my time. So I was considering those other classes I'd thought about before..." Before I left my husband. Before I left my home. Before I left my garden. Before my life fell apart.

Abby patted my hand. "That sounds sensible."

"Sorry I didn't tell you sooner," I mumbled.

"Don't be ridiculous. After what you've just been through, I'm impressed you're already sitting in front of me. Anything you need, I'll try to help. I already hired the new cashier though, so I'm not sure I can take you on again right now."

My job at Abby's was never a necessity once Frank and I were married, but as much as Frank had teased me about financial matters, a couple of motherly lessons somehow stuck. As a child and teen, Mom constantly pushed me to pick something to save for. "It gives you something to work towards and look forward to," she'd say. She also preached about the feeling of security that comes from knowing you have some money stashed away. She even encouraged me to keep some money separate from my husband when I got married. Frank never once asked what I did with the paycheque I earned at the garden center and had no idea I squirreled it away in a high interest savings account. It wasn't much, but I was fortunate enough to have it, and I could survive until the end of the year on that and the income I would earn teaching the gardening classes. I couldn't imagine having to beg Frank for money right now. At least that was something.

"That's not why I came," I said, even though some shifts would have helped. "I'm here to figure out some more classes so I won't end up living in a box."

"Hardly. You'd stay with me first," Abby said, tugging at the elastic corralling her hair into a ponytail. Most women Abby's age wore their hair short and slathered it with chemicals to hide the white. But Abby kept her hair in its natural state. Long, straight, and streaked with gray, it was most frequently seen protruding from under a bandanna. Although she didn't bear the title of Mom, Abby had become like a second mother to me ever since my awkward, lanky, fifteen-year-old arm had nervously held out an application. I had worked for her ever since.

I smiled. "I should have listened to you about charging for the transition to the gardening club–which we're in desperate need of a name for, by the way." With my change in circumstances, I regretted not figuring out some form of compensation for the club when we first came up with the idea, even with the slight padding I had around my financial middle. When we first discussed it, Abby and I had intended the club to be a group working project where we would go to each other's homes and work collectively on the gardens with my oversight, tutorials, and advice. After a few sessions though, it had turned more into a bitch-and-stitch knitting session without the needles. We chatted and drank wine without the gardening grime.

"There's already a North Toronto Horticultural Society," Abby said. "Quite formal with some very serious gardeners, so not quite like your casual group. You'll figure out a name. Maybe Becky can help, although she'd probably call it something pink. And yes, you should have charged. They'd have to fork out a fortune for a professional landscaper or gardener. Trust me. Your expertise is valuable. You have to stop letting people take advantage of you," she said, tapping the back of my hand with a black finger.

I stared at the hundreds of tiny pots arranged on the table, her statement hitting home more than she realized. Or maybe she already knew.

"Well, if it doesn't work out with that one," Abby said eventually, pointing at the door, "you'll be first on my list to call. You would have been anyway. Regardless, anytime you want a distraction, come over and fiddle with some seedlings. Or pop in for a chat."

Tears prickled. "Thanks, Abby. I think once the shock wears off I'm going to be desperate for a distraction."

"Really, Rose, anytime. I've been through it. I know how hard it can be. But it happens to the best of us, so don't let that part bother you. In the meantime, let's chat about those classes and get you busy."

I brought up giving herb and vegetable classes, grateful she seemed to sense my reluctance to talk. "Do you think it's too late? We're already into June."

"We have some seedlings left. This year stick to veggies that don't need advance planting. Expand next year. You can discuss planting over the course of a few weeks to have constant crop production during the summer like beans, carrots, and beets. Herbs can be transplanted from pots anytime, so that's not a problem, and you already have a separate class for them, so maybe just touch on those. What about mixing in some recipes?"

"And that's why I came to talk to you. Great idea."

We picked next Thursday for the veggie class and posted the sign-up sheet.

I sauntered down to Starbucks with a grin. I had a lot of work to do.

*****

Two women shoved strollers through the tight seating arrangement in Starbucks before disappearing to order. One peek at the pink bundles and all the enthusiasm I had acquired with Abby evaporated.

I glanced at the mothers. Oblivious, they ordered their mocha frappuccinos. I could have been a crazed baby snatcher. I peeked back at the babies, desperate to stick my nose in their strollers and breathe in their powdery scent.

The women returned and I forced a brief smile to cover my interest, refusing to strike up a conversation about their pink bundles. They resumed rocking the strollers and began an incessant comparison of infant accomplishments.

Blocking out their conversation proved impossible. First smiles and roll-over ages punctured my ears. I wished I had my iPod.

"Shit," I cursed under my breath. My iPod was still at home, my old home.

The stroller mommies whipped around and glared as if their babies could pick up swearing at six months. I tucked my nose back into my coffee. Now that would be something to brag about.

A blast of heat washed over me when the door opened. I breathed a sigh of relief. The two women who entered were stroller-less. They weren't even sporting watermelon stomachs.

"John's sperm count is worse than Janine's husband," the blonde said loud enough for the entire coffee shop to hear. Maybe the entire country.

Then again, maybe there were worse things than gurgling babies or pregnant bellies.

"And he's still smoking and drinking?" replied the redhead, her over-plucked eyebrows reaching the ceiling. "At least my hostile uterus is my own issue and I can control what I do. Charles would never change anything. Thank God our fertility issues aren't his problem."

The blonde sighed, ordered, and resumed their rapid fire before collecting their beverages.

"Are you sure this is decaf? We can't have any caffeine. We're trying to get pregnant," the blond barked at the barista while the redhead pried the lid off and looked into her cup like she could tell the difference by looking at it.

"Let's sit inside. It's too hot to sit on the patio," said the blonde before dropping down in a chair on the other side of me.

All of Starbucks succumbed to a collective sigh.

Couldn't they continue this conversation over coffee at home? Even the stroller moms looked offended. Sperm-Challenged eyed the babies like a wolf leering at a chicken coop, slyly plotting its next move. Hostile Uterus observed the tiny bundles like a woman on a diet staring at a tray of brownies she was desperate for. I snatched my coffee and bolted before a showdown ensued.

I hustled down the street to the grocery store, their looks haunting me with every step. Would I ever be boasting about my baby? Or was it too late? Would I leer at infants like a wolf, doing everything in my power to get what I want, or would I curl up in despair and gaze at them with sorrow?

If I hadn't been stupid enough to marry Frank, I might have found a loving husband, a wonderful man who would have jumped at the chance to have a child with me. I might have been pushing a stroller or dragging my kids to play group or school instead of this solo trip to the grocery store. I'd wasted years, and now I was old and alone. And even though I knew I could do it on my own, I didn't want to. I wanted a partner, an extra set of hands to help with the late night feedings and to hold mine during ballet recitals and baseball games. I wanted someone to cradle me during the scary times, a man with infinite patience to teach how to ride a bike, hold a hockey stick or baseball bat, and how to use a hammer and screwdriver. I could barely tell the difference between the tools, let alone give lessons.

I stopped and sat on a bench outside the grocery store to collect myself. Eventually, the thoughts petered out to a dull throb, and I stepped inside the store. After stopping to scan my list, I looked back up. Bright globes of red, yellow, and green assaulted my vision. Zucchini, the first vegetable I had fed my picky soon-to-be husband, appeared before me. It turned out to be his most loathed vegetable, something we laughed about for years, because he actually ate it. And discovered he liked it. A stack of Frank's favorite cookies towered beside me on sale. A sign for the ice cream he loved fluttered under the air conditioning.

I shivered. What was he eating? He couldn't even boil water.

Cooking for Frank had never been an aggravating chore. Even the grunts in between shovels of food and his hand dragging across his mouth instead of a napkin didn't bother me. The first meal I ever prepared for him had almost ended in disaster after too many glasses of Chardonnay to calm my nerves. Unsteady hands placed the plate in front of him, and he pulled me down for a kiss before inhaling the pasta carbonara. After devouring the last bite of cheesy soaked bread he'd wiped his plate clean with, he gathered me in his arms and plied me with kisses. He pushed me down on the sofa and whispered how I would make some lucky man a wonderful wife. I basked in his compliment and felt my cheeks turning rosy at the mention of being a wife and all the things I knew his fingers would do as they weaved up my thigh.

A tantrum-throwing toddler jolted me back to reality.

I pivoted, but my flip-flop twisted in my haste and I pitched sideways. I flailed my arms and caught only a box of chocolate chip cookies before my leg caught up and swung around with me. My hands slammed onto the floor and my feet karate kicked out sideways like I was some kind of kung-fu fighter.

A box of cookies hit the ground beside my head and suddenly it was raining cookies as the tower crumbled around me. I was drowning in one of Frank's favorites.

"Please don't let this end up on YouTube. Please don't let this end up on YouTube," I chanted, scrambling to my feet. At least I'd left the huge sunglasses on.

A pimply teenager in a uniform ran up to me. He was exactly the kind of kid who would put this on YouTube. Fabulous.

"You're going to have to pay for those," he said, pointing to the decimated display. "We can't sell them now, they'll all be broken."

I pushed the sunglasses up on top of my head and looked the little twerp in the eye. "I fell because there was something slippery on the floor."

"Impossible. There was nothing there."

"There was. Give me a minute to move these and I'll show you," I said, beginning to shuffle boxes around to clear the floor. There were hundreds of them.

"You'll have to pay for them," he said, his voice wavering.

"Ow, my back." I stood and gripped my lower back with both hands. "I should sue."

His eyes widened at the thought of this happening on his watch and I felt sorry for the kid.

"I don't think…" he started, running a hand through his floppy hair.

"Actually, I have an idea…" I said, cutting him off.

Ten minutes later I rushed out of the store, snaked my hand into my purse, and pulled my phone out of its pocket.

It dinged. I looked down.

Frank.

His first contact since I'd left.

I clicked the message with trembling fingers. "I miss you. We need to talk. Where are you?"

My fingers coasted over the keyboard. "I'll come by tonight." I hesitated and then pressed send.

55

CHAPTER FIVE

"I'm going over to see Frank," I said, taking a swig of Cabernet. We had just finished the pasta and salad I managed to prepare once Becky brought home the ingredients.

"What?" Becky shrieked, holding my arm down to prevent me from raising my glass again.

"He texted me earlier, told me he missed me and wanted to see me. I told him I would go by later tonight. To tell him it's over," I added quickly.

"This is so not good. You had a shit day. Your Starbucks trip alone could be listed in the dictionary under epic fail."

"Even with all the horrors though, I didn't call him today so that's something. And I need things like my iPod to drown out stupid people. I need to tell him it's over. I need to rip this Band-Aid off in one shot, not hair by hair like I'm doing moping around here day in and day out."

"Are you really done? One-hundred-thousand percent sure?"

I nodded. I was treading water at Becky's. Decisions needed to be made in order for me to move on, and the sooner the better. "I think the thousand boxes of cookies I had delivered to him says something."

"Excuse me?"

"Add epic fail definition number three," I said, telling her about my karate feet and cookie trauma.

"So I made a deal with the kid. I'd pay for them and give him a hundred bucks if he delivers them to Frank and leaves them on his doorstep. I even went back after Frank's text to tell him to deliver them tomorrow so he doesn't go by when I'm there telling him it's over. A last parting gift."

"I can't believe you did that," Becky said, clinking her glass with mine. "That's the last thing I expected from sweet Rose."

"It felt incredible. I wish I could see Frank's reaction when they're delivered. Today was a sign. I could have burst into tears at the grocery store and fled. I could have crumbled and melted with Frank's text, especially after the day I'd had. I could have arranged to meet him earlier and kept it from you. But I didn't do any of those things. I called you instead and rattled off a grocery list."

Becky beamed.

"I do still feel a bit wobbly though, so first I'm going to sit here and have you rhyme off all the reasons for my decision as further fortification. Then I'll have a squirt more wine. And then I'll go."

"I'll come with you."

"I'll be fine."

"I'll sit in the car. Just in case."

"Don't be silly."

"I don't know, Rose. I still don't think this is a good idea," she said, pulling a lock of hair at the nape of her neck and twirling it around her index finger.

"Just tell me the reasons again."

Becky rattled them off, one by one, while I nodded and agreed with each statement. I added my own interpretations and ideas.

I stood to leave. I had to do it. I had to get it over with.

*****

Frank looked the same. He hadn't grown two heads or horns and his face wasn't green. He didn't look like a monster, he looked like a man. Like the man I fell in love with, the man who'd taken my heart. And then stomped on it.

I stood in the foyer and shifted my weight from foot to foot. Frank dragged a hand through his dark hair, the same gesture he had made when he'd first asked me out that frigid, rainy November day. We had bumped into each other, or rather the unruly umbrellas we both wielded against raging winds and sideways sleet did, while we both sought shelter under a toy store awning. We flattened ourselves against the display window, full of Christmas decorations and gift ideas, and thrust our umbrellas out to create a shield.

"Do you think we can risk getting to the coffee shop without drowning, or should we stay here and risk becoming icebergs?" he said, pointing to the water pooling at our feet.

My teeth chattered as I laughed. He was so handsome, and after we chatted easily over hot chocolate, saying "no" wasn't an option when he ran his hand through his hair and asked me to meet him for dinner the following evening.

It felt like centuries ago.

He plucked at the side of his glasses and raised them.

"You're wearing your glasses?" I said, surprised because he avoided them like they were the same wedgie-inducing instruments of his youth. Frank had to be freshly shaved, contact-lens wearing, and impeccably dressed at all times. He was a thousand times worse than a woman primping before a casual dinner, let alone a special event.

He shrugged. Either he had lost a contact, didn't care about my presence, or wanted me to think he was comfortable, that we were comfortable. I couldn't decipher which.

I released a long sigh.

"I'm so sorry, Rose. I don't know what I was thinking. I should have told you. About the money, about everything." His face flamed crimson. We both knew what "everything" meant. And we both knew he would never have admitted that, even with his saying it now.

"It's over," I said, shocking myself with the absolute finality my voice carried.

"But we can work on it. We can get counseling. Don't give up on us," he pleaded, reaching his hand out.

I flinched and yanked my arm to my side. I looked away and noticed a paper-wrapped bouquet on the kitchen counter.

Frank's eyes trailed mine.

I strode down the hall and stopped. The kitchen sparkled. The dishwasher hummed. My houseplants hadn't shriveled. Had he hired a cleaning lady? There was no way he did this himself.

Frank picked up the bouquet. "I'm really sorry, Rose. I got your favorite flowers."

I shoved the package away. My eyes landed on another item cluttering the counter.

A Tiffany's box. And it was far from tiny. The more substantial the gift, the more colossal the transgression.

Frank picked up the package and held it out with a wide grin and slight shrug of his shoulders.

I smacked the box out of his hand, turned, and stalked back down the hall. Frank's guilt gift squealed across the ceramic tiles before bouncing off the wall with a thud.

"Rose? Rose, wait," he said, jogging to catch up to me.

I whipped around. "I need to come back and get some more things. Maybe this weekend. I'll leave the key in the mailbox. It would be better if you weren't here."

"But…"

"Did you ever even love me, Frank?"

Hurt flickered across his face. And then fear. "I did. I still do. Please, Rose. Don't do this. I need you. I love you."

I stared at him for a moment before speaking. "I don't believe you."

I wrenched open the door and stumbled to the driveway. The sound of our front door slamming echoed down the street. I lurched to the truck and snatched at the door handle, terrified of an untimely encounter with a neighbor. My sweaty fingers slipped.

"Shit. Fuck," I swore like Becky was inadvertently teaching me to while I hopped around flicking my wrist. I'd hacked off half of my index fingernail. Across the street, Mrs. Mendleson's lilacs wiggled. I froze, petrified she would saunter over and comment on my absence. I sneaked a peek while reattempting the handle. Emerald eyes and black bangs.

"Becky," I hissed.

"Just thought I'd go for a walk," she said, rushing over and pushing me around to the passenger side. She shoved me up into the seat and buckled me in. I slumped forward and moaned the entire way home while Becky rubbed my back.

Frank didn't even bother coming outside.

*****

The flame of confidence I threw at Frank when I told him it was over extinguished in one breath on the ride home. The thought of tearing my beautiful home in half while I selected which belongings to take and what to leave behind felt like my heart was tied to two Mack trucks driving in opposite directions. I didn't want to have to think of our life together while I tore it apart. I didn't want the reminder of the lies while I shoved items in boxes. I didn't want to recall the good times. And I particularly didn't want to wonder which of the fabulous memories were fiction. Or exactly how much of my life was lies.

"But you need things. Don't end up like me," Becky warned, gesturing to the two camping chairs we were crammed into, our bodies contorted to their shape. Becky had dragged me, the chairs, and four beers outside to the twelve squares of concrete constituting the patio and started talking once my sobbing had subsided. She refused to let it go.

"I don't care about things. I'll buy whatever I need," I said above the sizzling grills and laughter traveling down the townhouse patios. I already missed not having a grill and I'd only just begun cooking at Becky's. How many other things would I miss?

"Yes, honey. You do care. You need the rest of your clothes, kitchen stuff. You'll want your books, movies, gardening equipment. Hell, take the bed. You don't want to sleep on that lumpy futon forever, right?"

She had been harping for twenty minutes. Nothing seemed worth involving people and a large moving truck. Until she mentioned my bed. The sensible bed I'd splurged on hoping to get a decent night's sleep after years of putting up with Frank's Fred Flintstones Flips. The lure of my luxurious, king coil, center-dividing, pillow-top mattress snapped me out of it.

"You're right," I said with a long sigh. "I want my bed."

"That's my girl." Becky whooped and reached for her phone. She tapped the screen.

I watched her with curiosity.

"Saturday's a go. I'll text you later with the exact details." She dropped the phone back down beside her. "My brother. When you left, I called him to ask if he was around to help you move stuff. His friend's available too."

"How…"

"I figured if you told Frank today, you'd need to get it done quick. Now, do you want to go over during the week to pack? I could take a sick day?"

"What time did you tell them?"

"Noon."

"No, we'll go over in the morning. Thank you." I smiled and bobbed my head in wonder at this woman who was barely even an acquaintance a couple of weeks ago. "We do need to talk though."

"You're not breaking up with me, are you?" Becky smirked and pulled her hair back into a ponytail.

"We need to talk about where this is going," I said with a grin.

"What's up?"

"I know you said I could stay here, but you just got it together. This is your first place and I'd hate to intrude. I'll move to my mom's. It's probably for the best. I'll move on faster if I move there instead of getting used to hanging out with you all the time. You may never be rid of me then."

"Bring that enormous TV of yours and a couch and cook a few more dinners like you did tonight and I'll never ask you to leave."

I laughed. "I wanted to talk about it before moving my things," I said, trying not to choke on the words.

"I like having you here. But you have to stop cleaning up the place. I don't want you to feel like you have to. This is Rosie Time. You need to go out and do everything you've always wanted to. Skydive, rock climb, take a bee-keeping course. Whatever it is. Just don't start slaving over me. I don't want to be your surrogate husband."

"Am I really..." I trailed off and guzzled my beer. Had I replaced Frank with Becky?

"I'm not complaining. But don't expect me to perform husbandly duties. I don't swing that way."

I laughed again. How many times had I giggled, even through tears, since staying at Becky's? Living with Mom would never be this much fun.

"Thank you for bringing that to my attention and clarifying your position. So, how does roommate sound then?" I asked, reaching into the bag for another handful of chips.

"Awesome."

"I'll pay you rent. And I'll bring the TV and a couch."

"My little apprentice. I'm so proud of you. You're finally sticking up for yourself." Becky squealed and almost fell over during her leap out of the awkward chair to hug me.

After hammering out a roommate agreement we were both happy with, I promised it wouldn't be forever. "I'm realizing it's time I stood on my own two feet and I'll try to do that as soon as possible."

"Take your time. Make the right decisions. No one's forcing you to do anything anymore. Those days are over. And for the record, it took me an entire month to peel myself off my brother's couch. Literally. I clung to Buddy the Beagle, watched crappy daytime television, reality TV, and alternated between Doritos and Toblerones. One day I snapped out of it. I bought this place two days later. Best decision I've ever made, but you seem a bit more of a planner. Hopefully you're not mooning about on the couch forever, though. I'm trying to help you avoid that."

"I assume your chirpy wake-up calls are a part of your anti-moping program."

"It's for your own good."

"I usually crawl back into bed again after you leave, you know."

She swatted at me. "Well, I guess it's early still. You'll figure it all out. Your life is a blank slate now. You can do whatever you want."

I tilted my head back and gazed up at the stars, barely visible through the city's haze of lights. I could do whatever I wanted. I didn't have to consult or compromise anymore. I ran a finger under my eyes to stop stray tears from falling, unsure if they were from grief or relief at this revelation, or both. My life was mine to create. I could manipulate and mold it into whatever I wanted. Maybe it was time to start dusting off my dreams.

CHAPTER SIX

The house smelled the same. It was the first thing I noticed when I pushed open the door. The second was how tidy it still was. I had expected dishes littering the counters, a filthy sink, socks and underwear strewn haphazardly around the room, and chip crumbs surrounding Frank's favorite spot on the couch. Especially now that he knew I wasn't coming back. But the house was spotless. Why?

I ran my finger along the granite counter top searching for clues that my husband missed me. Based on the immaculate house, it didn't look like he had. At least not to clean up after him, anyway. Then why had it become my job in the first place? I slumped onto a stool and flipped through a stack of mail. Take-out menus tumbled out. Maybe he missed me after all. But maybe he was happier ordering the curries I loathed every night, like I realized I could eat ice cream for dinner daily if I wanted to.

I wandered over to the patio doors. Tiny weeds had already sprouted in my absence. I heard Becky grunt before her steps faded again as she continued carting boxes inside with the fervor of a ferret. She had nudged me down the hall with instructions to go reminisce, that I only had a few minutes before we needed to start packing. Initially, I had objected, desperate to focus on something else, but she had been right. I needed to say good-bye.

I resisted the urge to pull on my gardening gloves and climbed the stairs instead, my legs laden with lead. The photos lining the walls remained mute as I searched them for answers. I hesitated outside the master bedroom and stared at the fully-made bed, complete with the throw pillows Frank hated, remembering the first time we had made love on it, fueled by desire. And the last time, succumbing to our Friday night habit. I walked over and sunk into the luxurious mattress. Frank had returned the wedding photo I tipped face down to its proper position. I plucked it off the bedside table and cradled it in my lap.

There were no Photoshopped lies here. Glowing cheeks, sparkling eyes, and lips that practically touched my ears in a beaming smile preserved the happiest moment I had ever felt.

A single tear splattered onto the glass frame, blurring my face and altering my bursting smile into a grotesque grimace.

How did this happen?

"He was a jerk," Becky said in a voice reserved for funerals with both its volume and tone. With the exception of her words, it was appropriate on many levels and I appreciated her solemn, yet stern, statement.

I swung my eyes to the hall and found her leaning on the door frame.

Tears fell fast and furious like a sudden storm and washed over the photo like the rain that was supposed to be lucky on your wedding day. Only there was no good fortune here.

Becky walked over to the bed. "I often fell asleep cradling my wedding album, wondering the same thing I presume you are now. 'What happened?'"

A strangled whimper escaped me. I tucked my chin to my chest and clutched my stomach, where grief gripped my bowels.

"You may never figure it out, honey," she whispered, running her hand in circles on my back. "I could only gather bits and pieces, but I'll let you figure out your own story. We need to hustle though before the boys get here with the truck. You can cry later."

I let myself be pulled up and relinquished my hold on the frame. It bounced off the rug with a dull thud as we walked away.

"I've been rummaging through your cupboards," Becky said, dragging me into the kitchen. "I think we can make better use of all of this than he will."

Strewn across the counter were serving platters, pots and pans, several over-sized mugs, espresso cups, and even vases. My tiny jars of spices were lined up like tin soldiers next to my Kitchen Aid mixer and Cuisinart. The espresso machine crackled and the sweet scent of real coffee filled the room. Becky grabbed a mug, swiped the cream out of the fridge, and spooned sugar into my mug like she lived there.

By the time we finished with the kitchen, ten boxes filled with assorted kitchen items were stacked in the corner.

"How do I have so much stuff?" I asked, grateful I'd listened to Becky, who insisted on cramming as many liquor boxes as she could into my SUV.

She grabbed my shoulders and guided me into the living room. "It's fine. We'll make quick work of it. DVDs?"

I shook my head.

Becky ripped off one of the hot-pink sticky notes she had stolen from her office, slammed it onto the TV, and began wiggling around the room. They were to help her brother and his friend identify what to load into the truck, she had told me earlier after digging them out of her purse.

"Sorry if I can't catch your enthusiasm," I mumbled.

"Sorry." At least she had the decency to look sheepish.

"It may not be with you for long, so try not to get too attached."

"A joke. Good for you," she said, patting my head and making her way to the bookshelves.

"Not the bookshelves, just a few books," I said. I hated those bookshelves. Dark and gaudy, they would be another reminder of Frank, who had insisted on the hazelnut shade of stain.

Becky turned around and eyed the two couches. "Which one?"

"Doesn't matter. You choose," I said, scanning the shelves and yanking off recipe tomes, gardening encyclopedias, and my favorite novels.

Becky continued drilling me as we moved from the living room to the dining room to the basement, where I found even more items I would have missed if I'd forgotten to check downstairs. Executing a move was never an easy task, but the extreme pressure to rush and make snap decisions was grueling.

Another sweaty hour later, we stopped for a glass of water.

"There is no way I would have been able to do this without you."

"My pleasure," Becky said, dropping onto a kitchen chair. "And it would have been even more pleasurable if you had let me mix cayenne pepper in Frank's hemorrhoid cream."

I felt heat creep up my neck at the thought of Becky picking through our medicine cabinet, one of the most intimate areas in a home, but I was grateful I didn't have to see Frank's lone toothbrush or battle the urge to pick up his cologne and inhale.

"Too bad I already have a kitchen set. This one is lovely," Becky said, running her hand along the table.

"It wouldn't fit anyway."

"It'll be sad to see the patio furniture go too."

I stared at my favorite possessions and couldn't imagine a summer without lounging endlessly on them. "What the hell. The chair and love seat might fit. If not, we could always put them inside somewhere."

Becky bounced down the hall to find her pink Post-its while I choked back laughter and tears. On her saunter back through the kitchen, I grabbed one from her and slapped it on the indoor garden rack towering in the corner. The plants residing on it had lived there for the length of my marriage.

"I hope you don't mind a floral infestation," I hollered behind me while carting the massive philodendron I had rooted from Gram's as a teen to the living room. The foliage obstructed my view, but I didn't miss a step. I would have been able to walk the hall in my sleep. Would I ever feel that comfortable somewhere again?

"Sorry, but I don't have a floral delivery," said a deep male voice.

My scream echoed off the walls and seemed to go on forever. Dirt, clay, and leaves bounced off my legs when the clay pot shattered on the hardwood floor. I stared at the front door.

Peering at me, looking apologetic, were the same emerald eyes as Becky, only they were accompanied by short, dark curls and two perfect dimples. My heart raced at warp speed.

Becky sprinted down the hall, wielding a knife she didn't look afraid to use. "What the hell are you doing? You scared the shit out of us. It's a good thing I don't have a gun."

"Good to see you too," he said, dropping down to kiss Becky's cheek.

He was so tall.

"Rose," Becky said, turning to me. "Oh shit. Rose? Are you all right?"

"Erm. Hi," I said, forcing my jaw to relax and my mouth to shut. I removed the hand that had slapped it to stop my screeching and ran it over my hair. Damp strands at my temples greeted my fingers. How had so much hair spilled out of my ponytail?

"Sorry I startled you. I'm Scott," he said with a little wave, a gleam in his eye, and dimples flaring.

"Rose," I mumbled.

"You're sure you're okay?" Becky said, shooting a glare at her brother.

"Yes, yes. I'm fine. Just a bit of a shock. Going to splash some water on my face and try to compose myself." Maybe I'll apply some mascara too. There had to be an old wand of it somewhere.

I returned downstairs to find not one but two gorgeous men lugging the TV down the hall. Stuck on the stairs as they made their way past, I blinked at bulging biceps protruding from T-shirts. This could be a business. Gorgeous, muscled men moving divorcées. It would make a killing.

"Rose, this is Adam," Becky said from the living room where she was guiding them down the hall in full drill sergeant mode.

"Hi," I said with a nod.

Adam grunted in response and readjusted his grip on the TV.

"Put it down a sec, Adam," Scott said, stopping in front of my position on the stairs. He lifted his shirt to mop his already sweaty forehead. I coughed and spluttered to try and hide my gasp at his abs. They could have easily grated cheese. Had I died and gone to heaven? Overwhelmed with the desire to lick every inch of them, I averted my gaze. It landed on Adam, who was grinning over the TV at his friend.

"C'mon, slacker," Adam taunted with a smirk that probably had women drop to their knees on a regular basis.

"Okay, okay," Scott replied with a wink in my direction.

My grip on the banister could have produced freshly-squeezed orange juice if I'd been holding an orange. What the hell was wrong with me? I was moving out of my marital home. I should have been weeping or screaming. Not consumed with the sudden desire to have a threesome. I definitely couldn't ask Becky where this oddity fell on the leaving-your-husband-scale. One of them was her brother.

I approached the front door. Thoughts of abs and dimples and how well they would be paired with peanut butter and melted chocolate vanished. A massive yellow moving truck glittered in the sunshine like a lighthouse in a storm. I glanced across the street. Mrs. Mendleson's curtains fluttered, her gaunt face disappearing behind them. Her neighborhood nickname of "Mrs. Meddlesome" was well deserved with her prompt delivery of various street news, including break-ins, births and deaths, and for-sale and sold homes. The only way to increase her gossip delivery speed would be to put her on Twitter. By dinner, Frank and the entire neighborhood would be aware I had vacated the premises and that two gorgeous young men and one beautiful, foul-mouthed brunette had helped me.

I shrank back inside and embarked on one last round of the house. Still surprised nothing had been shattered, shredded, or burned, I darted from room to room, eager to get the hell out.

I paused outside Frank's office. Dread boiled in my belly. I didn't think there would be anything I needed inside, but I took a deep breath and opened the door. Everything remained as I left it, with the exception of a few new bills added to the chaos. He hadn't cared to clean it, to hide his lies. Maybe he was glad we were over. Maybe he was relieved.

I swallowed down the thought along with the nausea that accompanied it and scanned the room. A patch of pink poked through the blanket of white paper. My fingers grazed the pale pink corner. I squeezed my eyes closed and tugged, unsure why I wanted to twist the knife in my heart around once more.

I opened my eyes and dropped the card like a hot potato. Scrawled in script on the front was "To my Husband on Our First Anniversary." I reached out a tentative finger to flip open the card, my mind buzzing with thoughts of another wife and another life. But it was my name scribbled at the bottom, complete with multiple Xs and Os. I exhaled in both relief and frustration.

Would I ever stop wondering where Frank's lies ended?

I stumbled out of the office, down the stairs, and returned to the kitchen. I whipped open the fridge, grabbed a case of Heineken and the bottle of vodka from the freezer, then doubled up two plastic bags before tossing the entire contents of the freezer inside, including a large package of hamburgers and buns.

"Boys. Follow me," I said, sliding open the patio door and marching outside to move one last thing into the truck.

*****

"I can't believe you snatched the grill," Becky said, her legs dangling over one side of the wicker armchair and swaying back and forth like a pendulum. Both pieces of outdoor furniture were squashed intimately onto the patio alongside Frank's prize possession.

"This is one hell of a grill. Good job," Adam said, flattening a burger with the stainless steel spatula I had also pilfered. Flames shot up and the smell of charbroiled burgers filled the air.

My stomach grumbled, my appetite resurfacing for the first time in weeks.

"Inflicting the last deadly wound, taking a man's barbecue. That's low," Scott said, distributing another round of beer before dropping next to me on the love seat. His arm grazed mine and my stomach flipped like a flapjack. "But I kind of like it. Feisty."

Although I was flattered and confused and more than a little bit smitten, Scott had just helped me move out of my marital home. He was Becky's brother. And I had only left my husband two weeks ago. He couldn't be flirting with me. There was no way in any universe anything would happen, that anything could happen. Bobbing in the undertow of his delicious dimples was a nice distraction though.

"Well, technically I didn't even take half of what I was due, so he can't complain. Thanks again for helping me move, guys. Adam, you didn't have to cook up those burgers after all that work. We could have ordered pizza."

"And miss the opportunity to take this bad boy for a spin? Are you kidding me? We rock-paper-scissored on the way over here to see who would drive it first. Grills are forbidden on both our balconies. Condo regulations."

"You can always come here and use this one any time. If Becky doesn't mind," I added quickly, still unsure about her relationship with her brother. She always spoke so fondly about him, yet grumbled about their history too. I wasn't sure what to make of it.

"Are you kidding? Between the grill and the TV, we'll never leave," Scott said.

"Boys and their toys," I said, a story about Frank's sports car shooting to the tip of my tongue before I bit down on it. Where did that come from?

"Bring the food and promise you won't come by only to watch the big games and you're on," Becky said.

Adam nudged Becky's foot with his own. "You know what we haven't done for ages?"

She scrambled out of her chair, folded her arm at her waist, and bowed in front of Scott. "Brother, we challenge you to a game of Euchre."

Scott stood and bowed back.

"Do we need dueling swords?" I asked, laughing.

"We're a little competitive," they said simultaneously.

"You owe me a beer," Becky shouted and punched Scott's arm.

"Do you play cards, Rose? Euchre?" Adam asked.

There was a collective pause.

"It's been a while," I said. "That's the one with trump, right?"

Becky and Adam slapped their hands together in a high five. Scott groaned. "At least you know what trump is. I'll teach you as we go. You'll be my partner. These two won't ever switch."

"I'll grab plates and the next round," Becky said. "Why don't you guys get the table in the basement?"

The wicker groaned when Scott and I shuffled off as directed.

"Are you sure you want us here all night?" Scott asked while we dusted off the card table. "It's been a tough day for you."

"I think the distraction is exactly what I need, and a little Euchre ass-whooping would cheer me up immensely. And it had better not be us getting our butts kicked. You know the rule about playing your highest trump first when I call it, right?"

Scott grinned. "You're nothing like the little, broken bird I expected Becky to bring home to mend."

"More like a tough old bird."

"Nah, you've had a wing clipped. You'll fly soon enough."

I smiled.

"You're sure you don't mind us staying? Although with those two having their minds set on kicking our butts, you're better off agreeing. There won't be any stopping them now. Becky probably sent the two of us down here so they could plot our demise.

Although you could teach her a thing or two about subtlety. I would never have guessed you could play from your reaction."

"I'm fine with it. Thank you for asking though. And it's all a little fun. Becky's so cocky sometimes. It serves her right."

Scott laughed. We hoisted the table and began carting it up the stairs.

"Becky, why have you been hiding this downstairs?" I asked, distracting myself from how wonderful it felt having a man consider my feelings for a change, and such a handsome one too. "We could have been using it for a dining-room table."

"That's tacky."

This coming from the girl who used camping chairs in her living room.

"Becky, what did you sit on to watch TV before Rose arrived with the couch?" Scott asked, shooting a wink my way.

He had better not be able to read all my thoughts.

"Camping chairs… Oh, shut up," she said, swatting at him. "So I'm not as fancy as the rest of you, but I still know good taste. It was only temporary."

"Of course it was. Play nice, you two," Adam interjected.

Our natural, easy banter continued through the evening. The four of us chatted, teased, and laughed like we'd been doing it for years, and I sent a quiet thanks to Gram for teaching me the game. They told me of the Euchre years when the three of them played weekly along with various girlfriends and boyfriends filling the fourth spot. The losers had to provide dinner before the next game. Now I filled the fourth spot, partnered with Scott.

"Why didn't you ever hook up with Adam?" I asked Becky later, while we cleared the table. Over the course of the evening, I had noticed their subtle flirtation. They praised each other for hands, gloated their wins with more high fives over the center of the table, and joked about us losing and having to provide dinner the next time. Scott was oblivious.

"Scott had forbidden it," she replied.

"What? Why?"

She shrugged. "An older brother thing. I was never allowed to date his friends."

"Does that mean you have the same rule about your friends?" I blurted out, and almost sent the load of beer bottles and wine glasses I carried tumbling to the floor.

"What? You have the hots for my brother?"

"No way. I'm nowhere near ready for anything anyway. Probably never again. Besides, he's your brother. I wouldn't jeopardize losing you."

"That's good. I don't know how I'd feel about you two together. Talk about awkward," she mused, draining the dregs of her glass.

CHAPTER SEVEN

I stretched and rolled over to curl up behind Frank and found his side was cold, empty. I opened my eyes. Pink walls, not mocha. I moaned and yanked the covers over my head, the progress of the last week obliterated with my brain backsliding at the change from the lumpy futon back to my regular bed. I had hoped my days of waking up only to remember all over again had disappeared.

I remained cocooned in an attempt to avert reality, but eventually the scent of hazelnut wafted through my downy shield.

A few minutes later there was a soft knock on the door. "Coffee? I set up your espresso maker, so it's not the hazelnut-flavored stuff I know you hate. You'll still have to put up with the smell though, cause I love it," Becky said before lowering herself down and sipping from her mug.

I exhaled in relief and sat up.

"I'll let you mope around all day if you want, but I was thinking of going shopping. Do you want to come?" Becky asked.

I shook my head.

"Another time. Maybe just get settled today. We didn't give you a chance last night. Do you want help?"

"I'll be fine. Unpacking will keep me busy."

Becky eyed me like a psychiatric patient she wasn't sure she could leave alone. "I won't be long. A couple of hours."

I waved her away before propping myself up to take a sip of espresso and surveying the room. A ceiling-high stack of boxes lined the opposite wall. Based on the scribbles, most contained books, while some held china and other mementos. Two boxes were labeled "photos". I flung back the covers, determined to sort through them and pack up anything I didn't need to store at Mom's.

I heaved a box onto the bed and flipped it open. Piled high were albums, framed photos, and envelopes full of snap shots. My life's history in a box. Smiling faces at special events and reminders of tragic ones lurked. The first framed photo I pulled out contained a snapshot of Dad sitting in a fold-up lawn chair with frayed plastic stripes. He sported a wide grin, a bottle of beer dangling from his fingers. He had just finished the new patio and was "proud as punch", as Gram would say. I placed it face down on the bed, unable to handle his disappointment. He wouldn't have been proud of the decisions I'd made, that instead of having "doctor" associated with my name, I would carry the label of "divorcée." I realized with a jolt that Mom had said Gram would have been proud of me, but said nothing of Dad. She knew it too. But Mom was proud of me. That's all that mattered now.

I lifted out the stack of frames and also set them face down, unsure I could handle any of my favorite pictures from the past. I traced my finger around the edge of the silver-plated frame I knew held Gram's smiling face before turning back to the box. I pulled out two large albums. Our wedding photos. Frank had brought home two black leather albums to showcase them and insisted I transfer our photos from the wedding-white album the photographer had provided. Who puts wedding pictures in a black album? Maybe we were always doomed.

Without even cracking their morbid covers, I gathered them in my arms, walked to Becky's room, and dropped them onto her bed so she could deal with them for me. At least once she emptied them, I could re-use them and organize all the other random pictures stuffed in envelopes. What would I do with all the wedding photos though?

"What's this?" Becky called out shortly after I heard the familiar crinkle of shopping bags.

"Can you take out all the pictures for me?" I asked, dumping the contents of a black garbage bag onto my bed. Sweaters, jeans, sweatshirts, and T-shirts tumbled out. An hour earlier I had unearthed a stack of the photographs taken the year Frank and I met. Our first Christmas together. First Valentine's Day. Birthdays. A weekend trip to Niagara. My heart ached, knowing the last of every occasion lurked in the depths of the boxes as well. I slammed the lid shut, kicked the box into the bottom of the closet, and moved onto my clothes.

"Bonfire?" she asked, grinning when she wandered into my room, flipping through the pages.

Desperate to avoid my designer dress and beaming face, I concentrated on folding T-shirts. "I don't think so."

"First you won't let me mess around with his hemorrhoid cream and now you won't let me help you burn his pictures. You're too nice, Rosie."

"I can't wrap my head around getting rid of them. What if..." I stopped.

"What if he changes and you get back together?" she finished for me.

I whipped my head away from my clothes to look at her.

"I know. I had the same thoughts," she said, shoving aside my lump of clothes and pulling me down to sit beside her.

I stared at my hands. If I destroyed the photographs by whatever ritualistic means—burning or shredding came to mind—and we reconciled, any visual record of our time together before would be destroyed. The gap would be a constant reminder of this desperate time in our marriage.

Not that I'm going back.

"Not that I'm going back," I said out loud. "I don't think it's all sunk in yet."

"Of course it hasn't. You're still in shock," Becky said, throwing her arm around my shoulders. "It will and when it's time, we'll have a burning party."

I shrugged off her arm and nodded at my closet. "That's a lot of pictures to burn. How do I get rid of them all? If I toss away every one he's in, or that even reminds me of him, I'll have nothing left. No memories of the last ten years." I knew I couldn't keep them forever. Who would want to get involved with a crazy lady who kept her old wedding photos? Still, it couldn't hurt to keep one. Could it?

"But not every memory was a good one."

"But they weren't all bad. Surely I'll look back at some point and it won't be all bad, right?" Memories of our honeymoon and subsequent trips were documented somewhere in the boxes as well as when we welcomed our new nephew into this world. Frank's nephew now, his sister's child who I would never see again. The one he doted on, cuddled and coddled and spoiled. The one that solidified the idea Frank would be a fabulous father in my mind.

"He wasn't all bad," I said, somehow defending my soon-to-be ex-husband. I realized at the same time that I had taken all the pictures. Frank had none. No photos of his nephew. Maybe I should drop some in his mailbox?

"They never are, honey. There has to be something there to make us fall for them. It's called charm."

"Haven't we already had this conversation?"

"Just making sure you're listening. Did you get it this time?"

I frowned. "I don't know what happened. It was so subtle. It practically grabbed me from behind."

"I wish someone would grab me from behind."

"Seriously? That's what you got from that?"

"We should go out," Becky said, leaping off the bed.

I shook my head back and forth so vigorously I could have given myself whiplash.

"No way. Not yet."

"Come on. It would be good for you."

"Not yet, Becky."

"If I don't get laid soon, I'm going to shrivel up like a prune," she moaned, flopping back down on the bed with the back of her hand covering her forehead. Becky had missed her calling as an actress.

"Give me a bit more time."

"Fine, let's go for a walk instead. You need to get out of here for a while. And besides, I want to meet your mother."

*****

"Please tell me this will get easier," I said to Becky as we walked in the direction of my mother's house. Somehow I had managed to land within the same thirteen-block radius of the city I had spent my entire life in. I was grateful, yet wary of Frank living so close, and twitched every time a reverberating sports car rumbled, fearful of bumping into him.

"It takes time. You're going through withdrawal. It would be the same if you'd given up cigarettes."

"Too bad there isn't a patch for it."

"It's called finding a gorgeous man and having loads of incredible sex. Replace it with something else. Smokers eat a lot of crap when they quit. Sex is the crappy food for breakups." She grinned, seeming pleased with herself.

I blinked away the image of dimples and abs. While that kind of distraction might help the frequent bouts of doubt I had when cradling the phone, one digit away from dialing Frank, it might also send me scurrying back to my old life.

"You're right about it being easier to stay," I said.

"I know. Do you miss Frank? Or do you miss your life?"

"My life," I replied without hesitation. It wasn't Frank I missed as much as my tidy house, expansive gardens, gleaming kitchen, massive master bedroom, Jacuzzi tub, and the quiet. It was the most encouraging sign I had made the right decision.

"Good," she nodded, pumping her arms.

"I can't believe he hasn't called freaking out about the bed or the grill and that he didn't trash my things."

"Of course he didn't. He can't do anything or he's screwed. You've taken his bed and his grill. You sent him a thousand boxes of cookies. The poor guy is probably shitting himself that you're going to go postal on his Facebook wall about his sexual deviance or what a lying asshole he is. He's probably scared you'll call his mother, sister, ex-girlfriends, and his new ones when they appear. If you wanted him to get down on his hands and knees and bark like a dog, I'm sure he would."

I held up my hand. "Please, no dog-collar images. Do you really think so?"

"Hell yes. He's shaking in his designer shoes."

I considered the potential leverage. "I still can't believe the cookies. I've never done anything like that before."

"Instead of a natural disaster, you've had an emotional disaster going on in here," Becky said, twirling her index finger around her temple. "Pain, shock, upheaval. You're taking stock, acting out of character. There will still be aftershocks though, so be cautious."

I formed a fist and knocked. My hands were clammy, from both the heat and nerves. I hadn't brought anyone home to meet my mother–boyfriend or girlfriend–in well over a decade.

"Rose, dear. Oh, hello," Mom said, offering her hand to Becky. "I'm Susie. You must be the mysterious Becky I've heard so much about. Would you like a cup of tea? I just brewed a fresh pot."

Becky swiped her brow with the back of her hand. Not everyone shared my mother's English enthusiasm for tea on sweltering days, so I decided to save her from being polite. "Actually, Mom, I think we're too hot from our walk. I'll whip us up some iced tea instead."

Mom guided Becky on a tour of the back gardens. My stomach clenched as I watched her beam at Becky's compliments. I didn't visit often enough. At some point Frank stopped joining me, except for special occasions, and my own visits petered out. We still had our mid-week lunch, but dinners became rare. I was a terrible daughter. It wasn't like I worked long hours or we lived miles apart. Mom not only lost her own mother a few years ago, but she also lost her little girl.

"So, are you taking care of my girl?" Mom asked after we'd settled on the patio sipping our respective teas.

"Sure am trying."

"She can be stubborn, so tread cautiously."

"Don't I know it," Becky said, filling my mother in on the cleaning compromise we had come to that morning, consisting of Becky placing her coffee mugs in the dishwasher every evening and her ban on my sweeping dust bunnies until a week had passed. I twitched every time I walked by one.

Mom laughed. "Her room was always so tidy as a teenager I actually worried."

"Hello," I said, waving my hands in the air. "I'm sitting right here."

They looked at me and then turned back to each other, chatting like they'd known each other for years.

CHAPTER EIGHT

Becky bounded into the room when she returned home from work and sent her heels bouncing under the kitchen table. I had yet to comprehend how she commuted with a twenty-minute walk in each direction, plus a subway ride, in the three-inch contraptions. Two hours at a wedding and I couldn't wait to kick my heels off.

"What, no cleaning service today?" Becky asked, dropping her purse on the table.

I stared at her.

"Tonight? Garden Club?"

"Oh no. No. No. No. I'm so sorry. How could I forget?" I had promised to tidy up but got lost planning my classes and meandering about online.

She laughed and grabbed a bottle of wine. "Whatever."

"We'll make quick work of it," I said, gathering three pairs of her shoes colonizing the space under the kitchen table. I raced down the hall and flung them into the closet.

"I don't mind," Becky said, following me down the hall, dropping down on the bottom step and setting my wine glass beside her before sipping her own.

I hid my horrified look in the closet. Becky was entertaining and refused to tidy? But I lived here now, too.

"This is me," Becky said, waving her arm around. "People can take it or leave it. You love me in spite of it, don't you?"

I envied her nonchalant attitude and couldn't help but grin. "Seriously though, someone might trip over these shoes and sue you."

She laughed and shook her head at me. "So serious, Rosie. You have to loosen up. It doesn't matter if the house isn't spotless. I don't care. And neither should you." Becky pulled me off the floor where I had continued tossing her shoes into the closet. She led me into the kitchen.

I immediately began packing up my laptop and tidying the papers and notes I had scattered all over the kitchen table.

"Were you working on your classes?" Becky asked. "You could try them out on me if you'd like."

"Really? What a great idea."

"Now if only you would take my advice about cleaning," she said, smacking her hand down on mine as it swiped the sponge over the counter in front of her.

"Let me get the dust rats out of the hall and I'll stop."

"Fine. But remember, I don't want a housewife. And you don't want to be one either." She leveled me with a stern gaze before walking back down hall.

I shuffled behind her, fully chastised.

"I get it. I get it," I muttered, and watched her climb the stairs before racing to grab the Swiffer, broom, dustpan, and dust rag. The downstairs living area was small and I could cause some serious damage to the dirt in the thirty minutes I knew Becky would take to get ready.

*****

"Happy Housewarming," Martha said, handing me a miniature cyclamen, profuse with scarlet blooms.

"What? You didn't have to…"

"You moved. Your housewarming," she said, embracing Becky.

"We were just having our first roommate disagreement," Becky said, uncorking another bottle of wine.

"What happened?"

"Rose was busy all day and forgot to clean for tonight. When I came home, she jumped up and started tidying up after me."

"But…" I started.

"I told her I didn't want a housewife," Becky continued, ignoring me.

They both laughed. I remained silent.

"You should see my place most of the time. Between the kids, my husband, the dogs and cats, I can never keep it clean."

"But…" I said, trying to interrupt again.

Martha held her hand up. "Yes, I cleaned when you came over last week. But we're old friends now, right? No more tidying up for each other."

"It's not me you have to convince, it's this one," Becky said, jerking her thumb at me before distributing the wine she had poured. What about Becky's messy issues?

"I don't know why we all do it," Martha continued. "It's ridiculous. We all know no one lives like that. If we didn't have to run around like lunatics cleaning whenever someone comes over, we'd all be much more relaxed. So, no more with us, right?"

"Amen, sister," Becky said. They clinked glasses and looked at me expectantly.

"Fine," I grumbled and hoisted my glass. I couldn't help wondering what exactly I had missed in my bereaved state last week and what alternate universe I had stumbled into.

"Great. It's settled," Becky said, sliding the patio door open.

"How old are your kids again?" I asked Martha. "Sorry, last week was kind of a blur."

"Twelve and ten. They run me ragged. I'm not looking forward to the summer holidays."

If Martha felt exhausted at her age, how would I feel in another decade? I'd be pushing fifty when they turned those ages if I popped out a baby right this second, never mind the extra year if I found a man and got knocked up tomorrow. I trampled down the thoughts and chased them with a gulp of wine. "They must love having the dog."

"Sure, but they rile each other up. It can get a little hectic. You should see me try and answer the door. It's such an ordeal I can't be bothered anymore."

"My brother has a pup. Buddy the beagle," Becky said. "He doesn't have too many doggie friends. Maybe they could play together sometime."

"The more the merrier. Maybe we'll do a barbecue or dinner soon. We've been wanting to get to know more of our neighbors, but haven't had the chance with unpacking and everything. But now that we've adjusted to the neighborhood and the boys are settled in school, it's time we got to know some folks."

"Do you live far?" I asked.

They stopped talking and stared at me, wineglasses suspended mid-sip.

"Right. I was at your house last week." I fanned at my face, which felt like it had gone up in flames.

"Rosie, it's okay," Becky said, patting my arm. "When I left my asshat ex-husband, I went to my old house after work instead of Scott's for weeks."

"When my mother passed away a couple of years ago," Martha said, "I kept picking up the phone to tell her a story about the boys. Sometimes I couldn't even remember if I'd fed them and had to ask if they'd eaten. Don't worry, it takes time."

They hadn't made me feel stupid or embarrassed. Not like Frank, whose initial patience had waned a couple of weeks after Gram passed away. Not even a month later, he demanded I attend a corporate dinner and turned a shade of ripe tomato, his eyes almost popping out of his skull, when I asked his colleague about his wife. The gentleman mumbled something into his tumbler and turned to the dinner guest on his left. I remained oblivious to my transgression until we climbed into the car and Frank unleashed his fury. The couple had split up. He continued berating me even after

I pointed out I hadn't wanted to attend in the first place. But these women hadn't made me feel stupid or embarrassed. They understood. They cared.

"Thank you," I whispered, my vision blurring with tears.

The doorbell chimed and Becky shimmied to the front door.

"It does get easier, so don't be too hard on yourself," Martha said.

"Come in, come in," I heard Becky say at the door.

She hadn't mentioned anyone else coming tonight. Our Garden Club of five had dwindled to three since our first meeting. How had she recruited more members?

"Your home is lovely," I heard a familiar voice state. I bolted down the hall. My mother was here? What was wrong with my mother? I stumbled into a stunning bouquet of buttery yellow and deep violet irises. Mom handed it to me and Abby grabbed my arm and pointed to an enormous terra cotta planter on the tiny front porch, overflowing with at least a dozen varieties of flowers. It added yet another burst of color to the front of the house.

"Happy Housewarming," she said. "I wasn't sure if your home had sun or shade so I shoved everything in."

"It's beautiful. And so are the flowers, Mom. Thank you both," I said, embracing her and Abby before guiding them through the kitchen into the yard. Martha winked at me while I made the introductions. She was in on it too.

I made my way inside to pour two more glasses of wine. I couldn't help but grin at Becky's devious nature. Her secret-keeping ability should have landed her a job in the CIA instead of the crappy admin job she grumbled about.

The doorbell rang again while I uncorked a new bottle.

I cocked my head, confused. Becky didn't know any of my other friends. I barely did anymore. I made my way out front.

"Happy Housewarming," Scott and Adam cheered. They parted to expose an enormous urn overflowing with herbs. Basil, oregano, thyme, chives, parsley, and cilantro spilled out of various holes.

Overwhelmed, I blinked away tears and reached out to hug each of the boys. I ignored the heat worming its way down my body when my body flattened against Scott. "You didn't have to."

"Yes we did," Adam said. "We're going to be spending a lot of time here. We need you to like us."

I laughed.

"You're a slippery one," I said, slapping Becky's arm.

"You deserve it. Besides, we can't have a Garden Club without veterans." She paused. "And the muscle to help us carry out our gardening dreams."

Everyone laughed and a wave of happiness glided over me. The Garden Club wouldn't be three women sitting around gossiping. Maybe we would actually make something of it.

"So," Becky said, clapping her hands together. "Are we going to talk gardening or what?"

*****

"Here's to another week you've survived post-Frank," Becky said, raising her glass.

"This was a much better week," I mused, bopping my head along to Bob Marley's "Everything Gonna Be Alright" while chopping cilantro and garlic to slather onto mahi-mahi fillets dowsed in lime. I'd overheard the song during a successful trip to the grocery store earlier in the week, and took it as a sign after it bounced around in my head for days, reminding me over and over things would be all right. I finally downloaded it to a playlist so I could listen to the real thing instead.

"Don't be so optimistic. This is what you have to look forward to," Becky said, interrupting my trip outside to light the barbecue by yanking me down to sit beside her. She pivoted the computer screen.

I felt my eyes widen in horror.

Becky clicked again.

"It's like a train wreck. I can't look away," I squealed, slapping my hands over my eyes but leaving my fingers splayed so I saw every inch of the screen. Becky continued scrolling through the images. Each one was worse than the one before. She had been browsing through online dating profiles when one particular user, IAmAGod, sent her a link to his private photos. And private they should have remained. The first shirtless shot should have tipped us off after it revealed a six-pack, multiple tattoos, and a Fu-Man-Choo mustache.

"Are mustaches making a comeback?" I asked, suddenly concerned about my dating future.

"Ugh. I hope not," Becky replied, scrolling further down his profile.

Another photo. Again shirtless, his tight black jeans were unzipped, revealing a trail far from neat and trim.

"Say what you want about Frank, but he was always a fan of manscaping."

"That's the first good thing you've told me about him. Although trimming is a notorious sign of a man's concern over his endowment."

"Really?" I replied, wondering briefly if she was right before becoming distracted by the images on the screen. "Seriously? These are the pictures he uses?"

Each pose looked more ridiculous than the one before. There were flexed muscles from the front and back, two guns drawn pointing to the unzipped forest, and then my personal favorite, slouched on the couch with his arms crossed behind his head, lying in wait for a woman to kneel before him. Still unzipped.

"Turn it off. Turn it off. My eyes are burning."

"Who are these losers?" Becky said, blocking zipper-less fu-manchu from access to her profile. She closed the laptop.

"I wonder who took these pictures for him?"

"Who cares? Maybe online dating isn't for me." Becky released a long sigh and tugged another bottle out of the wine rack.

"Then it's definitely out for me. Whenever that day comes."

"Let's go out. We can go laugh at these morons in person. The bar isn't far. We'll leave whenever you want."

"Fine."

"Seriously?" she screeched, grabbing my arm.

"Yep."

Becky whooped and raced down the hall. "I thought I was going to have to drag you out by your hair one day."

"For the record," I hollered after her, "I'm going, but I'm not really into this and when I want to leave, I'm leaving. With or without you. And when I'm finally ready to get out there and you already have a fabulous man, I'll demand you come out with me instead of spending quiet nights cuddling at home with him."

"Fine. First dibs on the shower," she shouted down the stairs.

Had the last sixteen years of my life even happened? I felt like I was twenty, hanging out at my girlfriend's apartment near the University of Toronto's downtown campus, fighting over the bathroom before getting ready to go out clubbing, and picking up boys–instead of having just left my husband.

Becky had stayed in enough nights babysitting me, though. Scott and Adam were on a camping trip, so they weren't around for distraction. I knew if I didn't take the caged animal out, I would never get any peace. And based on the way she had commandeered my laptop every evening to browse for men, she was desperate for a night out.

Besides, after the week I had, what could go wrong?

CHAPTER NINE

A tussle over my outfit, several cocktails, a plate of cheesy nachos, and two investment bankers later, I was left to reap the benefits of my good-friend behavior. But the silence I had craved at the bar turned into moans that would have made a porn star blush.

I flipped over and slammed the pillow over my head, trying not to listen, trying to drown out the thoughts of whether I'd ever have sex again, when I would be ready. I wasn't like Becky. I couldn't jump back on the horse. Or on a random investment banker.

"Sorry," Becky said, not looking the least bit apologetic when she sunk down next to me the following morning. "I forgot how much fun that is."

As if I couldn't tell from her rosy cheeks and glowing face.

The pipes groaned and we both glanced up. Someone had turned on the shower. Becky grinned so wide she could have fit a slice of watermelon in her mouth. And not one of those tiny genetically modified ones either. Apparently, the banker hadn't bolted last night, and he had shower privileges this morning. Interesting.

"Can you take me shopping today for some new clothes?" I asked. "The pencil skirt and blouse won't cut it again, as you pointed out last night. Several times," I reminded her, in case she'd forgotten in her wine haze.

Becky hesitated for a second too long.

"Don't tell me you're spending the day with him now? Should I prepare for a wedding next week?"

"It's just brunch. Maybe later?"

"Don't worry about it. Come back here. Waste the day in bed with the sexy banker. I'll go to my mom's. Watch your chin, though. If you make out with him anymore his five o'clock shadow is going to hit bone."

Becky laughed and grabbed me in a hug before bolting back upstairs when the shower stopped running.

*****

Becky flipped radio stations like a sugar-infused ADHD child in the car. She bashed buttons until she discovered something tolerable, and then cranked the volume one or two notches only to abandon it seconds later. If a dance-worthy song played, however, she'd flick up the volume until conversation proved impossible.

I had forgotten about this when Becky bounced into my room the next morning and dragged me out of bed to go shopping against my hungover will. I struggled to remain patient until the ibuprofen kicked in, but the pain in my brain thumped along to the beat. Combined with Becky's perkiness after spending another night with the banker, I itched to pull over, yank the passenger door open, and shove her out to the curb. At least they had stayed at his condo last night so I didn't have to listen. I was, however, left alone with wine. Two bottles of it. I should still be under my duvet. Sundays were for sleeping in. Frank rarely stumbled downstairs until noon, unless golf was involved. I often used to crawl back into bed with him and wake him up...

"Spice up your life," Becky hollered, singing along to the popular Spice Girls song. She removed me from my Sunday morning thoughts. But instead of the present, I flew back to my wedding day. I had been speaking with Frank and a few of his colleagues at the reception when I noticed Gram hauling Mom by the arm out to the dance floor. "Go ask Gram to dance," I had whispered to my handsome new husband. Without many extended relatives, my side of the family attending was virtually nonexistent, and I felt guilty Gram had no one to dance with.

When Frank followed my gaze, the pair became separated by other dancers, and Gram stood stranded on the dance floor. The music switched from a crooning Elvis to bopping Spice Girls. Gram's royal blue dress shimmered under the lights. She twisted her head to listen before beginning to shuffle her feet along to the beat. I giggled when she waved her hands in the air at the chorus before completely abandoning herself to the music. Mom watched with a bewildered face as the crowd gathered around Gram and formed a circle. Frank's lips drew together in a tight line while he tugged at his collar. I'd dropped his hand and raced over as fast as my wedding heels allowed.

I heard Becky say my name. I blinked. The traffic light had turned green.

"Are you okay?" She asked, turning down the volume.

I snickered and swiped a tear. "Never better. Just remembering my wedding…"

"Oh no. Don't do that," Becky interrupted.

"I was remembering my grandmother dancing to this song at our reception."

"Spice Girls?"

"Yep." I grinned.

"Seriously?"

I nodded and filled her in on the story.

"Your Gram sounds cool. I could totally see your mom doing that too."

"Maybe age removes inhibitions? I don't know about Mom, though." I tried not to think about how old she would be when I had a daughter or son old enough to get married. And if they waited as long as I did…

"Is your Gram still around? I'd love to meet her."

"She passed away five years ago," I whispered. "But at least she got to see me get married. And doesn't have to witness my life falling apart." I gripped the steering wheel. The 1.5 carat princess-cut diamond I still couldn't bring myself to remove glinted in the sunshine.

"Shitty. It sounds like she was a lot of fun. She would have supported you, honey. One day I want to see that video."

"I doubt I will ever let it see the light of day again. Sorry." Another wonderful memory tainted by the dissolution of my marriage.

*****

"Something more age appropriate, Becky," I hissed, struggling to wiggle out of a tight spaghetti-strapped sun dress without tearing it. At Yorkdale, Becky paraded me through various stores and tossed dress after dress into my arms. I rejected them all. We were both losing patience.

"Come on. At least try."

"If I get stuck in one, and you have to remove it with scissors, you're paying for it," I said under the hot glare of the lights and assumed from the silence that she had disappeared again.

I shimmied in the current reject and it was halfway up my arms when another dress sailed over the door, this time landing on my head between my locked arms.

"This one's age-appropriate," Becky said, her sing-song voice trailing off before I could ask for help.

Unable to remove either the dress I was in or the one she'd flung onto my head with my hands, I hopped over to the corner and bobbed my head above the bench. Becky's latest offering sailed down, and I giggled, almost splitting the seams of the dress I was stuck in. When I finally freed myself, I picked it up and discovered it wasn't only a loud, floral print, but a floor-length A-line shaped gown with sleeves. I couldn't fathom why it lived among the skimpy ones. It was hideous.

"How's it going?" Becky asked. "I think we're almost out of options in this store."

"This one is perfect," I said.

"The midnight blue one?"

"I love it." I flung open the door and draped myself over the frame. Wrapped in the floral dress, I ran my hand down my side and smiled.

Her hand flew up to cover her mouth but I could still see her lips twitching.

I burst out laughing. "You should have seen your face. Your eyes almost popped out of your head."

Our howls brought the prim shop owner running. She darted evil looks from beneath her leopard print bi-focals as we wiped tears from our eyes.

"She probably has the same dress at home," Becky whispered when she walked away.

The teenage assistant snorted and slapped her hand to her mouth. She nodded in confirmation before running out front, which set us off again.

"Point taken," I said.

"Here, try this." Becky handed me a black dress she'd been cradling in her arms.

I held it up. "Looks promising."

I wiggled into it and began parading up and down the change room. Becky nodded in satisfaction. I didn't slouch, pull at flimsy fabric, or feel naked. "This is it."

I held out my credit card and avoided looking at both Becky and the teenage girl. I didn't want another giggle fit. But it wasn't giggles I needed to worry about. When the cashier's fingers grazed my card, I snatched it back and struggled to breathe while reality bombarded like a blitz attack. Although I may have saved and kept money separate from my husband, all our credit cards were joint accounts. What if he canceled them?

"What's wrong?" Becky whispered. The manager glared and motioned to the other patrons in line behind me.

I ignored her and fumbled around in my wallet for my remaining cash. Becky grabbed the change and steered me out of the store. She weaved me in and out of Sunday afternoon shoppers while I realized the extent of my credit blunder.

Frank was right. I was stupid about money. It hadn't even occurred to me to get my own credit card yet. It hadn't occurred to me to do a lot of things.

*****

Days had passed since the shopping debacle, and as much as Becky had tried to cheer me up that evening, she left for work the following morning and tiptoed in late at night. I received just a brief text stating she was going out with The Banker. She repeated this daily. I stifled my sobs to avoid her attention when she returned to sleep or shower or gather clothes and pretended to be asleep on the rare occasions she poked her head in.

My lack of financial foresight, distress at the thought of dating, my misplaced attraction to Scott, the loneliness at the bar while Becky flirted, and her disappearing trick after her newfound lust with The Banker had brought clarity to my situation and shoved my shock and denial off a cliff. I landed in a sea of despair.

I rolled over and stared at the little black dress hanging on the closet door. The tags dangled, taunting me about my financial blunder. I turned away and flicked on the tiny TV. Becky hadn't even noticed I'd carted the ancient relic from her bedroom into mine. Propped up at eye level on two vodka boxes not even two feet away from my bed, the blinding light and booming volume did nothing to drown out my thoughts.

The TV flickered unnoticed while I remained tangled in my duvet and rode the wave of memories.

Frank the Liar was becoming hazy.

Maybe it was because I'd lived with who I thought was Frank the Good for years, not Frank the Liar who I'd only discovered the day I left. Maybe Frank the Liar hadn't been around long enough in my consciousness to sink in, or maybe I was rationalizing, because even though I saw through his manipulating gifts, moods and attitudes, I was determined there was still good. There had to be. Why else would I have married him?

My phone dinged. Becky.

"Can't make it 2nite."

My fuzzy brain noted it must still be daytime. I glanced at the television for confirmation. A talk show. TV was my only reference point. Other than the requirement to emerge from my dark cave to relieve myself or binge on whatever junk food I could find. The clock had been covered by an empty bag of Doritos since Monday.

I couldn't believe Becky was ditching Garden Club. Scott and Adam were away, and Martha had kid duty due to a work event her husband couldn't get out of. I called Mom and Abby in quick succession and left voicemails, almost dropping to my knees in gratitude when I didn't actually have to speak to them. I bailed too, claiming the flu and told them they were on their own.

I channel surfed, waiting for the emotional ping-pong to end and the urge to crawl back and bury my head inside my marital home to disappear. I burrowed beneath the blankets in an attempt to avert disaster. But in the end, disaster found me.

My phone dinged again. I reached over. What other bad news was Becky going to impart?

But it wasn't Becky. It was Frank.

The first contact after weeks of silence. Was he going to yell at me now for taking the bed, his TV, or the grill? Why wait so long? Was he going to ask me back?

I opened the message with a wobbly index finger.

"I miss you."

My fingers flung open like they were spring activated and sent the phone crashing to the floor. I launched myself back onto my pillow, yanked the duvet over my head, and pulled my knees up to my chest to shield my heart from further pain.

Another ding.

I snaked my hand out from under the blanket and snatched the remote. I turned whatever talk show blazed on the screen to an ear-piercing volume.

Ding. The repeat alert. Or it was a new message?

"No, no, no, no, no." I sounded like a wounded animal.

I swiped my hand around the floor beside the bed and eventually grazed the phone with my fingers. I pulled it under the covers with me. The message alert popped up on the screen, illuminating my dark cocoon and blinding me. I unlocked the phone after my eyes adjusted and poked the text message button.

"I love you."

"No, no, no." I threw back the covers and bounded to Becky's room where I chucked the phone on her bed. It bounced in a high arc off the mattress and landed with a thud and crash somewhere on the other side. At least I wouldn't be able to find it in the mess, I thought, vaulting back into my warm bed–the bed that still had pillows arranged on Frank's side so it wouldn't feel so empty.

*****

I crawled around on my hands and knees and ignored the impulse to start tidying Becky's room during my search and rescue mission. I lay flat on the floor, using my fingernails to pluck up the bed skirt, loathe to discover what lurked beneath. I had assumed the phone wouldn't have bounced off the bed and landed below it, but there it was, glaring at me. I sneezed. Dust bunnies the size of tumbleweeds stampeded out around me. I shuddered.

The screen lit up. Another message.

I stretched to reach it. I ignored the putrid scent wafting from beneath my arms. I couldn't wait to be rid of this disgusting room. This unclean house. This life. It was making me lazy. Unclean. I hadn't showered in four days.

I wanted my old life back.

I leaned against Becky's bed and dropped my head in my lap. I forced air into my lungs. A paper bag would have been helpful. My phone lay on the floor between my knees, chirping every few minutes with Frank's text message love song.

I read each one as it rolled in, never hitting delete. My butt grew numb.

The curse of the messenger app we used meant he knew I was reading them. His bombardment continued. I sipped whiskey from the tumbler I'd poured before attempting to locate my phone. No ice.

He still hadn't called.

Forty messages later, the onslaught ended as abruptly as it began. I remained immobile except for my finger, swiping through his messages while I read them all in sequence.

"I miss you." "I love you." "Give us another chance?" "I bought some of your favorite wine by accident the other day." "I think about you all the time." "We should talk." "I miss you."

The next ding startled me after twenty minutes of silence.

"I'm sorry."

Frank had never sincerely apologized for anything. He bought apology presents or said sorry in passing, only to turn things back around to his way. How sincere was a text message apology? And what was he sorry about? Would he change? The phone vibrated in my hand before its next ding.

"I'll change."

I poked at the device still resting on the floor and gulped for air. "Starbucks. 7:00." I hit send and thrust the phone away like it had contacted Ebola. It slid across the hardwood and became tangled in a pair of Becky's yoga pants.

What the hell did I just do?

CHAPTER TEN

Prone to being prompt, I had arrived fifteen minutes early, ordered a latte, and perched on a stool at the counter lining the window. I'd spent more time primping for this meeting with my husband than I did our first date.

I'd showered, shaved, and plucked. I blow-dried my hair, slathered makeup on a face that hadn't seen daylight in days, and painted my fingernails and toes a pale pink shade I found in Becky's room. I tossed multiple outfits aside before selecting a pair of capris, a form fitting T-shirt, and flip-flops. I hadn't wanted to wear something he bought me, nor did I want to wear something new. If I could read into the implications of both, so could Frank.

After my text, he responded "Our house?"

I'd refused. There were too many memories, too much of a chance of falling into old patterns.

I drummed the counter top with my pink nails and bit my lip to prevent a cackle. It was 7:15. If there was any occasion to be on time you, would think this would be it. Frank's disrespect at being late used to irritate me, but now it solidified how stupid I was to think meeting him would be a good idea.

Did I actually believe I had misunderstood, that he would have answers? Did I think he had a valid explanation about everything and that he would change? What was wrong with me? Was I really going to forget the lies, the manipulation, and the disrespect? I should have called Becky for reinforcement, and to rattle off the reasons why I'd left him in the first place. They'd grown fuzzy, as if strangled with mold. But now they had more clarity than the diamond still sparkling on my left hand.

Frank obviously didn't care and had just proved his unwillingness to change. He probably figured I'd leap at the chance to be back in my mutated 1950s housewife role, serving his favorite dinner, finishing his laundry, and cleaning the house.

I almost toppled my stool when I hopped off and kicked it back. A man I hadn't noticed sitting next to me smiled. Handsome, I thought as I brushed past him. I should have introduced myself, flirted, and taken him to my bed. That would fix Frank, banish any fantasies of Scott's abs, and provide me with some much needed tension relief. His blond hair and blue eyes would have been a welcome escape from the dark men I seemed to fancy.

I stalked to the door and froze. Now twenty-five minutes late, Frank sauntered up the street, his lips puckered in a whistle. I launched the door open and stalked out to the sidewalk.

"Sorry I'm late. I came straight from work and there's construction on Yonge," he said, tossing his hands in the air.

"I guess I'm not worth being on time for?" I said, shrugging.

"Come on, babe. You know there's more traffic with all the summer construction."

"You could have adjusted your commute time. So much for changing."

We stared at each other. Two feet physically separated us, but a gorge miles wide stretched between us emotionally.

"Forget it," I said. "This was a terrible idea. There's no way this is going to work."

"Rose, don't be like that. We're here. Let's talk," he said, catching my arm as I pushed past him.

I yanked my shoulder back to dislodge his hand. It didn't budge.

"Don't run away from me," he said, his fingers clenching for emphasis. His voice carried a threatening tone I had never heard from him before.

Speechless, I took in his white knuckles and the skin on my arm blooming with blotchy red patches beneath his grasp.

"Excuse me," said a deep male voice. "Do you need some help?"

I swiveled my head to find the same icy-blue eyes which had twinkled and crinkled when he smiled at me in Starbucks now conveying alarm.

We all looked down at Frank's hand cemented around my arm.

Aware of the scene unfolding–and presumably the implications of our separation–Frank thrust my arm away. It swung back and forth by my side. "My wife and I have some things we need to discuss, so if you'll excuse us." He snaked his arm around my waist and propelled me down the sidewalk.

My feet shuffled forward until my brain caught up, and I rediscovered my voice.

"No. I told you we're done," I said, my thundering voice stunning several sidewalk patrons. Others gawked. I didn't care. I was grateful for the public arena. I wrenched myself away from Frank's grasp and stalked back to my rescuer, who appeared ready to charge. I adored him already. And I didn't even know his name.

"We're separated," I said, approaching Blue Eyes. I turned around to face my spluttering husband. He may as well have been foaming at the mouth, he'd grown that repulsive to me. "Frank. Leave."

"But..."

"Now."

My knight in shining armor pulled out his cell phone.

"I'll call the cops," he said, rolling his thumb over the numbers.

"You don't have to. There's one right there," I said, pointing south to an idling blue and white police cruiser stuck in traffic. I also noticed the construction signs. Frank hadn't been lying. But he sure made his point. I rubbed my throbbing arm.

"You'll regret this, Rose."

"Is that a threat?" I said in unison with Blue Eyes. He draped his arm around my shoulders. I leaned in for comfort. And maybe a little bit of spite.

Bug-eyed, Frank turned on his heel and stomped down the sidewalk.

"Do you want me to call someone?" Blue Eyes asked after we watched Frank storm down the street and climb into his sports car.

"Rose," I said, turning to face him. "My name's Rose. Thank you. And really, all I want is a drink. Can I buy you one?"

*****

Becky burst into my room.

I remained mute as she surveyed me, and then the room. Half-empty mugs lined my night stand and were accompanied by empty water bottles and the crinkly wrappers that had once contained chocolate and chips. I had devoured every snack I could find that Becky had stocked in the house.

Becky sniffed and wrinkled her nose.

I rolled over and faced the wall to avoid her wandering gaze. Five days had passed since meeting Frank and stumbling home after drinks with my hero. I had barely left my bed since–and not because I'd brought Blue Eyes home to it.

I heard Becky's bare feet slap the stairs. The front door slammed.

Twenty minutes later I heard her return. I rolled back over to face her and found my mother standing in the door clutching her pearls. Becky's face popped up over her left shoulder.

Mom lowered herself down beside me while Becky stood rocking back and forth in front of the TV, nibbling her thumbnail. Concerned glances darted between them. I picked up the remote, punched mute, and slumped back down, resigned to my lecture.

"Rose, honey. I know this has been difficult. You're certainly allowed to deal with it however you choose."

"Uhm..." Becky tried to interrupt.

"Let's have you go get in the shower today," Mom continued, ignoring her. "Then you can crawl back into bed."

I nodded and pushed back the covers. I would have done anything knowing I had permission to go back to bed.

When I returned, my night table was void of all emotional crisis debris, the curtains were flung back, and the window opened. Mom finished tucking the last corner of fresh sheets on the bed and handed me pajamas without saying a word. I dressed while she fluffed the duvet and folded it down.

I crawled back in.

"Cup of tea?" she said, pulling the blanket up over my shoulders and kissing the top of my head.

I nodded and reached for the remote.

*****

The sound of voices wafted up from downstairs the next night, along with the scent of my mother's roast beef. My appetite roared back with a long, low grumble. I pulled on my robe and shuffled downstairs. I stopped outside the kitchen. Becky and Mom chatted and laughed as they chopped and stirred.

Mom pressed a hand over her heart and exhaled when she saw me. "Feel up to joining us?"

Becky grabbed another wine glass and waved it around with a hopeful smile.

I nodded and took a sip when she passed it to me. It felt like battery acid on my empty stomach.

I set it down, placed both palms flat on the counter, and glared at them. "You both lied to me. You said it would get easier. It's not. All I've wanted to do is run back to him. And I almost did…" I trailed off, shaking my head.

"But you haven't," Mom said. "You're strong and you'll get through this step. This is the hard part. You don't have to believe me now, but it's true."

"Cheers, Rose. You've made it out of bed. Pretty good timing too. Your mom's roast smells out of this world. I should have given her the key to check up on you earlier," she said, practically drooling. It was no wonder. I'd left her without dinners for a while. Then again, over the last few days I never knew when she'd be around.

"Where's The Banker?" I asked, unable to keep the hurt from my voice.

Becky studied the floor before looking up at me, her eyes glistening. "I'm sorry. I didn't think. I shouldn't have left you here all alone. I didn't even think to call your Mom."

"Well, I suppose you shouldn't have to babysit me."

"No. But you're my first real friend in years and I ditched you. I ditched you for a guy like a love-struck teenage girl. It seems I still have a lot to learn too."

"Fine," I said, leaning over to embrace her. "We both have a lot to learn. It probably still would have happened though. I might still have gone to meet him."

"Excuse me?" Becky said, shoving my shoulders back to make eye contact.

"Oh, dear," Mom said, the sound of her pearls twisting echoed in the silence.

"What have I done? What did you do?" Becky screeched.

"Relax. I was just really stupid. Another item to add to my epic fail list."

"Oh my God. Did you sleep with him?" Becky demanded.

I shuddered and shook my head.

"Thank God," Becky said, reaching for her wineglass and tipping it back to drain half the glass.

"That would have been a terrible mistake, dear." Sex was not a topic Mom and I used to discuss, but Becky's uninhibited chatter had bridged that gap. I still wasn't sure if I was a fan.

Instead of the shadow of silence I had stumbled around in for a week, I was relieved to have someone to talk to again and the story tumbled from my lips, from Frank being late to the hours I spent tucked away in a booth at the local pub with Blue Eyes.

"I'm a shit friend. I shouldn't have abandoned you, especially knowing how terrible the first couple of months are," Becky said after we finished laughing at the timing of the police car.

"I think it needed to happen. At least now I can see him clearly without the haze of 'what ifs.'"

"You still should have called me."

"I know. I didn't…" I paused, unsure why I hadn't. "You're right. I should have. Maybe I'm not used to having a best friend around I can depend on either."

"You girls," Mom said. "You're very lucky to have found each other. Don't ever lose that."

With a wide grin, Becky grabbed my hand and squeezed. "We won't."

"And you can call me too, Rose," Mom said, her voice faint and tinged with hurt.

"Oh, Mom. You're right, I should have called you, too. I'm sorry," I said, grabbing the hand that had resumed the pearl twirling and giving it a gentle squeeze.

She sighed. "I didn't want to intrude. But I should have checked in with you more frequently."

"Not forcing me to do anything but shower and go back to bed yesterday really helped."

"That was Gram's technique. After your dad died, when she told me to stay in bed as long as I wanted, I turned around and did the opposite. I hoped you'd do the same. It seems we all have a little stubborn streak in us, not wanting to do what our mothers tell us."

"Preaching to the choir over here," Becky said, waving.

"Well, whatever you did, it worked. So can we all stop feeling guilty about what we did and didn't do, learn from it, and move on? Because I think I'm going to go have another shower now and I'd love to hang out down here today if you two giggling girls don't mind."

"Thank God. Now I don't have to question my decision to take you in off the street," Becky said, smacking my ass on the way out.

*****

"So, what's he like, this blue-eyed guy?" Becky asked, shoving a chunk of roast beef in her mouth.

"His name is Alex. He's nice. Thirty-seven, never married, loves dogs and kids. Has a niece he adores. He even showed me pictures. Not a workaholic, but loves his job."

"Hot?"

I nodded and told them everything I had learned about Alex. He was born in England in the same town as Gram, and moved to Toronto when he was two. He told me he still tries to visit as much as possible. We talked about our European travels and how we both loved the idea of sitting on the beach as much as a sightseeing adventure. He kept fit through running and cycling. Not one for the gym, he told me, sipping his Guinness. I had to force myself to look away from his understanding and compassionate gaze more than once. Our conversation flowed, along with the rounds I kept buying, and I managed to temporarily forget about my interlude with Frank.

Becky held her glass up in a toast after I filled them in. "He sounds perfect. Please tell me you exchanged numbers."

I nodded. It had been the only awkward part of the night. He asked if he could call me and I suggested I get his phone number and call when I was ready.

"Good girl. Now, does he have any single friends?" Becky asked, tipping her chair back.

I shrugged.

"You're going to call him, right?"

"Wait, what about The Banker?"

"Just keeping my options open."

I rolled my eyes. "Maybe at some point. It's still too early. I need to wrap my head around everything with Frank first, figure out how not to make the same mistakes."

"Plenty of time for that. But don't make him wait too long," she warned.

"I know, I know," I said, fully aware it was too soon, but wondering if I'd ever be ready. Alex seemed perfect. We had a fantastic connection. It wasn't awkward or uncomfortable. He didn't push me to talk about Frank. He was a perfect gentleman, holding doors and offering to walk me home. He never once suggested anything inappropriate. When I left him on the street corner, unsure about having a stranger know where I lived–however nice he seemed–I felt a pang of regret. I wished the timing had been different and that he hadn't seen me at my worst with Frank. He hadn't seemed bothered by it though, and maybe that was better than having to explain it all to a relationship contender.

If I ever got up the nerve to call.

CHAPTER ELEVEN

"You need to get these in the ground," I said, pointing at the multi-colored flat of impatiens wedged into the corner of the backyard. I had kept them alive with regular watering since arriving at Becky's and was tired of staring at their sad existence. I wouldn't be able to resist the urge to plant them much longer. They were begging for a permanent home.

"If you plant these, I promise I'll go to my mother's tomorrow night and let you go out with The Banker in peace. Then you won't have to wait until Saturday to see him."

She picked at her lip and remained silent.

"Becky? You're not thinking of ditching Garden Club again this week are you? Or cards? Adam will be devastated if he can't gloat all night about your latest win and Scott will be disappointed at not being able to grill. Plant these. Go out with The Banker tomorrow. Surely you can survive the following two nights without him."

"Maybe."

"Maybe what? That you won't cancel or that you can't survive without him?"

Becky stared off in the distance, her eyes glazing over. "He's amazing."

"Obviously."

"I don't want to lose him."

"By not seeing him for two days? Unless he's a sex addict, I don't think you have anything to worry about."

"The sex is insane," she said, her voice full of wonder like she'd discovered the meaning of life. More like the Kama Sutra.

"Glad to hear it. Or, you know, not hear it now that you stay at his place."

She giggled. "I'm having issues with the pink. It clashes with the red door. Maybe I should go buy more? Maybe red and white? That would look great for Canada Day, although it doesn't give them much time to grow. Then I can arrange all these ones in clumps by shade of pink back here?"

"A lot of people bunch them together regardless of color. It can be pretty."

"Sure. But I'm not most people," she said, kneeling down in front of the two flats.

"You most certainly are not. One woman I knew had what she called a holding garden. She planted everything there until she knew where its final destination would be. Mainly for perennials."

"Those grow each year, right?"

I smiled. My instruction wasn't a dismal failure. "You'll be a gardening pro in no time."

"You're a great teacher. Sorry if I'm making you crazy."

"You're not. And thanks."

"No, really," Becky said, settling back on her thighs. "It suits you. You'll be a great mom."

The dregs of the bottle of beer I'd been sipping went straight up my nose. I spluttered and coughed.

"Sorry," Becky said, tossing over her bottle of water.

"No one has ever said that to me before," I said when I recovered. "Not even Frank. What husband doesn't tell his wife she'd make a great mother? Unless he doesn't think she will be? Or maybe if he wasn't considering her to be the mother of his children? I guess my mom has told me, but that doesn't really count. Of course your mother would say that to you."

Becky grunted. "Not my mother. She's actually told me several times over I'd be a terrible mother."

"That's horrible."

"That's not even the worst of what she's said to me. We don't see our parents much anymore."

"I'm sorry. I didn't know," I whispered, mortified at my blunder.

"You're lucky your mom is so cool."

"I never really thought about it before, but I guess you're right."

"Right about what?" boomed a deep voice from inside.

I leaped off the love seat, somehow managing to stifle my scream. A bundle of fur and yelps bolted out and brushed past my legs. Scott followed.

"Can you please stop scaring the shit out of my friend?" Becky said, smacking her brother's arm before crouching down and covering Buddy the Beagle with kisses.

My heart throbbed at the fright. And maybe because I kept forgetting how good-looking Scott was until he reappeared. How tall. How sexy he looked in jeans and a T-shirt. How perfect his smile was. Or maybe I hadn't forgotten. Maybe after the Frank incident and the certainty I felt about my decision I was more fully aware, more open to ideas.

"Sorry, I didn't mean to scare you again," Scott said.

"You know you're not supposed to use your key unless it's an emergency."

A key? He had a key?

"It is. Rose needs cheering up. Becky said you were feeling pretty down lately, and you told me how much you loved dogs, so I thought I'd bring Buddy by for a visit."

I smothered my face into the dog, desperate to avoid thoughts of Scott unlocking the door and making his way up to my bedroom.

"Thanks. He's really cute."

"Adam wanted to come too, but he had a date."

Becky sucked the air in between her teeth. "That boy wouldn't know how to settle down if it smacked him sideways. You're two peas in a pod."

"I just haven't met the right woman yet."

Was he staring at me when he said that? I surrendered my attention again to Buddy, who was hopping around on his hind legs in front of me.

"You're very cute, Buddy. He's so tiny for a beagle."

Becky snickered.

"A little bit of a mix-up," Scott said, twisting the leash around in his hands.

"Buddy's a she." Becky burst out laughing. "Scott didn't find out until his first vet appointment."

"By then it was too late," Scott said, shrugging. "She already knew her name was Buddy."

I raised my hand to cover my mouth, hoping to hide my amusement. I didn't want to laugh at his expense. But Becky's laughter was contagious. Scott's lips twitched, betraying his composure, and when he succumbed seconds later I couldn't contain myself any longer. Buddy cocked her head and began running around us in circles.

"Buddy's a babe magnet," Becky said after we calmed down. "One walk along the boardwalk in The Beaches and he's got a dozen numbers."

"Well, not quite, little sister. It doesn't hurt though."

"Please," Becky said, waving his statement away. "A woman sees a single man with a dog and thinks 'keeper.' If he's mature and responsible enough to look after another living thing and is loving and kind to his pet, he'll treat her the same way."

"Really? Is that what women think?" Scott asked, turning to me.

Frank had never wanted a dog, or a pet of any kind. Was Frank responsible? Nope. Loving? No. Kind? Negative. Mature? Guess not.

"What do I know? I've been single all of two minutes. It does make sense though."

"Of course it does," Becky said, sliding open the door. "Do you want a sweater?"

"Please," I called out to her retreating frame.

Scott turned to me, his eyebrows furrowed. He cleared his throat. "It takes a while, doesn't it? I remember wondering if she would ever get off my couch. Buddy sure loved having her around though."

I could only hope Becky had spared him the gory details of my last week in bed. Particularly my hygiene lapse.

"You'll get through it, little bird. And you'll have guys falling all over you once you're ready to fly again."

"Thanks," I mumbled, staring at the patio doors and willing Becky to return.

"You will. I promise. And when you're ready..." Scott paused and leaned over with a hand raised. He smelled like cinnamon. I locked my knees to keep them from buckling and opened my mouth but no sound came out.

"Make sure you check your hair and face," he said, swiping his thumb over my cheek and pulling a maple key out of my hair.

I couldn't tell what burned more, my blush or his touch.

*****

That week, the Garden Club resumed at our place with all members present.

"Come for dinner on Sunday, Rose. I'm making a roast," Mom said. "You can help me pull out some more weeds."

"Sure."

"Every Sunday. You're all welcome to come. Just tell me by Friday so I can buy a roast that's big enough."

"Do we have to pull weeds too?" Adam asked, scratching his head. He looked like he was debating the torture of weed pulling in exchange for a home-cooked roast.

"Weeding is not mandatory."

Everyone laughed, thanked her, and said they might one day.

Martha pointed at me. "Monday you're mine," she said, reaching to slide a chunk of Brie onto a cracker before continuing. "I want to check out the new craft store and get some stuff for the kids. It might give me an hour of peace this summer. You're coming with me."

"Tuesday!" Becky said, almost spluttering her wine. "Reality TV drinking games."

"Wednesday," Scott said, nudging Adam who nodded in agreement. "We'll go mini-golfing or something."

"Thursday's Garden Club," Abby said.

"Friday is cards," I said, shaking my head. "What is this? An intervention? A prevention?"

"You're on your own Saturday," Becky said. "So no, it's not. We just thought you might like some company. You'll be alright Saturday though, right?"

"Of course she will be," Scott said, adding "Big Bird," under his breath.

I glared at him. "I'll be fine. I have you all on speed dial though, so keep your phones on Saturday night in case things get rough."

Buoyed by the Garden Club and a kick-ass game of cards the following evening where Scott and I regained the Euchre title, I spent Saturday evening at home. I curled up with a bottle of wine, a bowl of popcorn, and the latest Leonardo DiCaprio drama. Halfway through, Mom called. A text from Becky arrived twenty minutes later, shortly after which Martha phoned to confirm Monday, and then Abby rang to ask if I wanted to pick up a shift the following week.

I waited a few more minutes to make sure the interruptions were done before settling back into the movie.

Ding.

I hesitated before picking up the phone, still petrified every time a text message arrived that it might be Frank.

I unlocked the phone and felt a wide grin stretch across my cheeks. I opened the message.

A photo of Big Bird in all his yellow-feathered glory popped up on my screen.

I laughed a deep belly laugh that hadn't seen daylight for a while. Neither had the light, fluttery feeling of hope swirling around my heart.

*****

"What's for dinner?" Becky asked after kicking off her heels and slipping on flip-flops. She reached into the fridge and grabbed the bottle of wine I'd uncorked earlier.

"Chicken with wild mushroom and balsamic cream sauce," I said, watching her refill my glass and pour her own while I stirred. "Take it easy or you'll be hung over tomorrow after all the reality TV drinking we have slotted for tonight. The previews for *The Bachelorette* foreshadow some heavy drinking if I remember your rules correctly. I may need a refresher."

"Okay," she said, falling quiet while she sipped.

"Good day?" I asked.

"Mm-hmmm." She averted her eyes while I piled pasta onto plates. She didn't even lunge for her dinner when I placed it in front of her, but continued staring out the window instead. Her silence was even more unusual.

"What's going on?" I asked, my mouth running dry. Something was definitely wrong.

"Oh, nothing," she said.

"Come on, Becky. Spill it. We've been through enough not to be able to trust each other. Didn't we learn that last week?"

"I just don't…" She trailed off.

I refilled her wineglass. "Fortify your nerves."

"It's not my nerves I'm worried about," Becky mumbled.

I looked at her, confused.

She sighed, grabbed the bottle, and filled my glass until it was spilling over the edges. "Please don't hate me for this."

"You're scaring me now. What's going on?"

"Frank's on Singles Shack," she blurted out, peering at me over her glass.

"What?"

"Frank's on Singles Shack, the dating website I showed you last week. Remember? I recognized him from the wedding picture you were staring at when we moved your stuff. It's, uh, the same picture of him, actually…" She trailed off.

"What?"

"I wasn't going to say anything, but worried if you signed up without telling me you might stumble across him. Don't do that by the way. Don't sign up for any of these sites without me. There are some freaks out there. I'll help you sort them out…"

"Let me see it," I demanded, interrupting her babbling.

"Seriously?"

"Yes. Laptop," I said, pointing to it.

Becky obliged and pushed her plate to the other side of the table so she could set the laptop in front of her. She fired it up, logged on, and navigated to the site and her profile.

I stared at one half of the wedding photo I once cherished.

Becky extended two fingers out beside her where my wine glass hovered in mid-air. She touched the bottom and pushed it up to my lips. I gulped.

"And I thought my ex-husband was an asshat. I can't believe his sign-up date was just days after you left him."

The bottom flopped out of my stomach like it had been dropped down an elevator shaft.

"Excuse me?"

"Shit. I shouldn't have told you that part," she said rubbing her temples.

"No, I…"

"If you signed up and found him, you would have figured it out anyway, though."

"No, I…"

"Men are bastards."

"No, I'm glad you told me," I said when she finally shut up. "And really, we hate all men now?"

"Well, it shows the caliber of men on here. Not sure I want to have anything to do with them now."

"They can't be all bad. Can they?"

"Honey, you believe what you want. My experiences so far haven't been positive."

"Wait, why are you back on there? What about The Banker?" I asked.

The laptop emitted a high-pitched beep, signaling a new message on her profile.

"What idiot wants to talk now?" she said, opening the message. Her wine glass teetered precariously next to the keyboard when she lurched to slam the laptop shut. After her glance back at me she cursed, knowing she hadn't been fast enough.

"That was from Frank," I whispered, snatching her glass and downing it. I barely even registered her nod in response. "I saw the picture. Did he really write that?"

"Now I'm really going to close my account."

"He actually wrote that? 'You look like a screamer?' He wrote that to you?"

Becky let out a long, low whistle.

"Take this away," I said, shoving my plate at Becky. "And Jack me. Four fingers. No ice."

Becky complied with my command, spluttering off a string of expletives that would have made a sailor proud. She bashed Frank and cursed all men, stopping short of swearing them off altogether. When she finished her tirade, she regarded me for a moment while nibbling her thumbnail. "You can't sit here and stare at that screen all night. Forget *The Bachelorette*. We're going to see your mother."

She grabbed the uncorked bottle of wine she was about to open and dragged me out of my seat. By the time we arrived, the fury I felt could have fueled the entire NASA space program or ended the oil crisis. Possibly even both.

I bolted down the side of my mother's house and tumbled into the garden. I yanked, tossed, and slammed the trowel onto the earth until my back ached and my hands were raw and caked with mud. I heard the hushed tones of Becky and my mother and looked over to the deck. I shielded my eyes with a hand from the floodlights. Had that much time passed? I blinked. I hadn't asked for the light. I would have continued in the dark, the blackness keeping my angry thoughts company.

I sprung up and strode to the porch, my knees creaking with each step. I dropped into a chair and drained the bottle of water Mom handed me. She passed over a glass of wine. I slurped. My anger storm had blown over and I felt remarkably calm.

"I wish I never knew," I said.

"I'm sorry," Becky repeated, as she had over and over since divulging the information.

"Don't be," Mom snapped. "Rose, you needed to find out. It may not feel like it, but this will help you through the process. This, combined with last week, should cement your decision. I'm so sorry I never realized how bad it was."

"How could you? I didn't even fucking know. Sorry," I added for my colorful language.

"You didn't seem yourself after a few years, but I didn't say anything. I didn't want to pry and figured you would come to me when you were ready. I should have intervened sooner." She reached over and squeezed my hand.

"Mom, if you had, I would have pushed you away. I don't think I was ready to hear it."

"Maybe you're right. But I still wish I had."

Becky had watched the exchange in silence. "I wish my mother cared that much about me. Mine refused to let me come home after I 'trashed my marriage.' Divorce was never an option in my strict Catholic family."

Mom sighed. "Mothers make mistakes, Becky. There's no manual and it's the most difficult job in the world. I'm really sorry you didn't have the support you needed, though."

Becky shrugged.

"You're welcome here anytime if you ever want to talk to an old motherly type. I come complete without lectures."

"Thanks," Becky said.

"Your mother may have regrets," Mom persisted.

"If that's true, she could at least pick up the phone."

"It's hard to admit mistakes. Even harder to apologize."

Becky snorted. "I apologized for disappointing her, told her how terrible he was. She didn't listen. She didn't care. Marriages should end in coffins rather than divorce, according to my mother."

Mom's eyebrows shot up and she met my own worried glance. She turned back to Becky. "Did he hurt you?"

"I didn't mean it that way. We argued like crazy and there was a lot of screaming and it wasn't always his fault. He wouldn't have put me in a coffin though if that's what you're thinking. I meant it in a more 'death do us part' way."

"Thank goodness. Frank never did, did he?" Mom asked turning to me, her voice quivering.

I shook my head. "No. If he had, I would have bolted. This here is all the proof I need to solidify my decision," I said, my fingers tracing the yellowing bruise on my arm, the outline of Frank's fingers still visible. I pushed away thoughts of what might have happened if our meeting had soured in the privacy of our old home.

"I hope so, dear."

"No, I would have. Besides, Frank preferred compulsive lying, confusion tactics, weaseling, and manipulation to get his way. It was subtle. So subtle that I never noticed it."

"I'm glad you're rid of him."

"You and me both, Mom," I said, and for the first time since leaving my husband, I genuinely meant it.

CHAPTER TWELVE

I stared at the commercial, the remote hovering. A young couple strolls through lush gardens when he drops to one knee. She looks shocked, says yes. They beam. Diamonds are forever.

"Are fucking not," I screamed, launching the remote at the TV and somehow missing all fifty-two inches with my terrible aim. It bounced off the chair and fell to the floor with a thunk. I looked around, panting. With nothing else in my immediate vicinity, I yanked off my flip flops and chucked them too. They floated through the air and hit the ground without even a whisper, feet away from their intended target.

Bubbling rage rose up my throat. I quelled the desire to scream. Then I noticed them. My rings. They tore into the soft flesh on my hands as I pumped my fists. I clawed at them, my finger growing raw as I yanked, twisted, and turned the shimmering gold and sparkling diamonds. They wouldn't budge.

Maybe they were forever.

I scampered off the couch, snatched my keys, and marched down the street. I returned to the scene of my rage the previous night and dropped to the ground, this time at a different garden bed in Mom's backyard.

Frank was the most captivating, attentive, and charming man I had ever met. He wasn't a boy. He was a man. When we met he lived downtown in a condo he owned. He could cook and do his own laundry—granted, much of it went to the dry cleaners. He always refused any offer I made to pay. He opened every door for me, including the passenger side of his dark luxury sedan. His compliments extended from my beauty to my competence in the kitchen to how wonderful we were together in bed. And then there were his gifts. No one had ever made me feel so special, wanted, desired, and loved. I had been constricted in a charm cocoon.

I slammed and cracked the shovel down, eviscerating the hard clumps of dry earth until they became dust.

The changes were so subtle I never noticed them. Habits and routines became etched into our daily lives. Frank paid the bills and managed our money while I stayed home and managed our household. I washed his clothes, ironed his shirts, cooked delectable dinners, and kept the house and gardens tidy. I entertained his clients and even fetched him drinks at times.

The image of an immaculate 1950s housewife flashed. I leaned back on my heels.

I imagined her manicured fingers basting a succulent roast, her heels clicking and skirt swishing as she greeted her husband at the door with a crystal tumbler full of whiskey. The bottom of my stomach dropped out when I realized not only had I been responsible for every household chore, but most nights I did this too. Not always a roast, but I did have dinner ready, complete with a bottle of wine breathing. Sometimes even poured. I had done everything she did except look the part. The revelation hit me harder than a kick to the temple from a 1950s housewife's heel.

A shudder slipped down my body. I curled my toes to curb it.

Frank rarely stepped foot into the kitchen or laundry room. Once, after a rare trip away with Mom and Gram to England, he grumbled that our front-loading washing machine was more complicated than an aircraft cockpit. I had been secretly pleased he missed me, he needed me.

Do we all fall into roles that are reinforced and perpetuated over time? Or are there certain areas of expertise we gravitate toward and don't realize until it's too late and an irreversible pattern has been set? Did I do all those chores because I wanted to, or did I feel I had to, or was it simply because I worked part-time? Had Frank come to expect it?

What if I met another self-sufficient man when I started dating? Would I let it happen all over again? Or what if he wasn't? Odds were I'd meet someone who had been married. What if his wife had done everything for him? The curse of dating and mating in your late thirties—you no longer had to worry Mama did everything for him, but that his ex-wife did.

A desperate need for water surfaced. I glanced around, unsure how much time had passed. Mom watched me from the deck.

"I didn't want to startle you. You looked like you really needed that," she called out, descending the steps.

The moan I emitted likely set off every tom cat within a hundred-mile radius.

"Come have some water. I'll make tea," she said, taking my hand and leading me to the porch.

I sunk into a chair bathed in morning sunlight, allowing Mom a seat in the shade. I felt weak, drained, and had difficulty raising the mug to my lips when she brought it to me.

"Sorry," I said.

"Don't be daft. I've been expecting you."

I stared at her.

"You're just like me. And Gram too. You come from a long line of stubborn women who are too busy being strong and can't seem to ask for help. After your dad died, I was miserable for months, and then one day it was like the devil took me over and I wanted to smash everything. If Gram hadn't been there our house would have been torn to pieces. She led me out into the garden where I did exactly what you just did. Then I realized I had to pull it together for you."

"I wish I had someone to be strong for. I wish we'd had kids." My voice cracked and I blinked back tears.

"You need to be strong for yourself. I know you don't want to hear it, but you need to figure out why you were stuck in that situation for so long."

I winced. "He was... I had to...We..." I paused. "I was miserable. But I never knew it. He was terrible. How did I almost go back to him?"

"You were missing the old Frank. The one you fell in love with, not the monster he turned out to be. You missed your life, your home, gardens, having someone to talk to, make decisions with, and fall asleep beside. Someone to nurture and love."

"What if I didn't work hard enough? What if I let this happen?" I whispered.

"What could you have done otherwise to alter the outcome?"

"I don't...I don't know."

"If you'd stayed and let him get away with Lord knows what, you wouldn't have been happy. If you fought back, he would have pushed further and you would have been miserable. I don't see how it could have ended differently, and I think you made the right decision, especially after seeing everything that's happened since. I want my baby to be happy." Tears pooled in the corners of her creased eyes.

"I wish I hadn't been so stupid in the first place. Who knows where I'd be now."

"I can't help but feel responsible."

"How? I chose the bastard."

Her fingers flew to her pearls. She averted her gaze and looked up at the maple tree.

"So, how do I figure out why I stuck around for so long?" I asked.

"You lived much of your life centered around Frank. I'd start with that."

I gasped like she'd sucker-punched me. This realization had crept into my awareness in recent weeks, but that it was so obvious to her was a shock. "That's some tough love, Mom."

"Sorry. But it's for the best."

I nodded.

"You'll figure it all out. It takes time. And then you'll never make that mistake again."

"I won't?" I stared at the shadows and sunlight dancing together on the deck. I didn't share her confidence. Doubts swirled, and I wondered whether I would have the strength not to entangle lives and strangle out my own when I found love again.

"You won't," she said. "I think only good will come of this. You've clearly sailed through depression into the anger phase. Before long you'll find acceptance and move on."

I grunted.

"I'm confident good things will come from this. Like Gram…"

"What about Gram?"

"She had a secret and didn't confide in me until after your dad died. I think you need to hear it now, too. You need to know something good can come from the bad."

"What?" I said, exasperated by her further pause.

"When Poppa died, she was furious for having been left such a young widow with a teenage girl to raise. Our situations were remarkably similar. I'm so glad you're not having to go through that at least."

"Okay. I get it. What happened with Gram?"

"She never went looking for it, but it found her. She found love again."

"What?" I screeched.

"Close your mouth, child. You'll catch flies," she quipped, channeling Gram.

"You sounded just like her then."

Mom smiled. "I had no idea until she told me. They kept their affair secret. It lasted ten years, until sadly he passed away too. She wasn't angry then, but accepted her fate. She turned to the garden.

To us. You were her ray of sunshine and helped her cope more than you know. More than I ever realized. So there is hope, Rose."

"Gram. An affair." I shook my head, trying to take it in.

"Not an actual affair. They just kept it quiet. He was widowed too. She never even told me his name."

"Henry Stapleton," I whispered.

Her eyes widened.

"It must have been. I met him. I couldn't have been more than four or five. We went to Edwards Gardens. He held her hand crossing the lawn and she dropped it, saying, 'Thank you, Henry. I can manage,' when she caught me looking back from where I'd run ahead. He bought us ice cream on the way home."

"Really?"

"Double chocolate fudge. He wiped a smudge off my chin."

"It sounds like he was more familiar than you remember. I wonder how much time the three of you spent together that you can't recall."

"I wish I could remember more. Why did they keep it a secret?"

"I don't really know. She said it was because they were older, both widowed. He had a large family. They didn't think it was appropriate. Maybe they were embarrassed or maybe the secret was too sweet to break their silence."

"Gram wasn't too much for convention, was she? Then why would she have kept it secret? Are you sure he wasn't married?"

"As far as I knew, but she never told me who it was. You filled in that blank. She did tell me she preferred it. She liked not having to clean up after him and do his washing and ironing, but still enjoyed the benefits of a companion and lover."

I shuddered at the gleam in my mother's eyes and resisted the urge to cover my ears and yell "lalalalalala" at the thought of both of them…

"Oh stop," she said laughing.

"Did you ever…" I paused, unsure if I wanted the answer.

She shook her head.

"Why?"

"It never happened for me. I wasn't sure I wanted it to."

"Why?"

"You sound like you're two again with all the 'whys.' Remember what I said about not being able to see inside someone's marriage. Well, it's hard to see inside your own until you're out of it, which you probably realize now. My marriage wasn't perfect either, Rose."

My nodding at the hindsight of a terminated marriage swayed to questions, but she was already walking across the deck. The subject was closed. I reeled at Gram's hidden past and my own mother's apparent secrets.

I followed her inside, but knew better than to broach the subject. I wasn't even sure I wanted to know. "When you were angry, how long did it last?"

"It took a while. But this too shall pass, as Gram would say. Goodness knows I heard it enough. She was right about that. She was right about a lot of things…"

"Like what?"

"How quickly your teenage rebellion would end and what a wonderful woman you'd become. You may be misguided at times, but you're so strong, stronger than I could have ever been in your shoes. You'll figure it all out. But in the meantime, feel free to come over and abuse my garden any time. I could use the help. There are so many gardens here to tend to."

My interest flipped to worry. I'd never once heard her complain there were too many gardens. I glanced at her swollen knuckles while she washed our mugs. How many years did she have left in her to look after this house? She was too young for arthritis to claim her hands but there it was, as knobby as a tree trunk, and it would only worsen even with her medication.

"This too shall pass," she repeated.

I somersaulted into the past where she had stood rooted in the same spot, muttering the same words. The cabinets had become cream-colored, the trendy harvest-yellow appliances from the seventies had turned white, and the walls were now slathered in a rich buttery yellow, but everything else remained the same.

I had never witnessed my mother fall apart after Dad's car accident like she claimed, but I was dealing with my own grief at the time. Eventually our household shifted back to laughter, after long bouts of gardening, cooking, and talking. Gram led the charge, as Mom was guiding me now.

"This too will pass," I mumbled.

My mother's lips turned up into a smile.

*****

I declined Mom's offer for lunch and returned home. I had things to do.

I marched into the kitchen, filled a bowl with cold water, cracked a tray of ice cubes, and dumped them in. I took a deep breath and shoved my left hand in the bowl. When the tingling turned to burning I yanked my hand out and wrapped it in a tea towel. I slathered lotion on my red, blotchy fingers and snatched at my rings. They slid straight off.

I jumped when a car door slammed.

The world hadn't come crashing to a halt.

I stared at the rings that had encircled my finger since Frank crouched down on one knee in the middle of our favorite Italian restaurant on Yonge Street. Mortified by the attention and watchful eyes, it never occurred to me to say "No." The cheer after buoyed us. Two flutes of champagne on the house arrived. "What a great story to tell our grandchildren," Frank had said. If only I knew then that he wanted to wait so long to have children, I would have told him we might not live long enough to meet our grandkids to tell them the story.

The lavish diamond caught the late afternoon sunlight when I held it up. A minuscule polka dot pattern flickered on the wall as I examined it. I had tuned Frank out when he boasted about carat, cut, clarity, and color. I hadn't even wanted a diamond, with their value manipulated by supply and demand, and their impeccable marketing campaign which had been seared into my mind during an advertising lecture. I preferred small, understated rings such as an emerald, which was traditionally thought to preserve love and had long been a symbol of hope. Frank hadn't cared. He refused to listen. And while I worried about walking around with that much bling on my finger and had scolded him for it, secretly his generosity pleased me.

I shook my head, disgusted with myself. It's no wonder he walked all over me. I didn't even stick up for what I wanted as an engagement ring. But how do you tell the man you want to marry the ring he chose isn't what you wanted without offending him? Then again, he should have listened in the first place.

I jingled the rings in my palm, unsure of what to do with them. Do I shove them to the back of my jewelry box? Have the diamond set into a pendant? Did I want the memory of Frank dangling on my chest so close to my heart? Not so much. Do I sell them? Would anyone want to buy a used engagement ring and wedding band, or was that a bad omen? I wouldn't have wanted a used one. But there must be a market for it, especially in this economy. People can't afford to get divorced, so maybe they can't afford brand-new shiny engagement rings either.

I flicked on my laptop. These were questions only Google could answer. I plopped the rings down beside me and began typing. Pawn shops, ask.com articles, how to sell on Craigslist, how not to get scammed on eBay, and "how to sell a used diamond" blog posts flooded my screen.

An hour later, I shoved my chair back and clenched my fist around the rings. I stalked to the patio door, the sharp edges digging into my flesh. I had thought the rings might give me some extra time, but the hassle, aggravation, and constant reminder of my failed marriage while trying to sell them didn't seem worth it. Then there was the value, which Frank had always bragged about. The appraised value.

I could go down and chuck them into Lake Ontario and let someone else discover them and benefit from my bad fortune, I thought while climbing the stairs. Maybe I could bury them in the sand down at the beach and sit and wait for someone else to come across them. Maybe even post a twenty-first century treasure hunt online. I could feel my lips turn up into a smile, surprising myself that one appeared so easily after doing something I thought would be devastating.

I dropped the rings into the drawer of my bedside table and strode downstairs.

Life moved on.

And so did I.

I walked into the kitchen, plopped down at the table with a pad of paper and a purple pen, and began compiling a list of all the companies and accounts I needed to change my address with. I added submitting an application for a credit card and making an appointment with the lawyer about my will. I jotted down "Find a divorce lawyer" on a fresh page so I wouldn't have to look at the words–and so I could avoid the daunting divorce legalities a little longer. I also knew I would scribble way more than one page when I started that step.

Let's start with the easy stuff, Rose, I told myself. One mini step and then another, like I was learning to walk all over again.

I glanced over the list for a place to start. It was two pages long, plus the other page I didn't want to think about.

First, address changes. I started making calls. When the fourth chirpy customer service agent asked whether I wanted directions on how to change my name, I tossed the phone across the room. Then I tossed my cookies.

I clutched the toilet twenty minutes later, but remained determined and desperate to finish the task. I slunk downstairs, grabbed my stack of papers, and returned. I spread the paperwork over the bathroom floor should the violent reaction reoccur, and resumed my calls with the comfort of knowing the toilet was within projectile distance.

Apparently, separating a marital life was like splitting conjoined twins. Changing my name would add several more hours to all those I'd never get back. And then there were all those stupid hours

I had sported a goofy grin assuming Frank's name in the first place. Just as I had assumed I would never be anyone else again, that we would be together forever, and that my husband would uphold his wedding vows. *To assume makes an ass of you and me.* I definitely felt like an ass. A naïve, gullible ass.

When the last item was crossed off the first page, I decided I deserved a break. A champagne break.

"What did you do with your rings?" I demanded as soon as Becky pushed open the front door. From my perch on the stairs, I shoved the glass of sweating champagne at her and waggled my left hand in her face.

"What?" she said, dropping her purse on the bench, grabbing the glass, and sliding down the opposite wall.

"I took my rings off. Now what do I do with them? What did you do with yours?"

"They're upstairs, keeping my underwear company."

"What are you going to do with them?"

She shrugged.

"They're worthless, you know," I said. "Diamonds. About as much value as a car driven off the lot. No one wants a used one. And then there's the 'appraised value' versus the 'retail value,'" I said, contemplating the difference, suddenly wondering whether Frank had bought a used one, where my diamond was really from, and what its value actually was.

"Mine wasn't expensive to begin with, so it doesn't matter," Becky said, interrupting my destructive train of thought.

I told her about my modern-day treasure hunt idea and we giggled while toying with watching from behind some bushes or a tree to see who would be the lucky winner. Seeing someone else's joy at the discovery might have brought more satisfaction than pawning it for some change. Even though the cash would be useful, I would always consider it tainted, blood money from both the blood diamonds and Frank's world.

"I couldn't decide how to mark the occasion. I thought maybe an exorcism, or a fairy dance in the yard. But I think some champagne and good conversation would be best. And cheese. I picked up an assortment along with crackers. Maybe we can order something for dinner?"

Becky twirled her now empty glass in her fingers, her teeth munching her lower lip while she stared over my shoulder.

"What's going on, Becky?" I asked. I knew that nibble and faraway look.

"It's Wednesday. I'm going out. Scott and Adam are taking you mini-golfing. Remember?"

*****

The last thing I wanted to do was see Scott.

After Becky left I sulked out on the patio with my near-empty champagne bottle. Bubbles tickled my nose as I sipped. I was furious for not remembering the boys were babysitting me tonight. And there was no way I could cancel. Becky had made sure of that by calling Scott to confirm before she hopped in the shower. I even heard her state they had to wait here until she got home. I guess I was going to ruin her evening with The Banker after all.

"Rose? Are you back here?" Scott's voice boomed over the fence and sent me leaping from my seat.

I hoped my wobbling was from fright, but there was a strong possibility the last glass of champagne could be the real culprit.

"You're early," I called out, unable to hide my irritation. "Go to the front door."

I headed across the house. It might have been more of a wobble.

"Will you stop scaring the shit out of me..." I said, yanking the door open to a burst of color. Red, pink, purple, and white dahlias covered Scott's face. He didn't bring roses. I almost cried out in relief.

"Sorry to scare you again. These are for the first couple of times. I guess I'll have to think of something for this time," Scott said with a shrug. He passed me the colorful bunch.

"You didn't have to. Thank you," I said. One hand clutched the bouquet and the other smothered my chest to calm its thumping. I couldn't tell if it was from being startled, that he had brought my favorite flowers, or his presence.

"Beer?" I asked.

"Sure," he replied, removing his shoes and lining them up side by side. Frank only ever took his shoes off in the house when they were covered in snow. How did Scott inherit the neat genes and Becky the messy ones?

"Where's Adam?" I asked, to dispel any thoughts of Frank.

"Last minute change of plans. Sorry. You're stuck with just me tonight."

Unchaperoned, wobbly from the bubbly, and desperately depressed. This was not good at all. I snatched the champagne flute I had placed on the counter and drained the last half.

Scott raised his eyebrows and nodded at my glass. "Celebrating?"

I placed my palm flat on the counter and looked at my naked finger before pointing to it.

"You took your rings off. Good for you. That's a big step."

I nodded and attacked the package of flowers. The cellophane wrapper cracked and crinkled.

"These are gorgeous. Thank you. I've always loved dahlias. I always thought if I had a little girl it would be the perfect name," I blurted out. I had never told anyone but Frank my secret name. He'd always hated it. Damn you, bubbly truth serum.

"Dahlia. That's beautiful. Very unique."

I peeked at him from behind one of the strong blooms. His stared outside, his head tilted and his gaze unfocused. I shook my head to clear the image of us holding our baby girl for the first time and pronouncing her Dahlia. I fiddled with the flowers and forced myself to speak. "So, what's on the agenda tonight–besides ensuring I don't drink and dial or drink myself into a coma?"

"Adam wanted to go mini-golfing, but whatever you feel like."

"Can we stay here? I don't feel up to going out." What I really wanted was for him to leave so I could open another bottle of champagne. Or take me upstairs. Who was I kidding? I wanted him to pop open more bubbly and then bonk my brains out.

I shook my head. Stupid champagne. Speaking of alcohol. "I totally forgot to get you a beer. Sorry."

"No worries."

Becky's brother. Becky's brother, I repeated over and over again in my head as I handed him the amber bottle. Our fingers touched, shooting a zing up my arm and vaulting my chant to obsessive levels.

I tipped the rest of the champagne in my glass and shook the bottle to get the last drop.

"Hopefully the storm will hold off and we can sit out here for a while," I said after we settled outside. I swung my legs up onto the love seat and tucked my knees to my chest. "I hate being cooped up inside."

"This place must feel so small compared to your old house. You must really miss your gardens. How is everything? Are you managing here?"

I wrapped my arms around my legs and rested my chin on my knees, still reeling from our grazing fingers. Thankfully, Scott had opted to sit in the adjacent, over-sized chair. "Things are pretty great. Your sister's wonderful." It couldn't hurt to remind him. And myself.

"She is. All except her disgusting eating habits."

I laughed. "I thought it was just me."

"Nope. She's eaten like that forever. She would have made a terrible debutante."

"It's all part of her charm." When had Frank stopped making me laugh?

First the shoes, then the name, and now the laughter. Would I ever stop comparing?

*****

Scott asked about my classes and listened with more attentiveness than I had ever felt from Frank. Frank might have paid attention in the beginning, but the more I thought about it, the more I realized how much he twisted the conversation back to himself or deflected attention away from anything he didn't wish to discuss.

When Scott didn't have to keep up with Becky's banter and Adam's quips, his serious side showed up. It surprised me. I discovered more about his job as a web designer, how much he loved owning his own firm so he could make his own hours, and how it also allowed him to take on some pro-bono work designing websites for smaller charities, including a women's shelter.

"How's Becky doing?" Scott asked eventually, after we both darted glances at the blackening sky due to a long, low rumble of thunder. "How is she really doing?"

"Fabulous, other than work being a pain, which I gather is normal?"

Scott smiled. "She has a love-hate relationship with it, but for some reason she won't look for anything else."

"Her life altered dramatically a little while ago. Maybe she'll shift it again soon."

"You seem to be grasping the move-on attitude much more than she did. You immediately went to add more classes and now you're filling in whenever Abby needs you. You didn't even stop going to the Garden Club."

I shrugged. "I guess I needed to stay occupied. Maybe Becky's job is her way of keeping busy until the dust settles. She seems to be getting along well with The Banker though, so that's positive."

A dark shadow passed over Scott's face.

"What's wrong?"

"She gets carried away sometimes."

"Like ditching us for him?"

"Something like that," Scott muttered and stared at the grill. Ripples wandered over his jaw.

I looked up again. The storm clouds had mingled with the late twilight sky and created a greenish-gray hue. It was eerie.

"I think we should…"

A flash of lightening blazed, illuminating Scott's frown. He looked as shocked as I felt. I shoved my hands toward my ears, but I was too late. A deafening clap of thunder shook the house and set off car alarms.

"Shit," I screeched. Rain drops the size of quarters splattered the patio stones. I leapt out of my seat and snatched the cushion. Scott followed my lead, ramming me with his cushion from behind as I grappled with the sliding door, my dripping fingers slipping on the handle. I finally connected and we tumbled inside as Mother Nature released another round.

"That was crazy!" I shouted.

"More like stupid. We shouldn't have stayed out there so long."

"You were facing the storm front. You could have said something."

"And lose that game of chicken? No way. I would have looked like a wuss."

"Nah, you just would have been safe. Trust me, even if my initial reaction might have been to think you were a wuss, I definitely would have appreciated it after that display," I said, jerking my finger to the door.

I tossed him a tea towel and contemplated the situation. Scott had grown more attractive with every sentence, and not just physically attractive now, although the dark green golf shirt he wore intensified his eyes. I tried to ignore the hair protruding from the collar and the well-sculpted chest outlined beneath his damp shirt. Outside had seemed safer somehow, more public.

"Another beer?" I asked, reaching into the fridge. I felt giddy, almost wild. Maybe almost being struck by lightning did that to a person.

"Last one, I'm driving."

I pulled out two and twisted the caps off. I passed him one and brought the other to my lips, downing half of it before setting it on the counter. Rain pelted the window. I leaned over the sink to peek. The patio was a blurry mess.

I felt Scott brush up against me. I clutched the counter and stifled a yelp. I hadn't heard him over the storm.

We stood side by side and watched the rain turn to hail the size of golf balls and bounce high off the grill. It felt like a cave of long-dormant bats was whirling through my belly at his proximity and I forced myself to ignore the heat radiating between us.

Scott turned and flared his dimples. "Rose…"

I reached a hand out and grazed one of his dimples. His eyes went wide before the dimple grew deeper. I pressed my toes into the floor and raised my body to meet his lips.

We leapt apart when another house-shuddering clap of thunder exploded. I had no idea how long had passed. My ears buzzed and my lips burned.

"Is that normal?" I whispered. "How is it possible that I never… I don't… Wow."

"I know," Scott mumbled.

We stared at each other, panting. I looked away, suddenly wondering what the hell I was doing.

Scott didn't let me think for long. He gathered my hair behind me and kissed my neck. He nibbled his way up to my earlobe, my kryptonite. I gasped. He pulled away, his fingers cupping my chin. He searched my face and then reached down for my hands without breaking eye contact and entwined our pinky fingers.

"We don't have to do this," he said, pulling my hands up and beginning to kiss my fingers one by one. "I want to. I've wanted to from the moment you screamed in the hall. But we don't have to. Not now. Not ever if you don't want."

"Less talking. More kissing," I said, yanking his head back down.

Eventually, I tore myself away and took his hand. I lead Scott down the hall and up the stairs where I slammed my bedroom door shut.

Screw the consequences. I had always played by the rules and look where that got me.

CHAPTER THIRTEEN

Only two days had passed, but I couldn't handle it any longer. Guilt flared. Not only did I have sex with the first man I laid eyes on after leaving my husband–*while* leaving my husband–but I had sex with Becky's brother. I couldn't figure out which was more disturbing. Then guilt would transition to memories and daydreams. Flashes of Scott's body, his whispers, and our murmurs and groans, continued to propel heat to my cheeks and bottom out my belly. Attempts to banish them proved useless. They cascaded into my consciousness like gentle waves caressing the coast.

I wanted more.

I snatched my purse and hopped in the truck.

Becky was right when she said it would cure my withdrawal. Frank had barely broken into my consciousness since. But now I needed a patch for my patch.

I rang the bell and then pounded on the door. The barking frenzy further announced my arrival.

"I had sex with Becky's brother," I blurted out before Martha even cracked the door an inch.

"Holy crap." She shoved the dog aside and ushered me in.

"I really need to talk about this. Obviously I can't talk to Becky. Sorry to just show up. I should have called."

"Don't worry," she said, leading me into the kitchen.

I followed behind, silent.

"Lucky girl. He's damn cute," Martha said with a sigh.

My head bounced around like a bobble head. "Too cute. Total mistake. I can't stop thinking about him. What have I done?" I moaned, slumping into a chair. Buster rested his head in my lap and I ran my hand over his golden fur before scratching the sweet spot beneath his collar. His back leg began twitching as he leaned into my thigh.

"Maybe you needed to? To move on," Martha said with a shrug. She plopped the kettle on the stove.

"But with Becky's brother? I should have called that guy who saved me from Frank or started dating or even picked up some random guy. So stupid." I averted my gaze and landed on the refrigerator. Family photos, paintings, reminder notices, and colorful magnets dotted every inch. Would I ever have a fridge like that?

"So, what happened?" Martha asked, interrupting my downward slide into more disturbing thoughts. "Wait, when did this happen?"

"Wednesday, when he was supposed to be babysitting me."

Her mouth dropped open. "You hid that well during Garden Club yesterday."

"I can't believe you didn't notice. I could barely look at him, let alone stand in the same room. I bolted away every time he came near me."

"I didn't notice a thing. But that's probably because I had my nose tucked into the Brie again. Don't ever give me your melted walnut topping recipe or I'll have to kill you."

I blew out a breath. "Thank God you didn't notice. I've been worrying Becky might have caught on and I have another Academy Award to win tonight when the guys come over to play cards." I dropped my head in my hands. "What have I done?"

"Yes, what have you done? Fill me in, please."

As I told her, Martha oohed and ahhed in all the right places and asked for details I grew shy about revealing, but eventually divulged.

"Mmm. Good for you," she said, nibbling her lip and staring at the wall.

"Uh, Martha?"

"Sorry. Living vicariously. And that was better than my trashy romance novels any day. Too much information?" she added with a chuckle. "I guess we haven't known each other long. Oh well, no harm done. Sex. We may be of different ages, married or single, have kids or not, or have different hair and shoe sizes, but it's one of the common denominators among women... Speaking of which, how was his shoe size?"

"Perfect." I grinned.

"Fantastic. Nothing more disappointing than unwrapping a stubby pencil. What was I saying? Oh right. We may have kids and husbands or be single and chasing men, but it all comes down to sex. Married women talk about our lack of it and how a weekend away rekindles romance or how his doing the dishes revives a failing libido. Single women complain about not getting any, or it's all he wants and never calls once he gets it. We always want what we don't have. Single women want the sexual security of married life and married women long for the passion and spark of a new relationship. Women would have nothing to talk about if it wasn't for sex."

"We'd still have shoes."

Martha laughed. "Yes, but nothing bonds us more than a good gossip about our romps."

"Any ideas on how I can banish all my naughty thoughts of him?"

"Why on earth would you want to do that?"

"So I don't do it again."

"Would it be so bad?"

"No. It would be fantastic. That's the problem. Once is a one-off, it can be explained away. But twice? I don't think there's any going back from that. Besides, Becky would kill me."

"Are you sure?" she asked, eying me over her World's Greatest Mom mug.

"I'd be rebounding on her brother. It couldn't lead to anything good. I don't want to lose my first girlfriend in years."

"What did you tell him?"

"That it wasn't a good idea," I said, wincing at the memory.

I had untangled our entwined limbs before speaking. "You need to leave before Becky gets home. I'm a terrible liar and she'd know the instant she saw us. Please."

"Sure, use and abuse me."

Heat crept through my cheeks. I was far from that kind of girl.

He grinned. "Okay, Rosie. Are you going to call me?"

I groaned. "This was a bad idea, Scott."

"Just tell it like it is," he said, beginning to collect his clothes from the floor. "I'm a big boy."

I ached to kiss him again, but I knew the wonderful place we would end up. I also knew Becky might arrive home any second. I collected his socks from the floor and handed them to him. "Becky's your sister. It would be too complicated."

"You sure?"

"I'm not ready."

"Really? Cause this…" he said, pointing back and forth between us, "is intense."

I could only bob my head up and down to confirm my stance.

Scott frowned before dropping down and kissing my cheek. I remained motionless as he bounded down the stairs. When the front door clicked I bolted into action, petrified Becky would have some form of laid-dar and know what transpired the second she saw me. I splashed water on my still flushed face, rubbed cream and concealer into my raw chin, and ran a brush through my tangled hair. I ran back to my room, took a deep breath of the sweat-filled air one last time, and yanked open the window. I resisted the urge to crawl back into my bed and lounge in Scott's scent still lingering on the sheets. I pulled the duvet up instead and dropped down to relive the evening until Becky's key jingled in the lock.

"Are you sure this is what you want?" Martha asked, releasing me from my reverie.

I nodded and swallowed the lump in my throat away. "It's the only way. Now, I just need to get through tonight."

*****

The temptation to cancel cards by claiming an emergency with my mother so I could run over there to hide held immense appeal. But I knew I had to face the situation. I couldn't avoid Scott forever. And my mother wasn't a convenient cover. They might hightail it over there to check up on us.

I picked at a hangnail and sighed.

"I smell wood burning in there," Becky said, reaching over and tapping my head. My mother was rubbing off on her already. The phrase was a staple during my youth.

"Just thinking about the classes." I stood and dumped my coffee in the sink. I hated lying to her.

"Have you come up with any new ideas?"

"I'm stumped. There are only so many times we can offer the veggie and herb classes and introductory classes."

"What about more specific classes, like for roses and whatever?"

"Abby and I talked about that. I'll do it, but for some reason it doesn't hold as much appeal," I said, yanking open the dishwasher and jamming dishes inside. Where had my zest for teaching the classes gone? Was it possible the small scale classes had lost their appeal after I realized the plethora of possibilities before me?

"Rose doesn't know what to do with herself," Becky announced once we settled into our respective Euchre places, and proceeded to fill them in on my classroom boredom.

"Go back to school," Scott suggested, and threw down an ace with a wink.

My libido leapt and my belly danced a jig. I looked away from his golden forearms, tanned from rounds of golf and Sunday afternoon baseball games, and tried not to think how easily they flipped me over.

"School? Uh, no thanks," I said, wrinkling my nose.

"Think about it. What if it was the opportunity to do what you love and gave you freedom?"

"I suppose, but I'm way too old to be going back to school."

"You're never too old to learn something new," Scott said.

"That's what you taught during my first gardening class," Becky said in a squeal. Whether it was for proving Scott's point or winning the hand of cards, I couldn't tell. She high-fived Adam over the table.

I sighed. "I know, but that was a small class for fun. I've thought about it, and I don't think a massive educational undertaking involving years of study is what I need right now." The idea of landscape design courses or a horticultural degree had resurfaced in the last few weeks for the first time since mentioning it to Becky sometime during those early days. The days following my marital exodus had grown fuzzier than mold-covered cheese, but some thoughts and ideas grew ripe with age. I knew Scott was right, but I didn't feel up to starting over. I'd had enough new beginnings already this year.

"It's not bad. I did it," Scott said.

My look of surprise must have encouraged him, because he tossed down a jack and continued. "I took web design through night school and some marketing classes. Why don't you take web design classes and you can work for me? I'm starting to have to turn down clients."

"I'd much rather learn accounting, thanks."

"Then do it. Find something you want and do it."

"What is this, another intervention?" I said, shaking my head. I looked at Adam. "Help?"

"Don't look at me. When these two get something into their heads, you have no choice but to comply. They're relentless."

Scott and Becky looked at each other and shrugged.

"Just look into it. What else will you do? Do you want to be stuck in a cubicle all day long like this one?" Scott said, pointing at Becky.

She smacked his arm as he shuffled. The cards scattered onto the table. "Thanks for the reminder, big brother. It's Friday night. Don't get me going about work, please. Do something you want now, Rose. Do it while you can. You really don't want to get stuck in some horrible job like me. You'll shrivel up and wither away."

"We definitely don't want that," Scott said as we both reached over to scoop up the cards. His thumb grazed my hand. A shock surged up my arm and forked through my body. If that was how electric shock therapy feels, how did it ever fail?

"No. No, we don't," I said, sliding my hands back and organizing the cards.

"So you'll do it then?" Scott beamed and I couldn't help but smile.

"Fine. I'll look into it," I said, throwing my hands up in defeat.

"Told you," Adam said.

"And when you're ready to get started," Scott said, "I'll set you up with a killer website."

"You don't have to do that."

"It wouldn't take long. A simple site, no interactives. Maybe some "how-to" posts. You could even do some instructional videos. You could begin a gardening blog. You could even start now, build an audience. All you have to do is pick some topics and write about them. It wouldn't even have to be instructional. It could even be your thoughts and inspirations while gardening."

His eyes lit up as he talked and his enthusiasm was contagious. Frank had never been supportive in any endeavor I wanted to pursue.

"Hello?" Becky said, dunking a ruffled chip into the onion dip. "Mr. Website Big Shot. Aren't blogs out now?"

"It is a bit saturated, but if you're unique, post frequently, and network, you can find an audience."

"Sounds like a lot of work," I said, suddenly worrying I wouldn't be able to follow through.

"It's not really difficult," Scott insisted.

"And you have all the clients from the garden center to start with," Becky said. "You can use your notes from your classes to find ideas to write about."

"Just give in, Rose. They won't let up until you do," Adam said.

I wasn't used to being the center of attention, or having so many people invested in my future. I fretted about disappointing them. It was so much easier when no one else showed any interest. But my friends were encouraging me to do what I wanted, not what they thought I should or shouldn't do, or what was in their best interest like Frank would have done. The difference was enormous.

"Okay, okay. I'll think about the blog. Definitely no videos though. And I'll look into school. Anything else you guys want me to do?"

Scott cocked an eyebrow.

"Never mind," I practically shouted, before hopping up to refill the chip bowl.

"Why don't you find a way to help the food bank?" Adam asked.

I turned back around. "What do you mean?"

"They're always looking for ways to increase their donations. What if there was a way to garden, teach, build an audience, and help the community all at the same time?"

I dropped back into my seat and stared at Adam like he had just invented wine.

CHAPTER FOURTEEN

I donned sunglasses, even with the overcast sky. My eyes blazed from the hours I had logged staring at my laptop, and I didn't need the sun searing them further should it poke through the gray. I reversed the truck and zipped through the side streets before turning south and heading downtown.

During my two-week Internet investigation of all things gardening-related, from blogs to schooling, I discovered a landscape design program at George Brown College and decided to investigate. Unfortunately, with the fall semester weeks away, starting this year wasn't an option. This, combined with the tuition fees and full-time schedule that left little room for gainful employment, was enough to justify not exploring it further, especially with preferring planting, but I decided to check out the course to be sure. And to get the intervention monkeys off my back.

The blank slate that was now my life initially terrified me, but the more I considered it, the more breathless I became. I didn't have to share decisions or listen to anyone trash my ideas. I decided where to live, what furniture to buy, whether to teach or go back to school, or find another job. Even when to have children. I was solely responsible for my own fate. It was only if I met someone that I would have to relearn the art of compromise. The thought of just how much I'd deferred to Frank rolled around in my head like the clomping of a caveman with a square stone while I researched. Would I be able realize my mistakes and redesign my future, like they were able to invent the wheel?

My resolve flourished like a weed, and I vowed to keep pushing upwards regardless of being stomped on, plucked, or sprayed. My marriage to Frank was like temporary weed control. Regardless of how much he trampled down, I kept trying to surface, and now that his pesticide-induced fugue had evaporated I could grow and blossom.

I cruised down Avenue Road toward the land of college dreams, where the boys and girls would be so young they would be clueless about life without laptops, smart phones, and DVRs, and I would be too old to comprehend their lingo and new texting language. I still used full words in every text message I sent. I bopped and sang along to the retro lunch hour. They would definitely be too young to remember any of these songs. I crucified "Push It," and attempted to ignore thoughts of how out of place I would feel. I also ignored the distressed glances of pedestrians while idling at a stop light. For the first time in months, years even, I felt fantastic. The interventionists might have been right. Maybe I did need some focus.

I hammered the accelerator when the light changed. The SUV lurched forward and belched smoke. I slammed on the brakes, my heart whacking in my chest. Horns blared. I scanned the rear view mirror and debated whether I should attempt to pull into the side street a few feet ahead. I tapped the gas. Another cloud erupted from under the hood, but the truck sustained enough momentum for me to coax it around the corner and pull up to the curb.

I wiped my hands on my jeans before clawing around in my purse.

The cell phone took the brunt of my frustration as I stabbed at the tiny screen. With a jolt, I punched delete. I threw my head back, bouncing it off the headrest. In my panic, I almost dialed Frank.

I looked back down. The battery alert notification flashed across the screen and spurred me back into action. I had seconds before the battery died. I scrolled through my contacts, noticing for the first time how few there were, and jabbed the one number I knew could help.

After barking out the situation and location, the line went dead. I cursed myself for not purchasing a car charger for my phone. I cursed Frank for refusing to arrange some form of emergency towing package, and then cursed my own short sightedness for not taking care of it myself after leaving. Then I cursed because I didn't even have a mechanic. Frank had looked after anything car-related, and I discovered another gaping hole in my life I'd have to take Polyfilla to.

Thirty minutes later a black truck pulled up. I clambered up off the curb, stretched, and released a long sigh of relief, grateful the phone had enough power to allow my desperate call for assistance to be heard.

"Thank you so much."

"I sure could get used to rescuing you, Rosie." Scott smiled and dropped down to kiss my cheek. "Let's have a look."

He popped the hood, bent over, and began fiddling with the engine. I pulled my tank top away from my skin to fan myself, suddenly quite hot.

With both hands planted on the SUV, he angled his head to look at me. I swiveled my eyes away from the mesmerizing sight of his behind and returned his gaze. He winked.

Crap. He'd caught me.

"It seems to have overheated. And it looks like you have a leak. I'll call a tow truck and bring you home," he said, wiping his hands on his jeans. Was there anything sexier than a man that could get his hands dirty?

"Oh, I…" I trailed off. It was a sign. Landscape design had never felt right anyway.

"Don't worry about it. I don't have any other appointments today. We can talk about that blog of yours," Scott said, dialing his phone. He explained the situation, gave them the address, and holstered the phone back on his belt.

Alone with him, without a chaperone, was exactly the kind of situation I wanted to avoid.

"Thanks again. I'll have to repay you somehow."

His dimples flared.

I rolled my eyes. "No. Stay for dinner. I'm making pasta carbonara, trying to teach Becky how to make it, actually. Not sure why I'm bothering though. She's useless in the kitchen. Her noodles turn to mush or cement."

"Not quite the reward I was looking for, but I guess if I have to share you with my sister…"

"You're sure you don't have to be anywhere?" I asked, cutting him off.

"Nope. I cleared my schedule when I got your SOS. I'm at your service."

I sneaked a peek at my watch and performed some quick calculations. Even if the tow truck took an hour, we would still have several hours alone before Becky arrived.

"Thinking of all the commands you'll give me?" Scott said, smirking.

I bit my lip and pretended to be looking down the street for the tow truck. "Actually, I was considering what I need at the grocery store. Do you mind if we stop along the way?" It was a useless trip. Our fridge was fully stocked. I only suggested it to shorten the time we would be alone together before Becky arrived home.

Scott shrugged. "Sure."

I scoured my mind for other errand excuses to delay our transit time, but couldn't find any. I could only hope my willpower would hold.

*****

"You guys got to me the other day. I've been researching like a mad woman," I said, trying to find a topic that wouldn't invoke indecent thoughts while we unpacked the groceries. I pulled out the vegetables and placed them on the counter.

"What did you find?"

"There are a lot of blogs out there, but I'm considering it. I looked into George Brown for landscape design. That's actually where I was headed this afternoon."

"You should have told me. I would have taken you down there."

"I don't think it's the right fit anyway. It will take years and I don't want to wait. I have a bit of a patience problem sometimes."

"You don't say," he said, spawning those dimples I wanted to suck honey out of.

I couldn't risk a repeat lunge at his lips so I picked up the bundle of spinach and turned on the tap to wash the leaves. It was earlier than I'd usually prep dinner, but it gave me an excuse not to drag him upstairs. Not that he'd be kicking and screaming from the grin he still tossed my way.

"Inspiration struck while I was sitting on the curb waiting for you. I'm going to talk to Abby about it this week," I said.

"What is it?"

"I'm not going to disclose the idea yet, in case it doesn't work out. But keep your fingers crossed, because it would be perfect."

"If you're as excited as you seem from that smile, then it'll work out. What you're most invested in yields the greatest rewards."

"I suppose. I just hope…"

"Don't hope, Rose. Do."

"It can also yield the greatest heartbreak, though."

"But then at least you've tried. You can't know unless you try." His eyes conveyed the double meaning.

I nodded and inspected the spinach for dirt. It took every ounce of concentration to ignore the warmth spreading through my chest from his encouraging words, and how much I yearned to kiss him again and nestle in his arms. "I'll just finish the salad and then we can sit outside and wait for Becky."

"I doubt we'll be doing that," Scott said, appearing beside me.

My breath hitched.

He pointed at the window. "Another storm's rolling in," he said, pulling a knife from the drawer at my hip and reaching for a cutting board.

I stifled a sigh. It wasn't exactly what I was hoping he'd reach for. "Oh, right. Stuck inside again. That sucks." I babbled. What happened to the easy banter we had while playing cards?

"Thanks for the help," I said, enjoying the company and assistance in the kitchen. Scott's capability was evident from his dicing skills. Becky lacked in the helping department, and Frank had failed miserably at both. I hoped Scott wasn't helping to rush the task so we would have more time alone. Without anything to do.

"I have ulterior motives."

This time I didn't stifle my sigh. "Of course you do. Scott, we can't."

"Why?"

"Do you really need me to tell you all the reasons why?"

"Yes," he said, picking up the cucumber.

I paused, almost forgetting all my reasons. I wasn't sure where to look. Definitely not at the cucumber he was wielding.

"One, you're Becky's brother..."

"So?" he interrupted.

"It makes things complicated."

"How?"

"Because it could end badly. It could ruin our friendship, my friendship with Becky, the games of Euchre, Garden Club."

"It wouldn't have to. And it wouldn't end badly."

"I just had a relationship end badly. *My marriage.* Why would you want to get involved with me? You'd be the rebound. I wouldn't want that for anyone I care about, and I care about you. I like and respect you. I'm certainly not ready for a new relationship yet and I don't want to get involved with you for a bit of fun. No matter how fantastic it was."

"I can't see how it's a bad thing," he said. "There's so much I like about you, from your ability to carry on an intellectual conversation to you grabbing me and dragging me upstairs and everything in between. And what we did up there." He let out a low whistle while gesturing at the ceiling with the knife.

I remained silent.

Scott lay the knife down on the cutting board and placed his hand over mine. We locked eyes across the island.

"I… I can't…" I whispered.

"I'm not Frank. I'm nothing like him," Scott said, matching my hushed tone.

Lightning flashed. I looked past him and watched the rain thundering against the window. Scott's thumb began moving in circles over my knuckles and fingers, whispering encouragement.

"I know," I said, my voice catching in my throat. The simplicity made me wary, yet held immense appeal. Avoiding disastrous dating and the treacherous online universe with worries about married men, liars in general, or men seeking desperate divorcées would be a serious bonus, but I couldn't help but worry about making the same mistakes I made with Frank. There was no chance of casual dating with Scott. We'd already slept together, and because of our intertwined relationship with Becky, it could never be slow. I would be vaulted into another relationship and regardless of ease, I knew I wasn't ready. I knew I didn't want to start another relationship like that. I hadn't even fully processed my broken marriage yet.

I looked down and discovered my own thumb fondling with a mind of its own.

I finally raised my eyes and met his. "I'm sorry."

Scott's shoulders slumped and his face went slack.

The fluttering butterflies that had appeared when Scott's hand covered mine turned malicious. They flew at my chest and delivered a wing beating that left me breathless with regret.

Thoughts of tugging his hand toward the door lingered, but my feet remained cemented to the floor.

I slid my hand out from beneath his. It grew cold as it fell to my side.

CHAPTER FIFTEEN

I pried Abby away from the garden center to ask her advice.

"Would you only want to design gardens or design and maintain them?" she asked while we nursed coffees, perched on stools inside Starbucks.

"Just the planning and implementation, I think. Continued maintenance might be too much work, too much scheduling and hassle. Or maybe just one or two? I already have Mom's garden to look after."

Abby tilted her head. "What's wrong?"

"She's starting to grumble about how much work it all is."

"I can't believe she never let on during Club. I dread that day. It won't be long before I reach that point myself." She sighed.

"You're far from it."

"It sure doesn't feel like it some days."

"Unfortunately, Mom seems to be prone to the same arthritis Gram was."

"Kryptonite for gardeners. Stops you cold." She shuddered and rapped her knuckles on the counter. "Knock on wood it doesn't inflict its pain on me."

"It won't. Besides, I don't think you'll let it."

Abby smiled. "Well, if you're assisting her with the garden, you could help a few others and maybe start there? There are a lot of seniors who might pay you for some form of low-budget gardening service. You could do that until you secure more clients interested in design; maybe even design some low-maintenance gardens for seniors who want to keep a beautiful garden without the hassle? You'd have the website sorted courtesy of Scott. Now you just have to figure out how to get through this winter in case you get off to a slow start."

A young woman with a basketball belly shuffled past with a toddler in tow. I swallowed hard before turning back to Abby. She shot me a sympathetic smile. Abby never had children, and I often wondered why, or if she regretted it—especially in the last few months. But I never had the courage to ask.

"It gets easier," Abby said, tapping the side of her paper cup. "I always wanted children, but after years of nothing happening, we found out it wasn't meant to be, at least not naturally. We didn't have all the options that are available now. Adoption was the only viable choice for us, and when we started investigating the process, our marriage fell apart. Single parent adoption wasn't considered back then. My heart shattered every time I saw a pregnant woman or a baby carriage after I found out I couldn't conceive, and then again after we separated, knowing I'd lost my chance."

I remained silent. I didn't trust myself to speak.

"You have options though. You can get a sperm donor. You can adopt. You can be a single mother."

"Why didn't you get married again?" I asked, even though I wasn't sure I wanted to hear the answer.

"The thought of confiding I was incapable of having children was enough for me to steer clear of dating. 'Who would want me,' I thought, so I stuck my head in the dirt and tended to my seedlings. They became my babies instead, and after a while I gave up. I was pretty stupid." She took a sip before continuing. "I was terrified. I can see that now. Don't let fear consume you. It may not be for the same reasons and it's only natural to be scared after what you've been through, but don't let it grab hold and take over. Learn from what happened."

"It's just hard sometimes," I said, dabbing a wayward tear with a napkin. If I was younger, it would have been easier. But creeping up to forty, I could hear the baby door creaking as it began to close.

"I know. But after some time has passed and things seem easier, you'll realize how many options are available and how much love and support you have if you decide to do it alone. In the meantime, focusing on yourself and your career will help. I don't think you'll have difficulty meeting anyone, especially with this new venture. Who knows, maybe you'll find some lovely man who hires you to design his garden."

"Not if I'm tending to the elderly," I said with a snort. I didn't feel hopeful, especially after shoving Scott away. We clicked so well it would be easy to fall into a life with him, maybe even get to the point of a baby. But then would I have learned anything? I wouldn't have even taken the time to breathe.

"If you ever want to talk about it, you know where to find me. I'm quite enjoying this little coffee break. I should do it more often."

I laughed. Abby rarely took more than five minutes for lunch or dinner over the years, let alone a coffee break. "So, what wise wisdom were you imparting when I ignored you to weep over a baby bump?"

"Wise wisdom? I don't know about that. I only asked about what you'd do over the winter."

"See, that's wise. I have no idea."

"A seasonal business needs serious planning. You've seen how few staff we employ over the winter. The majority of our sales come in May, June, and July. August drops off slightly and then we're into fall and winter, and with the brief exception of Christmas tree and wreath sales, October through April is tough. Spreading funds around over the year is paramount. Don't forget that. It might be different if you can design throughout the winter and implement your ideas in the spring. You'll have to see, though."

"I guess so. Maybe I'll do temp work over the winter to get me through."

"Great idea. Then you won't stress if you don't secure dozens of clients right away."

I nodded. "Thanks, Abby. You've been a lifesaver again."

"That's what I'm here for. And I meant what I said before. If you ever need to talk, about anything, please come find me."

"I will definitely take you up on that," I said. Even though Abby told me I could do it alone, she actually understood how the end of my marriage might mean the end of my baby dream. No one else had. Not Mom or Becky or Martha.

"I also had another notion about teaching and design I wanted to poke your brain about," I said, and began outlining my thoughts. I couldn't help returning Abby's grin as her eyes grew wide and she championed my idea.

*****

Vitalized by my conversation with Abby, I went on a mission. The Garden Club was in danger of collapsing, and I intended to save it. Armed with cheese and crackers for Martha, Abby, and Mom, beer and chips for Scott and Adam, and two bottles of wine for Becky and me, I traipsed home and plopped my goods on the counter.

While it was fabulous for getting to know some more people in the neighborhood and to make new friends, we hadn't added any new members and needed something more to sustain our meetings. Mention had been made of changing our weekly attempts to bi-weekly or monthly meetings, and although I was in agreement about possibly switching to bi-weekly gatherings because we weren't doing anything in particular, I was concerned it would fizzle out over time. We never did any work at each other's homes, and mostly congregated at the townhouse. People skipped because they were too busy and it didn't take priority. We weren't doing anything worth prioritizing for. I planned to change that.

I dragged the card table upstairs and slapped a table cloth over it to hide any embarrassment Becky might feel. I also wanted to create a more formal atmosphere than our usual wine, beer, cheese, and chat sessions. I placed a deep purple African violet in the middle of the table and set a folder with handouts, some paper, and a pen at one end before starting on the cheese platter.

When I ushered everyone into my impromptu meeting room they exchanged confused glances.

"Adam, I have you to thank," I said to him before turning back to address the group. "I sincerely hope everyone will consider helping, and I think Adam's musing the other day was bang-on. I believe our little club needs some focus, and I was thinking we might take on some volunteer work, something where everyone could donate their time and skill sets. We could be more productive than sitting around here every week. Not that I don't enjoy it…" Abby winked from her chair.

"Will there still be cheese?" Martha asked, reaching over for another slab of Brie. "I'll do anything if you have cheese. I'd pick cheese over chocolate any day."

"That's the craziest thing I've ever heard a woman say," Becky said, shaking her head.

Martha shrugged. I loved how unapologetic she was.

"Rose, what a fabulous idea," Mom said.

"The Garden Center is going to donate whatever we can and try to sponsor whatever we decide to do," Abby said.

Scott nodded and mentioned his agreement. It was the first time since he saved me from my SUV that I'd seen him. His BlackBerry had buzzed soon after I'd told him nothing could happen between us and he'd flown out the door. If it hadn't been an unplanned encounter that afternoon and he hadn't been in my presence the entire time, I would have thought he staged it, like one would to extract themselves from an obnoxious date.

"What can we do though? It's just gardening," Becky said.

"Help the elderly and disabled?" Mom said, wiggling her fingers.

"What about creating gardens in places where people might need their mood lifted?" Martha suggested. "Like hospitals, seniors' centers, or any urban space I guess. Who's behind all those wild daffodil gardens springing up all over the city in random spaces?"

"Good idea. I'll check," I said, jotting it down. "They're all great ideas, but I've been doing a little research and I think there's a way to help the food banks, like Adam said. We could help with any gardens they may have, assist in designing and planting new ones if they don't have any yet and have the space. But we might even be able to help if they don't have the space."

Everyone looked around, confused.

"What if we helped them build rooftop gardens? We could even help out with something else I uncovered. Potato barrels."

I whipped open my folder and handed them each a print-out of an article I'd written on the subject.

"It's so simple. All you need to do is poke holes in a large barrel or old garbage can and fill the bottom with soil and compost. You plant a few potatoes and watch them grow. Every time they grow six inches, add more soil to the bottom, and continue until the barrel is full. Once it flowers, you can tip over the barrel and watch all the potatoes tumble out."

"Geez, I could do that on my balcony," Adam said.

"Well, it might get messy, but if you were careful and had another barrel of similar size you could transfer the dirt back and forth each year, adding compost as you go."

Scott nodded, his lips pursed. He looked impressed.

"I'm so doing this with the kids next year. What a brilliant idea," Martha said.

"Maybe kids could help grow food and use it for their community service for school? Or maybe they can help with rooftop gardening once we sort ourselves out?" Mom said.

"What about schools themselves?" Adam said. "I'm a big brother to a kid in an underprivileged area. What about helping them? They could take the vegetables home. That potato barrel sounds like it would be perfect to start with. We could teach sustainable, local harvesting to schools."

"Incredible idea. I'll add it to my research list to see if it already exists. Anybody else have any other thoughts?"

"Wait, can the actual barrels be made? What if the shop class made them?" Becky asked. "Do they even have shop class anymore?"

Everyone began talking at once. I continued scribbling and felt a wide grin stretch across my face.

CHAPTER SIXTEEN

Two months prior I thought Becky was lying when she said it would get easier, but her words were true. I settled into a new routine and my old life with Frank faded. My days became so busy I sometimes wondered what I used to do all day until my husband arrived home.

I spent Sundays with Mom and anyone else that joined us. Monday and Tuesday nights consisted of reality TV with Becky, or over at Martha's if Becky was with The Banker. Wednesday evenings I taught my classes. Thursday was Garden Club and Friday we played Euchre. I remained home alone on Saturdays while everyone was out dating. During the days I prepped for class, researched like a maniac, read, and had lunch with Mom or Martha. I cooked dinners and cleaned whenever Becky wasn't looking. I even learned to let some of the chores go, becoming more inclined to leave shoes where they fell upon entry and allow the dust bunnies to build an army before sweeping them off the battle field.

Frank's fading also wasn't due to my patch. I managed not to obsess about Scott and somehow avoided falling back into bed with him as well, possibly because I always ensured we were chaperoned.

The days galloped past, and suddenly it was the beginning of August when I settled into the couch to catch up on my soap, which I'd neglected for weeks. Two minutes into *General Hospital*, their infamous HIV storyline resurfaced. Over the years I'd watched the show dedicate hours to raising awareness. I had even skipped classes at university to stay home and watch the young couple struggle with their diagnosis, bawling with my girlfriends when Stone took his last breath.

Awareness. I blinked as the scenario switched to another couple, this time a cheating scenario.

STD. Cheating. Whips. Chains. Lies.

I gasped for breath and dropped my head in between my legs where I forced myself to breathe instead of gulping for air. My heart ricocheted off my chest while I berated myself for the gap in memory. How could I not have remembered?

My fingers trembled when I was finally able to pick up my phone, and a few days later I found myself flat on my back, staring up at white and black speckled ceiling tiles. They're the opposite of a starry sky, I thought, while my doctor muddled around between my legs and rattled off the diseases now detectable through blood and urine, diseases I hadn't thought about in years.

I battled back tears while she poked and swabbed. Her patience astounded me. She took the time to ensure I was okay, and not just physically. She probably handled this kind of situation daily. The thought didn't help. Many intrusive questions later, including whether I was sexually active, which I felt like a tramp saying yes to–already sleeping around–she passed me the requisition forms.

I drummed my fingers on the novel sitting unopened on my lap as I waited for my turn to be pricked.

I had never called Frank at the office. I only used his cell phone for contact. He could have been anywhere, doing anything all that time. Had he been out engaging in behavior that terrified me, not only because of the acts themselves and what they meant, but because he might have been out picking up diseases?

And I had slept with Scott without even thinking about it. At least we'd been safe. All those lessons about safe sex pounded into my head during adolescence and early adulthood hadn't evaporated when I'd pledged my vows and said "I do" to Frank until death do us part. I could only pray Frank hadn't forgotten them, like he'd forgotten our wedding vows.

The scent of rubbing alcohol lingered while the lab attendant jabbed the needle in my arm and continued filling vials. I stared at a strategically placed abstract painting. Instead of brightening the clinical atmosphere, it only added to the sterility of the room. The plastic tourniquet snapped when released. Blood splattered into the vial dangling from my arm. She withdrew the needle, pressed a soft cotton ball against the puncture, and asked me to apply pressure. With a zip, she tore off white tape, patted it down over the crook of my arm, and yanked her hand away. She avoided eye contact while tilting the vials up and down several times before attaching a label.

I shelved any offense, preferring the anonymity today instead of the bubbly behavior I usually encountered with lab attendants. Maybe she was mimicking my own unwillingness to engage in inane conversation about the weather, or maybe I was imagining her quiet, impersonal attitude. Or maybe it really was the battery of blood work with horrific names–HIV, syphilis, gonorrhea, and chlamydia–putting a damper on our interaction.

I relived the fuzzy memory of Becky's drunken promise to remind me to get tested. A shudder tore through me. This should have been done months ago. I pushed down and leveled the fluffy cotton ball with my fingers, taking perverse satisfaction in the pain.

The last time I had blood work done, I was one week late. Thrilled I might be pregnant, I'd rushed to the doctor's for a blood test to confirm. I justified it to myself that blood work was more accurate, but it was really me, being cautious. I hadn't wanted to leave any packaging around for Frank to find. Although at the time I didn't want to believe it, I knew he would have accused me of trying to get pregnant without his knowledge. This time I was being poked and prodded because he might have cheated on me. I couldn't wrap my head around going from the joyous possibility of a cooing infant to a potentially deadly disease in a matter of months.

Through a film of tears, a hot pink blur handed over a plastic cup. She advised me to fill it between the lines marked. I willed my hands to stop trembling so I wouldn't miss and pee all over my fingers, and for my bladder to cooperate so I wouldn't have to come back.

"Thanks," I mumbled, placing my sample in the box and bolting out the door without waiting for a reply. She was probably wondering what my story was; cheating husband, slutty woman, cheated on her husband, all of the above? I tried to console myself that she probably performed those tests multiple times a day.

Again, it didn't help.

*****

The possibilities paralyzed me.

The suffocating silence that descended each nightfall shrouded me in a sheath of loneliness, confusion, and terror. I lay awake, obsessing about the results of the tests and dissecting my marriage. I wondered when I would be back in that sterile room; whether it would be soon due to a devastating call about my test results, or later, at some point in the future, with either joyous news about a pink or blue bundle or terrifying news about a future medical challenge? Would I have someone holding my hand?

Every time the phone rang, my heart paused for two beats before pounding in my chest, and by the time I gathered the nerve to peek at the call display, a cold sweat blanketed my body. I hadn't shared this new development with anyone. Becky would have been the obvious choice, but she barely stepped a manicured toe inside her own home anymore, and when I did see her, it was always in the presence of others where a private conversation proved impossible. Thankfully, no one picked up on my fear, so I didn't have to share. I didn't want to worry anyone, not to mention how embarrassed I felt by my stupidity. Instead, I munched my way through enough potato chips to cause a national shortage.

After two weeks passed and I had yet to hear from the doctor's office, I knew my tests were clean. I decided to celebrate.

I dialed from my slouched position on the couch.

"Miss Becky or Miss Rosie?" I heard after rattling off our phone number and address.

"It's Rose…"

"The usual? You different order from Miss Becky."

"Uhm, yes please. Kung Pao Chicken and Beef Fried Rice?" Apparently Chinese food wasn't just for celebrations anymore. They knew my order. How did that happen?

"You pay cash?"

"Yes."

"Thirty minutes."

Click.

Silence again.

I turned up the volume on the TV. Tears floated down my cheeks and dampened my shirt. I let them fall, hoping they would stop by the time the delivery guy arrived. I had ordered my favorite take-out and didn't want to lose my appetite. Enough meals had been wasted already in the last few months because of emotional outbursts.

I slunk into the kitchen and uncorked a bottle of Cabernet. I carried it into the living room along with the huge goblet we used to fight over–when Becky was home. I poured until wine sloshed at the rim and leaned down to slurp a few sips to avoid spillage.

I needed to embrace the loneliness so I wouldn't grab hold of the first man that came along, a life preserver saving me from bobbing and gasping for air. I didn't want to drag anyone down with me. It was why I hadn't called Alex to see if his damsel in distress act could morph into boyfriend material, and the reason why I couldn't be with Scott.

Another insight gleaned from my defunct marriage during my midnight insomniac sessions was why I latched onto Frank in the first place. The near-thirty fear had crept over me. My friends started settling down, getting engaged and married. My biological clock began thumping, begging for my attention. Loneliness lurked when my formerly single friends flocked in twos, fours, sixes, and whatever other pairings didn't include an odd number, an odd member that was me.

I couldn't let that happen again, even with every stroller sighting engulfing me in a flaming sweat that would instigate concerns about early menopause. It didn't escape me that abandonment into love would be much easier than sitting here alone again, too lazy to cook for myself or even get plates for the take-out, with my sole encounter for the day being a language-barrier-laden conversation with a Chinese food delivery man about change.

The doorbell rang.

I finished my sip of wine, grabbed the cash from the coffee table, and jerked open the door. A short man in a green ball cap held the bill up to his nose. I shoved the cash at him, snatched my food, and waved away the need for change before slamming the door.

I was alone again.

*****

Unsure about staging a full-out intervention, I called Martha over for some advice first. And maybe a little company.

"A rare Friday evening out. What a treat," Martha said, kicking off her flip-flops and propping her feet on the opposite chair. "I needed to get the hell out of my house."

I passed her a glass of Pinot Grigio and dropped into the remaining seat.

Martha sipped and let out a long sigh while staring into the wine glass she cradled. "My best friend, Pinot."

"What happened today?" I asked, laughing. Martha's tales of motherhood were always entertaining. I loved that she could laugh at her trials and that she recognized the need to run and have a break at times. She never gave me the candy-coated version of being a mom, and as much as it freaked me out at times, I loved every story.

"Oh, just the usual. The boys were bouncing off the walls after being cooped up all day with the rain. The dog puked, so Robbie threw up, which the dog then started to eat. Then the cat pissed on the couch, and as I tried to Febreze the stench out, Jimmy bounced right off it and smashed his head on the coffee table. His head gushed so much I thought he was going to need stitches. Thankfully, he didn't. I hope Mark remembers to get them to bed on time or he can deal with the cranky-pants fall-out tomorrow. And that he remembers to wake Jimmy at least once before I get home in case he has a concussion."

"I'm impressed he helps out so much. Frank wouldn't have done half the things Mark does. Quite possibly none of it."

"He's amazing. Even though I'm a stay-at-home mom, he never makes me feel guilty about it. He never expects or demands anything from me. He doesn't work late every night or play golf every weekend. He even sends me on spa days so I can have a break. These men do exist, but are apparently very rare. And after hearing my girlfriends moan about their husbands, I guess I won the husband lottery."

"You both won," I said smiling at her. How long could I wait to find my own Mr. Perfect?

"He's not perfect though," Martha said as if reading my thoughts; or maybe she was sending me a warning, saving me years of searching for Mr. Perfect. "I know his imperfections and he knows mine. We work through them together. We know our own strengths and weaknesses and each other's, and work around things as they come up. I wish I could say we never fight. But we do."

"I never fought much with Frank. I always tried to keep the peace instead. It's probably where I went wrong."

"I think it's important to fight. It clears the air. You work things out and find out what's important to each other. It depends how you fight though, I suppose. Name-calling, character assassination, and dredging up old buried stuff doesn't help. Someone should teach respectful arguing. I bet they'd make a killing."

"I'd take that class. I'm not much of a fighter." I stared out at the damp patio. Where did the feisty teenage girl that used to inhabit my body go? Somewhere along the way she vanished and took all her confrontational behavior with her.

"I think you have more fire in you than you think," Martha said with an encouraging smile.

I shifted in my seat.

"So, what's going on? You said you wanted to chat about Becky?"

"I'm worried about her. She hasn't only been skipping our club meetings, she's never around. She calls at the last minute to cancel our card games, leaving me and the guys sitting around staring at the walls with mounds of extra food. Last week we all blasted her, so at least she had the decency to cancel tonight a day in advance. She only comes home for clothes. It's like she's moved in with him already and she's only known him a couple of months. She apologized about not being around after my depressed week in bed, saying she ditched me like a love-struck teenager and still had a lot to learn, but she's reverted back. I don't know what to do."

"You need to talk to her."

"I suppose," I muttered into my glass.

"You do," Martha insisted. "Maybe she'll be upset…"

"That's what I'm worried about."

"But you have to try. She'll understand it's coming from a place of concern. Maybe not right away, but she will."

"I don't know," I said, shaking my head. "I've been on the receiving end of this conversation several times and I was always upset. And I never learned from it—no matter how many girlfriends I lost along the way. Not until now, that is."

"You're ready to look at your mistakes and learn from them now. Becky might not be. You said she recognized it before though, right? Maybe nudging her could be all she needs."

"I don't know," I repeated, uncertain. "Did you ever have any friends ditch you for boys? I can't imagine you were ever on the offending end."

"I think you get caught up in the frenzy of new love in the beginning. And I'm sure I've done it, but never for too long. I have seen friends dash off with their knights in shining armor though, and disappear. And it doesn't only happen with men. It can occur with women too, when babies appear or even when divorce comes into play. Relationships dissolve for many reasons. Friendship is particularly difficult, and takes a lot of effort when you're at different stages of life."

"What if I'm overreacting? It's still so early in their relationship. Maybe she'll come around once the honeymoon phase is over?"

Martha held up her hand. "Stop with the excuses. Your instinct tells you this isn't right, right?"

I nodded, amazed with her ability to see through my procrastination—and call me on it. "Based on what Becky's told me of her past relationships, I'm worried this isn't healthy for her."

"Your only option is to talk with her. It seems like you've resolved a lot since you left your husband. Maybe you can pass some of your insight onto Becky, help her now like she helped you in the beginning."

"I don't know if I've figured out that much. It's a work in progress. Becky kept telling me to go out, date, have lots of sex…"

"Check on the sex," Martha said, waggling her eyebrows.

I laughed. "Well, I did that and I can't take it back, but I still think it was a mistake. I don't think that particular piece of advice was the smartest thing for me. So maybe my advice won't be the best for her? I don't know, Martha. I'm still trying to sort through everything. I think if I'd gone out and gotten involved so quickly, I wouldn't have figured anything out."

"Smart woman."

"I'm trying. And I know Becky took some time away too, but look what's happened to her now that she's back on the dating bandwagon. She's practically moved in with the first man she's met. What if I do the same thing?"

I felt Martha's hand cover mine. "I don't think you will. You're much stronger than you give yourself credit for. You could have blamed Frank for everything and gone off and dated and not learned anything, like you said–but you didn't. You're sorting through it. You're evaluating your mistakes in the relationship. That's huge. I doubt Becky's done that."

I shrugged, unsure about her compliment or her faith in me, but as I trolled back through my conversations with Becky about her marriage, I knew I'd taken a different approach to the dissolution of mine than she had with hers. I sighed. "You're right. She hasn't. She's never mentioned anything about her marriage other than her ex's transgressions. She's not going to be happy if I confront her about this."

"*When* you confront her. And if she doesn't see it now, it will sink in later, when she's ready. All you can do is plant the seed. And I think that was already done several weeks ago. Maybe some fertilizer is all she needs to remind her."

"God, I hope you're right," I said.

*****

The moment it turned a decent hour the following morning I sent Becky a text.

"C U tomorrow?" I typed, hoping she wouldn't cancel yet another dinner at my mother's. I set the phone down on the counter and sipped my coffee while waiting for a response. When the screen remained blank, I looked around for a distraction.

The coffee-and-tea-stained sink spurred me into action. How did I let it go that long without giving it a good scrub? After the stainless steel sparkled, I steered my attention to the counters and the stove top before tackling the refrigerator. I removed all contents and tossed shudder-worthy discoveries into a black garbage bag.

After scrubbing each shelf, I returned all non-offending items and began attacking the cupboards.

I hauled the garbage bag to the dumpster and then flicked on the espresso machine when I returned. It was past three o'clock and Becky still hadn't responded. I dropped into a chair in front of my laptop. There was nothing left to clean except Becky's bedroom, and after my previous dust bunny assault I refused to engage them in battle no matter how much they needed conquering.

My phone dinged as soon as I settled outside with my espresso and laptop. I nibbled my already decimated thumbnail while peering at the screen and praying, as I had all morning, that I wouldn't have to convince her to come home.

"Will be there. Jay has a family dinner."

I felt like I'd been punched in the gut—and not because Becky was only coming because her boyfriend was busy, but because I suddenly realized how often I had committed the same offense in the past.

A screaming match between me and my best friend in high school, Jessie, came into focus. She had accused me of ignoring her for my boyfriend, Matt, and I walked away. Ten years of friendship lost over a boy in my life for only a dozen months. I lost my virginity to him and had no one to talk to about it.

I thought I knew it all back then and had decided Jessie was being possessive, jealous without a boyfriend of her own. I pictured my awkward high-school self kissing Matt in front of her after our fight to rub it in. I shuddered. How was I to know at seventeen that the exchange would foreshadow every relationship I would ever have until this point? Why didn't I listen to her? My life could have turned out so differently if I had.

I never knew whether Jessie's parents had forced her to attend my father's funeral, but she shuffled along between them in a new black dress she had bought without me. Mascara smudged the skin beneath her red-rimmed eyes. Her mom and dad approached my mother, leaving us standing in awkward silence, the bitter words of our last conversation lingering. Jessie offered wooden condolences while my tears and sobs dominated our exchange.

I never confided that in that moment they were more for the loss of her friendship than the loss of my father. I missed her so much. I knew I needed her, but in the weeks and months that followed, I was so lost in my own grief that I didn't reach out to her or even attempt to apologize. Matt eventually found another girl, one who actually smiled instead of crying all the time or lashing out at him, and Jessie began dating the swim-team captain. Alone, I anticipated leaving high school behind to start at the University of Toronto the following fall with a clean slate.

And then I did it all again. Another best friend–Samantha. Another boy, Chris. A fight. A friendship dissolved. Another broken heart when he dumped me. And again, no one to talk to.

I did it again with Frank.

I switched out my espresso for glass of wine.

I was supposed to be older, more mature in my late twenties. My head swung back and forth in disbelief.

"Never again," I vowed, promising myself I would never, ever, repeat that pattern. I also knew that no matter how difficult, I had to approach Becky and make her see it too.

I nibbled my lip.

Unable to sit alone with my thoughts, I flopped on the sofa and flicked through the upcoming movie selection. Were these Saturday night chick flicks for sad, lonely, single women sitting at home wishing their next first kiss will be their last first kiss? Or for sad, lonely, married women sitting at home desperate to remember the anticipation and butterflies of a first kiss?

My cell phone rang and I jumped.

"Hey," Scott's voice boomed.

I sat upright on the couch. "Hi."

"You doing anything tonight?"

"*Bridget Jones's Diary* and a side of Pinot Grigio," I replied with no pretense of an active social life. Scott already knew that, and I was past games. The ones Frank had played left an indelible mark.

"Shut that crap off. I'll pick you up in an hour."

"Okay," I replied without hesitation.

My answer was met with silence. "Scott?"

"I'm here. Sorry, just surprised I didn't have to use any of the multiple excuses I had ready to get you to agree."

So was I. The loneliness had its own agenda. I was desperate for some company; Becky's brother or not. "I think maybe it's time to see how the world lives on a Saturday night," I replied.

"Do you want to know where we're going?"

"Oh, sure."

"Are you sure you're all right, Rose?"

"Fine. Fine." I would need to be careful with him tonight. "Do I have to get dressed up?"

"Nope. Just as you are."

Definitely not. I hadn't showered and had been lounging about with bed-head in a tank top and pajama pants all day. No to mention the mad cleaning I'd done. I felt my nose wrinkle. "I'll see you in an hour."

I didn't ask again where he was taking me. I didn't care. As long as it was away from this townhouse and away from my thoughts.

CHAPTER SEVENTEEN

I bounded down the front steps as soon as Scott's truck rounded the corner.

"Hi," I said, climbing in. My cheeks could have split from the grin that had sprouted since he called. The muscles must have atrophied after years of not smiling.

Scott leaned over and pecked me on the cheek. Goosebumps popped and covered the length of my body. Damn it. My smooth legs would be stubble-bound in seconds from the puckering pores. I rubbed my hands vigorously up and down my legs to warm them. While slathering them with shaving cream earlier, I had tried to convince myself I would have cropped the forest regardless of where I was going. But I suspected it was a good indication of what I really wanted to happen. My Girl Guide training was still coming in handy more than twenty years later, and I was nothing if not always prepared.

"Is it too cold in here?" Scott asked, noticing my shiver.

"Maybe a little," I lied, clasping my hands in my lap and shoving them between my knees.

"Sorry, I love the cold." He reached over and flicked off the air conditioning.

"You prefer it cool?"

"Yep. I love the cooler nights of fall, the changing leaves, and the smell of the fireplace burning for the first time. They all signal winter is about to begin."

"You're crazy," I said. I had heard about people who love winter, but never actually met one. I thought they were an urban legend.

"Nope. As long as you're dressed properly and there's a steaming cup of hot chocolate and a roaring fire when you come inside, it's great fun. Skiing, snowboarding, skating, or snowmobiling. I've never been able to decide which is my favorite."

"I had no idea there were that many." I ignored Scott, who looked at me like I'd said I didn't know the Pope was Catholic, and continued. "I'd stay curled up in front of that fire with the hot chocolate and a book. Or somewhere with a beach or a swim-up bar. Summer is my season, when I can putter around in the garden." It was the first positive sign I'd made the right decision about him. There was no way love could bloom with such an opposite love of the seasons. Maybe I should get to know men before lusting over them. There was no point starting something headed down a dead-end street.

"The Caribbean isn't bad, but I prefer to spend a week up north. Winter or summer."

"Mmm-hmmm," I replied, distracted by my thoughts, which had turned dark and lusty since I realized we were too different for a relationship to work.

"I love Christmas too."

That snapped my attention back.

His grin faded into a grimace when he glanced at me. "Shit, sorry."

My fingers dug into my thigh and I shrugged, not trusting myself to speak for a moment. "It'll arrive eventually. My wedding anniversary precedes it, so maybe Christmas won't be so tough after that," I tried to joke but it ended in a squeak.

Scott's warm and slightly damp hand covered my own and squeezed, forcing me to abandon kneading my thigh. He didn't remove his hand when I stopped–and I didn't push it away.

This was a really bad idea.

"So, where are we going?" I asked, attempting to redirect the unpleasant conversation and distract myself from his fingers, which had entwined with mine.

"It's a surprise. You didn't want to know earlier, so now you'll have to wait."

"Give me a hint," I pleaded, turning to face him as we continued driving further downtown towards the lake.

"Nope," he said, smiling.

I forced my eyes forward.

Scott unclasped my hand and clutched the steering wheel. He jerked the truck to the left to maneuver around a car that had slammed on the brakes next to an empty parking spot. Frank would have cursed and squealed the tires in a dramatic swerve, but Scott wasn't fazed and didn't rant and rave about it for the next five blocks. It wasn't the first contrast I'd uncovered between the two men and their cars. Scott had told me about treating himself to the truck after landing his first large account. He worked hard and earned it. Frank had felt entitled to it. It was an enormous difference, and this new insight plopped into the spreadsheet of pros and cons and differences I'd been tallying in my mind.

Traffic congestion slowed us as we approached the lake. Scott grinned and tapped his fingers on the steering wheel.

We had to be close. I leaned forward and peered out the window for clues.

A teenage couple rounded the corner carting a life-sized teddy bear and an armful of hot pink cotton candy. The Ferris wheel appeared in the distance. "The CNE!" I squealed.

"Don't ever become a detective," Scott teased and patted my knee.

"I haven't been to the CNE in years, probably not since high school."

"I try to go every year. It's the perfect end to summer and gets me stoked for winter."

Images of him walking hand in hand on the midway at the summer fair with random girls surfaced.

"I usually head down with Becky."

The visions vanished. "We should have waited for her."

"She wouldn't have come anyway. She's too busy…" Scott said, his clenched jaw obliterating the dimples. "With him."

"You're worried about her?"

"She doesn't always make the best decisions."

"Is that you being a big brother, or are you legitimately concerned?"

His nostrils flared slightly before his eyes locked onto mine. "She's my little sister. I'll always be concerned about her. She chooses these shitty guys and gets all wrapped up in their lives and then I barely see her. Sometimes not at her doing. Sometimes they forbid her. And she goes along with it. They…" He slammed his hand on the steering wheel.

Even though I watched him do it, I still flinched. Scott didn't notice. He continued glaring out the window. I gathered my thoughts before responding. "When I met Becky, she seemed so determined not to get into a situation like that again."

"She says that every time, but she's a repeat offender."

"I was planning on talking to her tomorrow about it. I've been worried too. And now I'm even more concerned. Maybe we should stage one of those interventions you all seem to love so much." How hard could it be? They did it for me. And it was an addiction, right? Addicted to the wrong men. It would be so much easier if I had back-up.

"It won't work."

"We could try," I said, overcome with the notion that if I could help Becky, I would avoid my old patterns too. "We have to try."

He turned to face me, a tight smile on his lips. "Let's not talk about her anymore tonight, okay?"

I nodded and hoped the conversation wouldn't tarnish the rest of our evening.

"There better be a vendor with flip-flops in there," I said with a laugh to lighten the mood. Strappy sandals were definitely not appropriate for the hours of walking we were about to do, no matter how many women walking around us seemed to think they were.

"First on our to-do list. I didn't want to say anything when you climbed into the truck with those sexy shoes or I would have ruined the surprise."

I attempted to swat him and stumbled. Scott's arm slid around my waist and pulled me into him before I tripped and kissed the asphalt. We remained entwined and strolled up to the Princess Margaret gates.

*****

The front door glowed blood-red in the moonlight.

"I told you to stop after one round," I teased, nudging Scott as we strolled up the path. We were still giddy from the excessive sugar consumption, exhilarated by the rides, and buzzed off the crowds. I hadn't stopped teasing Scott about the sixty dollars it took him to win one tiny teddy bear and couldn't stop giggling.

"I can't believe I couldn't get three stupid rings on bottles. I'm a disgrace to my gender."

"The games can't be that easy or they'd never make any money. You could have bought half a dozen teddy bears for what you spent."

Scott shrugged. "My manhood was at stake. Besides, in for a penny..."

"...In for a pound." I glanced up at him and hoped my own grin mirrored his goofy one.

"Here, let me take those," Scott said, gathering the cotton candy in his arms and dangling my heels from his fingers when I had difficulty navigating my purse for keys. The teddy bear was already firmly trapped under my arm.

"Come in for a drink?" I asked, looking away. This non-date had been more romantic than any in my dating history, and I was loathe to have it end. In fact, it might have even turned into a date with some hand holding "so we don't lose each other in the crowd" and a breathtaking kiss at the top of the Ferris wheel, where I had to force myself to pull away with a reprimanding look. Scott had just shrugged and continued to stroke my cheek with his thumb. When his hand snaked behind my neck to guide me back, I didn't push him away. Dangling hundreds of feet in the air with a clear view of the lake, the sun setting, and a gorgeous man next to me who brought out long-forgotten fireworks, any thoughts of caution dispersed.

"Sure," he replied.

I shoved my key in the lock, but the front door swung open from the inside. I lurched back and screamed.

"Where have you been?" Becky cried. "I've been calling for hours."

"Nice to see you, little sister. Been a while," Scott said, pushing past me. He dropped my shoes on the floor, cotton candy in the basket, and strode into the living room.

"I needed you," she whined again, looking back and forth between us. She gave her head a quick shake as if to ignore what was right in front of her.

I dangled the teddy bear behind my back.

"It's always when you need something," Scott said, plopping down on the sofa. "What about all those games of cards when you blew us off? And have you thought about poor Rose here lately? Sitting home alone? We went down to the Ex."

I preferred to think he was just emphasizing his point and tried not to be offended by the "poor Rose" comment.

"You went without me?" she snapped.

"You'd just be busy with The Banker," Scott said, returning her glare.

"Stop calling him that! You know his name is Jay."

"We can go another time if you'd like," I said, overwhelmed with the need to fix the situation.

Becky whipped around and fixed her gaze on me. I would have been turned to ice if such a superpower were possible. She blinked at my sudden shudder, turned on her heel, and stomped upstairs. Seconds later, whimpering traveled through the vents.

"Sorry," I said, finally releasing the breath I'd been holding.

"Why are you apologizing? It's not your fault. I stopped telling her if I went with someone else first a long time ago because she used to get so pissed. But I'm sick of her antics, sick of never knowing if she's going to go with me or ignore me for whatever guy it is at the moment," Scott said, his elbows coming to rest on his knees. He leaned down and pressed his palms into his forehead.

I wanted to plop down and gather him in a hug, but couldn't help wondering who the previous mystery attendees were and whether I was just the woman of the moment. "Beer?" I asked instead.

He released his palms. "Please," he said, grabbing the remote. The TV flicked to life while I walked to the kitchen. How guys could shut it down emotionally by turning on the TV would forever confound me.

I fetched two bottles of Keith's, popped them open, and stood staring out the window above the sink. I couldn't believe our glorious evening had curdled in seconds.

I heard Scott walk down the hall. Moments later, his hands weaved around my waist.

"I had a wonderful time tonight," he said in my ear.

Shivers cascaded down my body from his warm breath.

He entwined his fingers with mine and twisted me around. The intensity of his gaze left me speechless, immobile. I couldn't blink if I wanted to. My head inched forward like he was the south magnet to my north.

A crash thundered above us.

I pulled away and flipped my eyes to the ceiling.

Scott stepped back and shook his head. "I'll call you next week. About the website."

He turned and walked away. My feet remained rooted to the floor.

Seconds later, the sound of the front door slamming reverberated through the house. I slid down the fridge to the floor, where I hugged my knees to my chest and wept.

CHAPTER EIGHTEEN

I glanced at the clock. Two minutes had passed since I last checked. I lifted the I Heart New York mug to sip my third frothy cappuccino of the morning and drummed my nails on the table top. When would Becky get up? The debate about delaying the "talk" until she was less upset, or whether last night offered the perfect opportunity to discuss the problem, still raged in my mind when I heard the floor creak above me. My stomach spiraled into a frenzy, like it was hosting a squirrel block party featuring peanut-butter appetizers. No amount of steady, deep breathing calmed the scurrying. The excessive caffeine intake probably hadn't helped.

I hustled over to the espresso machine and jammed the start button, having converted Becky somewhere along the way from the dreadful hazelnut. The kitchen drowned in noise while I frothed the milk. Becky still hadn't appeared.

With no indication she was coming downstairs, I dusted the top with cinnamon and left her mug on the counter. I resumed my position at the table, where I waited and worried. I worried she wouldn't come down at all, that she would come down screaming, that she would grab her purse and charge off to Starbucks, or even worse, that she'd bolt back to his place.

When she finally shuffled into the kitchen I remained silent, knowing I wouldn't get anywhere until she had her coffee. There was a strong possibility I might have been stalling. Becky didn't look at me. She only grunted at the cappuccino, which she grabbed before stalking back down the hall. I heard her moving around in the living room and seconds after she let out a long sigh, the TV screeched over the silence.

I wasn't prepared for her silent treatment. One of my legs danced a jig beneath the table while I sipped my cold coffee and debated what to do. With a deep breath, I pushed back the chair and stood. I wobbled and grabbed the counter for support. With another deep breath I used it to push off, like a raft shoving off from a dock, and stumbled down the hall, wishing I had Scott, Adam, Martha, Abby, or Mom there for support.

"Uh, Becky?" I said, lurking in the doorway to the living room.

She flicked her red-rimmed eyes to me but remained silent.

"Can we talk?" I asked in a hoarse whisper.

She released a long, sarcastic sigh. "What?"

"I just..." I hesitated, having hoped she would be more receptive. I didn't know where to start.

"Spit it out, Rose."

"Sorry about last night," I mumbled.

"Whatever. I know Scott goes without me anyway, so I shouldn't have been so surprised."

"Oh," I said, stunned by her perceptiveness. "Well, I didn't know. Sorry."

"Fine," she said, turning back to the TV.

Still leaning on the door frame, I tasted blood from where I'd been nibbling the inside of my cheek. The conversation wasn't progressing like I'd hoped.

"Can I ask you something?" I asked.

"God, I hate it when people say that. You're going to ask it anyway, so just ask the damn question, don't give me the option to decline."

Even sporting cotton pajamas, disheveled hair, and a bare face raging with irritation, Becky still looked beautiful. I desperately wanted to back out, say nothing and stumble upstairs, but Becky was my best friend, and I was concerned. And I wasn't the only one. Although maybe I was the only one who could get through to her.

"I think… I mean… I'm worried. I'm worried about you spending too much time with Jay. I think maybe you're doing what you said before that you didn't want to…" I trailed off, annoyed I hadn't expressed myself clearly.

"Really? You're worried about me. How sweet."

"Uh, I am. I don't want…"

"You know what I don't want, Rose? A fucking lecture. It's bad enough I get them from Scott…"

"But I'm not Scott. You can talk to me. I want to be there for you, but it's hard when you're never here. Please don't make the same mistakes, Becky. I don't want to see you get hurt."

She narrowed her eyes at me. They were like twin glaciers. "Maybe I have made some mistakes in the last few months, and maybe Jay wasn't one of them."

I gasped like I'd been sucker-punched and suddenly remembered why I loathed fighting with girlfriends, boyfriends, my husband, or anyone. I wanted to race away, but Becky's look of triumph at hurting me spurred me on. I had to get through to her. "Becky, listen to yourself. I'm your friend, but you're pushing me away. Is that what you want? What happened to Becky, my maiden in shining armor?" I forced a grin. It was a lame attempt to break the tension.

"You're attacking me. What the hell do you expect?"

"I'm not attacking. I'm trying to talk to you."

"Fine. You want to talk? At least I'm trying to get out there, not hibernating at home because I'm scared."

"Maybe, but I'm not ditching card games and Gardening Club. You said you lost all your friends before. What about this time? Do you want that to happen again?"

She snorted. "Just wait. You'll find a guy soon enough and you'll do the same thing."

"No. I won't."

"Whatever," she said with a dismissive wave of her hand.

After a few moments, Becky spoke again. "You know what pisses me off the most? You never even asked if I was happy. You sauntered in here and started harping about my making a mistake. What if Jay isn't a mistake? What if he's the best thing that's ever happened to me? You don't even know because you've never asked."

"You're never home to ask," I said, surprising myself with the sarcasm in my voice.

"No, I've been out living."

God she was good at this. My novice abilities were no match, but I kept trying. "Well, if you want to ditch all your friends again, far be it from me to stop you. I've only known you a few months, so I'll get used to not having you in my life. You might want to think about your brother, though."

"As much as you think about him?"

From the forest fire I felt engulf my face, I knew my blush would have toppled the Rosie Scale. I remained silent, flabbergasted by her observation.

"I'm not stupid. I watched you two come home last night. You were like giddy teenagers in love. Stay away from him if you know what's good for you."

I furrowed my eyebrows. "Is that some kind of threat?"

She snorted. "No, a warning. Even though you're apparently ready to throw our friendship out the window, I do still care about you. I don't want you to get hurt. He'll hurt you. It's what he does. Or you'll hurt him. Don't use him, Rose." Her voice was an arctic breeze that joined her frigid glare. There was that instinctive sibling protectiveness I had no experience with again.

"I don't want to lose this friendship. I just wanted to tell you what I thought. Friends do that."

"Fine. It's been noted," Becky said, resuming her channel surfing.

"And don't forget what I said about Scott," she called out when I finally peeled myself off the wall and skulked upstairs.

*****

Over the course of the following week, I worried and wept while Becky shopped and slept. I had expected her to disappear back into The Banker's world, but she surprised me and remained home more evenings than out, and I still had no idea why she was so upset the night we arrived home after the CNE.

Everyone said it would blow over, that she'd come around, but I couldn't share their enthusiasm. The Bubbling Becky they saw only came out when we entertained. The remainder of the time I endured cold shoulders, glares, and silence shrouding our home.

Even Scott seemed unperturbed when I brought it up again during a working lunch we had arranged to plan my website. "She'll just ignore you until she needs you."

I flinched. "We can't keep telling her she's doing something wrong. I think we need to be supportive so she feels she can come to us. If we keep pushing how wrong we think it is, she might keep seeing him like a teenager you tell not to do something and they run right out and do it anyway."

His jaw hardened. "She was always like that. There was never any controlling her. I have no idea what to do, Rose. I've tried everything. I've given her the space and let her hang out with these assholes. I've put my foot down, and she goes running back. It always ends the same."

"I don't think you can put your foot down. She's a grown woman," I said, the skin on the back of my neck bristling. Was that natural big brother-little sister protectiveness, or was it more? Was he controlling like Frank, but on his best behavior with me? Did I have yet to see his ugly side? How can you tell the difference between controlling and concern? Had he given me a huge clue so early?

I felt myself turn cooler, mistrusting and unsure.

Scott's leg bounced up and down under the table while he jammed his finger down on the mouse to navigate the website. I returned my attention to the screen. "So, how do I post something?"

"Click here and type whatever you want to say. Then hit post."

"That's simple."

"To dress it up a bit, you can add images with this icon, add a link with this one, and there are many options for fonts, text size, and color."

"Thanks for doing this. You didn't have to go to so much trouble. I'm not even sure I'll do this yet."

"You will."

He was so confident in me, so sure. I didn't know what to do with it.

"This was really nice of you, even after..." I trailed off.

Scott shrugged and ran one hand through his hair, mussing the dark curls. "It wasn't much work, so don't worry about it. You could have figured it out on your own. I only saved you a bit of time."

He hadn't flirted, brought up the Ferris wheel, or even tried to make a move. He was all business. Did last week's antics with Becky make him realize that a relationship between us was a terrible idea? I should have been happy he respected my wishes, but instead, over the course of our lunch I had grown frustrated by his lack of attention.

Until the comments about controlling Becky.

At that, I shoved my leaping libido off a ledge and forced myself to focus on his tutorial.

*****

The following Saturday afternoon, Becky shuffled into the kitchen in her pajamas. I stiffened in front of my laptop, the article on herbs I had been writing forgotten. When she approached the espresso machine, I remained committed to continuing the avoidance dance we had been performing all week. I stayed silent and began packing up my belongings to head upstairs when she spoke.

"I'm sorry. I shouldn't have yelled at you last weekend. I know you're worried. Scott too."

I swiveled around to face her. "What happened last weekend?"

Her emeralds sparkled with tears. "Jay told me I was being clingy and that he wanted a night out with his friends. I freaked. And then you weren't home and Scott wasn't around–although I know what he would have said anyway. And then you both came home laughing and happy while I was miserable. The timing was shit and when you said the same thing the next day about my spending too much time with him, you have no idea what a nerve you hit. But it wasn't fair for me to go off on you like that. I'm so sorry, Rose. Please forgive me?" she whimpered.

"I was going to talk to you last weekend regardless."

She released a sob.

"I'm sorry we weren't there. Scott is too."

Becky snorted, unconvinced. She wiped her nose with her sleeve. "Sure he is. He's seen me do this a million times."

"A million? That's a lot of guys, Becky," I teased.

"Well, maybe a baker's dozen." She grinned back and then stared off into space, suddenly serious again. Her voice wobbled when she spoke. "I did it again, didn't I?"

I approached her and gathered her in my arms. "You'll figure it out. We both will."

"I hope you're right," she said, her words trailing off.

"I am," I said, releasing her. "Cappuccino?"

"Please," she said, pointing at the machine. "That thing hates me."

I wrinkled my nose. "Is that why this household saw a return to hazelnut this week?"

She nodded and shrugged.

"And here I was thinking you did it to spite me," I said, laughing. Becky joined me.

"Screw it. It's after four, let's have wine."

"I'll grab it. Sit down."

"You're such a mother hen," Becky said, rolling her eyes as she walked past and plopped down at the table.

I yanked open the fridge and had to crouch to reach the bottle hiding at the back.

"So, what's my brother like on a date?"

My head bounced off the top of the refrigerator with a thud. "Oh, it wasn't a date," I said, waving my hand behind me, hoping to convey it was nothing. Grateful for the cover of the fridge to hide my blush, I attempted to determine how I could remain inside until it dissipated. The bottle of wine was right in front of me.

I glanced at Becky out of the corner of my eye when I emerged. She twirled her empty wine glass and looked thoughtful, an act that could only end in wine puddles once I filled it.

"It would be nice, the two of you together."

I plonked the bottle on the counter and dove back into the fridge. "There, open that. You hungry?" I called out, yanking open the crisper when I saw her approach with a mischievous grin. "It's not like that. It, uh…it wouldn't be right."

"That sucks. You could have been my sister-in-law and I could have been the crazy auntie to your babies."

"Do we have any Balderson's left? The aged cheddar would go great with this wine," I said, trying to deflect attention away from the conversation. I did learn from the master, after all.

"Yum. Cheese. I think we still have some crackers." She jumped up to retrieve them from the cupboard and I finally felt safe to emerge from the fridge. Hopefully, any remaining red tinge to my face could be explained by the cold.

We sat in silence, munching cheese and crackers and sipping our wine. The large clock on the wall was marking the seconds with loud ticks, a constant reminder that life marches on. I searched for something to say, but kept getting distracted by her blessing bombshell.

"Do you like him?" she asked, eyeing me over a chunk of cheese.

"He's nice. Very supportive," I said, gulping some wine.

"He hasn't been hanging around here to see me, you know. I've seen the way he looks at you."

Oh. OH!

"Come on." She nudged me with her foot under the table. "Why not?"

I stared at the fridge and wished for its cover again. I should have confessed everything, but didn't want to start another fight and I knew she'd be upset because we hadn't told her.

"Go for him if you want, Rosie. I'm serious. He's a great guy. I said all that bad stuff the other day because I was pissed. I always thought he was a bit womanizing, but maybe it's because he hasn't found the right girl. He might have in you, though. You'd be perfect together."

We hadn't hidden it as well as we thought. I took another long swig of wine and began chewing the inside of my lip. It was another obstacle removed when I wanted an impenetrable barricade.

"I know you think it's too soon, but if you're pining over him anyway, what difference does it make?"

Unfortunately, I couldn't find any fault with that logic.

CHAPTER NINETEEN

A few days later, still buzzing from Becky's blessing, I wandered in search of wisdom in my mother's garden. And maybe some of her insights, as well.

"Hey, Mom," I said, pushing the door open and calling out to avoid startling her. I bounded up the stairs to change into the grungy gardening shorts and a T-shirt I stored in my old closet.

My childhood bedroom was still the same shade of mauve I had slapped on it in high school, but the remnants of my teenage years had been replaced. Mom had swapped out my large desk under the window for a smaller table that housed a sewing machine. The Johnny Depp and Rob Lowe posters that had once stared down at me in large poster form had been replaced by a few framed prints. But my "Hang In There" upside down kitty poster somehow still clung to the back of my closet with twenty-year-old desiccated masking tape. While changing, I considered rolling it up and carting it home to stick up in my new room, but maybe Mom still needed a reminder once in a while too.

I found her sitting outside with a cup of tea and slid onto the seat beside her.

"I'm glad you're here. You can help me with the roses."

I swept my gaze across the garden. Several plump pink and red rose blooms had withered and waited to be pruned. More weeds had sprouted in my absence and several yellow-headed devils threaded through the lawn. "The only thing dandelions are good for is wine," Gram used to say and since the city had implemented the pesticide ban, I was surprised there hadn't been a dandelion wine-revival considering the fields of yellow.

I turned to face my mother. Dark circles marked the skin beneath her eyes. Her short dark hair had become streaked with white. Did I not notice because I saw her so frequently? Or was something else going on? My mind vaulted to the worst case scenario. "Are you all right, Mom?"

"I tire more quickly these days."

"Really? You're just tired?" I asked, searching her eyes. I had heard of parents not telling their children about a serious illness to spare them the pain. What if Mom was following that ridiculous notion? She nodded and continued staring at her overgrown garden.

"Have you gone to the doctor?"

"I'm just slowing down. I don't know how much longer I can keep up this place."

"I'll come over more often to help," I insisted, covering up my first thoughts. *You can't sell my childhood home. Where would you go? I need you.*

"That would be lovely, but I'm thinking of converting some of the gardens. Maybe you could help design some new ones. Something low-maintenance with shrubs and mulch. It would be great practice for your business. You could even take pictures and put them on your website."

"You want to get rid of the gardens?" She might as well have told me she wanted to take up skydiving or have plastic surgery. I had liked Abby's idea, but never thought Mom would be interested.

She sighed. "Sometimes you reach a point in life when you realize you can't handle everything. You need to ask for help or make changes. Surely you've figured that out in the last few months." She smiled, patting my hand. "Over the years I've made changes as I needed to. I hired a lawn care company and had you help with the gardens, but I think it's time for more." She hesitated. "I've been considering condos."

"I'll move in with you," I blurted out.

"You'll do no such thing. I certainly won't let you run from mopping up after Frank to babysitting your poor old mother. You need your own space now."

"Hire me as your gardener."

"I just told you I would. If I decide to stay."

"No, full time," I paused. "Never mind. That was stupid. I'd do it for free."

"I can't have you spend all your time here puttering after me. Besides, that's not what I want. I don't think I would be able to enjoy the gardens if I couldn't tend to them. I don't want to watch you do what I can't. But I don't want to take away your special place to come and think either."

"When I land a few clients, I'll have other gardens to putter in, so don't worry about that," I said, putting on a brave face as a landslide of memories crashed over me. My knee getting stuck in the banister, my first kiss on the front porch, and Mom tying the corset of my wedding dress all flickered through my mind. The happier memories turned into unpleasant ones of my father's scolding, my eavesdropping on their arguments long after they thought I was asleep, and my mother's howls upon learning of his car accident. Even Frank appeared, sitting on the front steps as we chatted eagerly about our future, his boasting during family dinners, and then his absence from the house when he gradually pulled away and dragged me along with him.

We sat in silence and stared out at the gardens that had kept us together over the years when many mothers and daughters drifted apart. I thought about leaving my own garden behind for a new beginning. It hadn't killed me. Maybe it was time for Mom to have a new beginning, too. Maybe it was time we both let go of the past.

"You should do it," I said, pounding my fist on the table. "Buy a condo. You could run their gardening club, plant their gardens, supervise even. You wouldn't have to think about all the maintenance this place is and you wouldn't have to do anything if you don't feel up to it."

"You'd still visit, even though there wouldn't be any gardens to play in?"

"Of course. As long as you move somewhere with a pool," I said, grinning. I hoisted myself up to go envelop her in a hug.

Her eyes glistened as she kissed my cheek and I couldn't help but wonder how long she'd held onto this place for me.

"Oh, Rose. I'm so pleased you're not upset."

"You need to do what's right for you, Mom. Don't hang on to this place if it's not what you want."

She nodded and raised her mug to her lips. "So, what's brought you over to pound in the garden today?"

I let out a long, heavy sigh. "Becky gave me her blessing to be with Scott."

Her mouth fell open. "How did that come about?"

I filled her in on our truce and Becky's approval. Somehow my marriage dissolving combined with Becky's contagious discussions of pretty much everything and anything had cranked open a window to allow my mother and I to talk more openly. I'd told her everything about Scott weeks ago. I had confided in her more in the last two months than during the last two decades.

"I'm so thrilled you girls came to your senses. And now you have nothing standing in your way with Scott," she said with a huge grin. "I like him. He's kind, considerate, and I've seen how he looks at you."

I groaned. "Not you, too. Becky's approval has made everything worse. I'm still worried I'll ruin my relationship with her or screw up their relationship, and I can't jump at the first guy that comes along. It's what I did with Frank, for God's sake, and look where that got me."

"I stand corrected. You have yourself standing in your way," she tutted. "Maybe you're avoiding him because you like him too much. You're scared of those feelings, scared to get your heart broken again. But you can't keep running away."

"But shouldn't I be cautious after what happened to me? I have every right to be scared."

"You can't live life scared, and you can't not trust for the rest of your life."

"But what about those controlling comments about Becky? He seems so charming and lovely, but what if it's too good to be true? What if he's just like Frank?" I asked with a shudder.

"Do you think he is?"

"My gut says no, but I don't think I can trust that anymore either."

"Scared is no way to live, Rose."

"But it's only been a few months. Don't I get some kind of pass for a while?"

"Maybe, but you can't keep hiding forever."

"I know, I know."

"You'll be fine. I know you will."

"I wish I had never met him," I moaned, dropping my head in my hands on the table.

"Which him?"

"Both of them," I said into my arms.

"Sometimes it takes years before you understand why something happened in the first place."

"Everything happens for a reason, right?" I said, peeling myself off the table.

"I don't know about that. I think it's random. It's what we learn from the situation or experience that's important."

"Why do you think I fell for Frank and stayed with him for so long?"

She pinched the bridge of her nose and sighed. "He was charming. He said all the things you wanted to hear. Your father was just as charming. I worry it's my fault."

"I told you before, Mom, I make my own decisions, however terrible they might be."

"Yes, but I'm afraid your father's criticism led you straight into Frank's arms when he told you everything your father wouldn't."

Rendered mute, I stared at her. Only the cardinals calling out broke the silence until she continued.

"Your father was more similar to Frank than you realize. You were a rebellious teenager when he died, so even though you stood up to him at times, you probably never knew how much I tiptoed around him. When you were a child I worried about the damage he might be doing but I didn't have the strength you did to leave. I'm sorry," she whispered, swiping at stray tears with the tissue she kept in her sleeve. "I've never been more proud of you than when you left that bastard."

I couldn't speak. Memories bubbled to the surface like lava and they burned while flowing into my consciousness. The first wave began with his last Father's Day, when I had cooked his favorite meal. He blasted me for lumpy mashed potatoes and dry meatloaf. I threw the apple pie I'd baked earlier that day on the table in front of him and stalked out the door. I marched down the street to Gram's, furious with myself for not bringing the pie for us to share instead. Or not tossing it in his face.

I flashed to the first memory of my father yelling at me. He'd taken issue with my accidentally kicking the soccer ball into my own net and screeched from the sidelines about my blunder. I was five years old. I sobbed the entire walk for ice cream, something Mom and Gram had insisted on. My father drove home. Alone.

I recalled his demands over the years for better grades. "How are you going to get into med school?" he used to shout repeatedly, regardless of whether I'd received the highest test score in the class. He continued even with the knowledge that I had no intention of becoming a doctor. He ridiculed my job at the garden center and mentioned my "lack of ambition" at any opportunity.

My attire as a teen didn't escape his wrath either. Shouts of slutty clothes and threats of cutting off my clothing allowance were frequent occurrences. Mom and Gram had slipped me twenties with an unspoken agreement not to mention it, and once I worked for Abby I began buying my own clothes. I wore them under things he approved of or changed at my girlfriend's houses. Some clothes I never even brought home.

Never once was I beautiful or smart, clever or funny to him. How had I never seen that before? Was it because I received an overabundance of it from Mom and Gram instead?

"Why didn't you leave?" I asked when I could speak again. I wasn't demanding or angry, just curious.

"I had no way to support myself and was afraid of what it would do to you. I think I'd also had enough loss in my life after losing my own father that I couldn't handle any more."

"I wonder if I would have stayed with Frank if I'd had children."

"I don't think so. You've always been much stronger than I was. You stood up to your father much more than I did."

"That was teenage rebellion, like you said."

"No, it was more than that. When you were four years old, you became obsessed with a hot-pink frilly dress Gram gave you, and when we were leaving for a barbecue at one of his friend's homes, he demanded you change. You crossed your arms, looked him straight in the eye, stomped your foot and said, "Daddy, I'm wearing this dress. You can't make me change." Mom smiled at the memory I couldn't access, even though I had starred in it. "You had fire in you even then, and if the flame dampened over the years with Frank's constant demands, the ember is still there. When you find that fire again you won't make the same mistakes."

I tried to nod. I felt like a damp log. How would I ever flame?

CHAPTER TWENTY

I approached Becky with the laptop clutched to my chest. I stood in the hall, my mouth turning dry. "Becky. It's time," I said.

"What's up?" she asked, tearing herself away from the TV.

"Singles Shack."

"Oh." She arched one eyebrow so high it rested on top of her head.

I stared at the wall behind her, my face flaming with guilt. "I need to do some dating. I can't dive head first. I need to dip my toes in the dating waters first." The conversation with my mother had made me even more determined not to use Scott as a guinea pig for my trust issues. Instead, I decided to sign up for Singles Shack. Even with Frank on the site, and his abhorrent message to Becky, I still refused to believe every man on Singles Shack was an arse.

"Name?"

"I'm sorry?" I thought she'd said "lame" because of my cliché comments.

"You need a user name. Something cute or quirky. Definitely not suggestive or you'll get all the losers."

"What's yours?"

"GTAQT," she said looking smug. She rolled her eyes while I stood there trying to figure it out. "Greater Toronto Area Cutie."

I bobbed my head. "Smart. How did you figure it out?"

She raised her arms over her head in a stretch while I hovered by the door. "It took ages. You can't access the women to see what they're using, which is frustrating, so I surfed through the guys' names and went from there. Eventually, it came to me. You may want to sleep on it for a while. Also, start jotting down some notes about what you want to say about yourself," she said, waving the converter in my direction before she resumed clicking, almost knocking her water off the side table in the process.

Where did the Becky go who had urged me to do this a few weeks ago? Was she trying to discourage me so I would go out with her brother? It didn't matter if she refused to help or screamed I was making a mistake, I refused to buckle or bend to the force of Becky and her dimpled brother. Or my mother.

I left Becky to her movie of the week and wandered upstairs. I tucked my legs underneath me on the bed and began typing up a profile so it would be ready when a user name popped into my head. Although I had struggled with it at the time, creating the "About Me" page on my website now felt like it had taken the effort of writing a shopping list. For Singles Shack I needed to appear cute and funny and convey the correct message. From browsing the men, I discovered online dating was tricky. No photo or having a fuzzy one, or one false word or oddball comment and potential dates would click off my profile. I knew because that's what I did. One good looking man's atrocious spelling sent me clicking away faster than Becky changed channels. I glossed over anyone who hadn't written anything. I moved on if there were no photos, because it was likely they were married.

The next day, on my stroll home from the small market shop, a potential profile name popped into my head. I stole Becky's beginning and added "girl next door" to come up with GTAGND. I danced around the kitchen while I unpacked the groceries. I twirled between the counter and the fridge, tossing fresh fruit and vegetables into the crisper. I resisted the urge to sing into a banana.

I poked the power button on the laptop and picked at my lip while it loaded. I typed in the profile name, hit enter, and slumped in my seat, holding my breath. If someone had already used the name, I would have to come up with something else. After several seconds, a new screen popped up, requesting my personal details. The breath I'd been holding tumbled out. Somehow, no one had used the moniker yet.

I leaned forward and completed the profile.

Seconds after clicking complete, an instant message popped up.

"Afternoon delight?"

I wrinkled my nose and blocked the user.

I tried to focus on writing another gardening article, but thoughts of dating consumed any available space in my mind. For the first time since leaving Frank, I really considered it. The term divorcée danced through my mind and the image of a high-maintenance, plastic-faced, middle-aged woman surfaced that I had difficulty equating with my situation. Even though I didn't fit my stereotypical image of a divorcée, it still didn't change the fact that I was going to be one.

Desperate to be prepared, I tried to figure out what to say about my marriage even though I wouldn't divulge the information too soon. First mention would gloss over it with clichés: it didn't work out, we fell out of love, and we weren't meant to be. They didn't convey anything, but would suffice. Who wanted to discuss that so early in a relationship anyway?

But if something serious bloomed, did I tell them Frank was an overbearing pig? That he was manipulative and a compulsive liar and that I left the second I found out? What about my part in the situation? It takes two people to manage a successful marriage and two people to tear it apart. I probably wouldn't believe anyone who said they didn't share any of the blame. But how did I explain my role? Did I say I was naïve and gullible or that I never stuck up for myself and let his questionable behavior slide? Would that risk my being taken advantage of all over again?

I watched the flickering laptop and waited for a date. I had assumed it would happen quickly. Who knew online dating was a game turtles could play? Unless you only wanted a hook-up, based on the dirty messages I'd already received, each one more delightful than the last. They were almost enough to make me delete my profile, but I thought it best to confer with the online dating guru first.

"Let me get this straight," Becky said when consulted. "It was 1:30 in the afternoon? On a Wednesday?" She tucked a hand over her mouth in a dismal attempt to hide her amusement.

"That's right."

"Of course you only got the creeps, you dumbass," she said, snorting with laughter as she sailed down the hall towards the fridge. "The good guys are all at work or on the golf course. The losers are at home, or checking at work–which is probably worse in my opinion."

After some grumbling, I came around to her amused way of thinking. At least she wasn't giving me hell for signing up.

"You know, I didn't get many dates from it."

"I thought you got loads of hits."

"Sure, some creeps, some great-seeming guys, but I found it pretty nerve-wracking to go out and meet someone I'd never met. Even after chatting with them online for a while."

"Oh."

"Don't worry," she added. "I'm sure Prince Charming is online."

"Maybe I should forget about it," I said, closing the profile that had taken me hours to perfect.

"What, because of your back-up plan?" Irritation replaced the amusement in her voice.

"I'm sorry?"

She remained silent and it dawned on me. "Oh no, Becky. It's not like that. I promise."

"Explain it to me then," she demanded, jerking open the dishwasher and removing two wine glasses.

I folded the laptop down, my hands lingering over its warm shell. "I don't know how."

"It seems pretty simple to me. You're ready to date, so what's the problem?"

"I want to start slow. It couldn't be slow with Scott. We already know each other. I respect him too much. And then there's the fact that he's your brother. I don't want to ruin our friendship. Even with your approval, I don't want to mess that up and I don't want to jump into something just because it seems easy. I realize now it's what I did with Frank, and you know how that ended. I don't want to make the same mistakes."

"A few bad dates and you'll reconsider anyway, so why bother?"

I remained quiet. I didn't know how to explain it any further.

She shook her head. "You've got this great guy right in front of you. You like him, and the feeling is mutual. Why are you making it so difficult? I'd kill for that kind of luck."

"I don't…"

"Think it's a good idea," Becky said, mimicking my previous explanation. "Fine, then date yourself into a stupor and leave Scott alone." She was all business. And controlling. It reminded me of Scott's extreme concern for her, which was the only reason I omitted from the list I'd spouted off to her.

"Geez, Becky. I know you're concerned about him, but give me a break. I know what I'm doing."

"Do you?"

I nodded enough to make myself dizzy, but I couldn't look her in the eye.

*****

I watched my mother smother a vase in bubble wrap and place it in a sturdy brown box.

"I don't know why you're bothering to have it painted," I said. "Some developer will just demolish it to build a monster home." Rage bubbled at Frank for convincing me we should buy a sterilized new home and I grew disgusted with myself for not piping up sooner about my preference for an older house full of charm and history, like the one I grew up in. Instead, I had lived on top of someone else's bulldozed memories.

I felt my face pull into the familiar pout I had sported as a child. I wanted to stomp my feet and scream at the thought of this house being leveled.

"Stop sulking."

I swallowed down my childish impulses and passed her more bubble wrap so she could continue de-cluttering.

"I know you've had to deal with a lot of change this year, but maybe getting it all out of the way at one time isn't the worst thing for you."

I stared at the steps, which had sent me to the hospital for ten stitches when I was five. My gaze stretched to the height marks etched in the kitchen door frame to mark my progress. They would soon be erased from history.

I knew Mom had to move on. I knew I had to move on too. But I was reeling from her recent marital admissions, subsequent thoughts of my father, packing up my family home, Becky's cool attitude since I signed up for Singles Shack, Scott's absence since our conversation about Becky, and all the dismal, hopeless men online. The seams of my life were coming undone, and I had nothing to stitch them up with. And soon I wouldn't have Mom's garden to draw out the poison. She had her eye on a condo a few miles away in Hogg's Hollow. I wouldn't be able to walk over to visit anymore.

I felt her stare, as only a mother could, and was embarrassed by my petulance. But I couldn't help myself.

"Why don't you look for a place? You could buy a condo too. We could be neighbors." She grinned.

"Sure, me and all the old folks."

"It's not a retirement home."

"Sorry. I know."

"You'll be fine financially, right?" she asked, her eyebrows drawing together.

I sighed. "I'll be fine."

"Just think about it. The focus might help."

"I should buy this house from you. We could both live here. You wouldn't have to move!" I said, rising and hopping around like a bunny. Why hadn't I thought of it before? "You wouldn't have to give up the garden. I can take over the cooking and cleaning…"

"Rose," she interrupted, clutching the picture frame she had just removed from the wall. "I don't want to be kept. And I want you to find your own way. I refuse to have you tied down to this old clunker of a house and all its bad memories. That would be almost as horrible as if you had stayed in the house you lived in with Frank. Now, stop sulking and help me clear up all the boxes in the basement that you've left gathering dust since high school."

Maybe she was right, I thought, wandering down the stairs. Maybe it was time for a move.

CHAPTER TWENTY-ONE

My face flared when Becky arrived home, multiple shopping bags in tow. I hadn't expected to see her before I went out.

She dumped her purchases on the kitchen table and turned to face me. Her eyes roamed the length of my body, from the tips of my strappy-sandal covered toes to the cut and styled top of my head.

I squirmed under her scrutiny.

"Hair cut?"

"This morning."

"New outfit?"

"Yesterday."

"Date?"

I nodded.

"Who?"

"Uh, remember Alex? The guy who saved me from Frank? I stumbled across him on Singles Shack, actually. We've been texting for a couple of weeks."

When Alex's friendly face had popped up as I trolled through profiles, I tapped a message out on my keyboard, editing it several times before settling on: "Hi. It's Rose. Remember me? You came to my rescue outside Starbucks? How have you been doing?" I hit send before I could reconsider. Why not start somewhere I know? I needed to get the double-whammy first date in ten years and first after-marriage date jitters over with. Then I could branch out to online dating. If I could ever weed through the men.

"Interesting," she said, eyebrows raised.

"What did you buy?" I asked, poking through her bags with the hopes of distracting attention away from my date and her obvious disapproval.

"New boots and some sweaters," she said, crossing her arms. She didn't fall for it and continued eyeballing me. "You look good, Rose. I know Scott would approve."

I flinched. "Come on, Becky. Please don't ruin this for me. It's my first date. You should be dancing with glee."

"I just thought after everything…"

"What?" I snapped, panicking that Scott had told her we slept together. Why hadn't I come clean with her?

"I had all these fantasies of you marrying Scott and becoming my sister," she said, shooting her lower lip out in a pout that would have put a toddler's to shame.

I gulped. "I don't even know if I'll ever get married again at this point. Do you?"

She shrugged. "Where are you going?"

"Picnic in High Park."

She nodded and pursed her lips in approval. "It won't be as fun as the CNE."

"I know," I said, the words flying out of my mouth before I could censor them. "Too bad you weren't with us," I added, trying to cover up my blunder.

"I wouldn't have wanted to crash the party anyway." The hurt in her voice couldn't cover her lie.

"You wouldn't have," I lied right back at her.

"Whatever. Are you sure about this?"

I nodded.

"Okay," she said. Her sing-song voice was clearly a warning.

*****

I pulled off my cardigan as we strolled through the park.

"What about here?" Alex asked, stopping at a grassy patch away from the heavy foot traffic.

"This is perfect," I said. Frank would have picked wherever he wanted without consulting me. No, scrap that. We would never have gone on a picnic in the first place.

Alex unfolded a Hudson's Bay striped blanket and sent it flying in the air before spreading it on the ground before my feet. I loved the Canadian heritage he displayed with the blanket and couldn't help but wonder if we'd be eating off red and white plates.

"What a perfect day," I said, angling my face into the late September sunshine, the last remnants before winter stole the warmth away. Barks and yelps floated over with the breeze from the dog park and brought a smile to my face.

"I haven't been to High Park in years," I said.

Alex rewarded me with a huge grin. "I love it here. We could wander over to the dog park later if you want. It sounds like they're having fun."

He opened the wicker picnic basket and removed cheese, crackers, crusty bread, and various dips and spreads. Then came plates, knives, a bottle of red wine, and two plastic glasses.

"Definitely. You think we'll run out of cheese?" I teased, unwrapping the first of five different varieties.

"I thought I remembered you loved cheese from our conversation."

"You remembered right," I said, flattered. I popped a piece of aged cheddar into my mouth. I could barely recollect what he'd looked like, let alone his interests. In my defense, it had been a stressful day and there were multiple alcoholic beverages involved. I did, however, remember the ease of our conversation, and it continued while we lounged in the sunshine nibbling cheese and crusty bread and sipping a vintage Merlot.

"This was a great idea," I said, looking out at the flocks of people enjoying what might be the last perfect day of the year. A woman close to my age caught my attention. She chased a toddler who squealed with delight every time she "almost" caught him. I swallowed hard and ignored the ache in my abdomen. I felt Alex staring at me so I plastered on a smile and turned to face him. He returned my smile and shifted his weight.

I knew what was coming. I'd seen enough movies to know he was about to kiss me, yet it didn't seem contrived. His lips were soft and gentle as they brushed mine. Romance films favored this scene for a reason, I thought. Although it didn't quite compare to the kiss at the top of the Ferris wheel. But maybe it was whose lips I was kissing. I pulled away with guilt at the thought.

The intensity of Alex's gaze startled me, and I wondered if he'd be able to X-ray my brain with those blue eyes.

"I'm glad you found me again," he said, squeezing my hand.

"So am I."

After we tucked the remaining cheese, crackers, and empty bottle of wine back into the picnic basket, we hit the dog park. Alex grabbed my hand and didn't let go. We laughed as the dogs chased each other with tongues flailing.

"I've always wanted a Chocolate Lab," he said.

"Why don't you get one?"

"It wouldn't be fair. I work too much and wouldn't want it to be home alone all day."

"There are dog-walking services, you know. Doggie day-care even."

"It's not the same. One day, though. When I get married, have kids."

"I've always preferred smaller dogs," I said, lost in my own what-ever-happened-to-my-dreams reverie.

"Don't tell me you're one of those types that would buy one of those ridiculous dog strollers they sell now," he said, nudging me, but his eyes conveyed concern.

"Of course. And if she's not in the stroller, then she'd perch in my purse and travel with me everywhere, sporting a pink collar and two bows."

"Cute," he said nodding and trying to look serious, but I could tell he was trying not to look horrified.

"I'm kidding," I burst out, unable to hold back my laughter any longer.

"Thank God," he said smiling, before leaning in for another kiss.

"So you don't like small dogs?" Alex asked when he pulled away.

"Not the tiny ones. Too scared I'd step on it. I've always loved beagles," I said, pushing aside thoughts of Buddy the Beagle and his dimpled human.

"They're not small dogs."

"I guess I like medium-sized dogs then, although I do love them all. They're always so happy to see you and easy to please," I said, pointing out two beagles chasing each other. They slowed and some serious humping started.

We chuckled as the humper was denied and his intended ran off with another, much larger dog.

"Let's get out of here," he said, grabbing the picnic basket and clutching my hand before pulling me in the direction of his car.

*****

"How are things going with Jay?" I asked Becky, approaching the subject like a yellow traffic light. I was eager to end our superficial conversations with our love lives off the table, so I had suggested a rare Saturday girls' night complete with dinner, wine, and chick flicks. Becky grinned and said she'd cook if I provided the wine and Martha brought dessert. When I tossed her a skeptical look, she flicked her hair behind her shoulders with a smirk and told me she'd been practicing on the nights I went out with Alex. These happened to be opposite the evenings she went out with Jay, which was the other reason I suggested the girls' night–our conflicting schedules. I missed hanging out with her.

Any doubts I held about Becky's newly-honed kitchen skills vanished. She diced red onions with ease while responding. "We're working it out. I'm trying not to be clingy and do my own thing, but then he doesn't understand when I say I'm busy, like tonight. I don't get it. It's like he wants it both ways."

"That's weird, especially after he said he wanted his space," I said, surprised and impressed by her follow-through.

"That's what I told him. But he said it's only once in a while when he goes out with the guys."

"How do you feel about that?" I asked, still treading lightly.

"I don't know. When I said tonight was a girls' night, he got irritated, and I had to remind him of his guys' nights. It's all so confusing because he said the clingy bit, and then you and Scott said it. I know you're probably right, but I don't know how to back off, especially when he gets aggravated if I have other plans. Which isn't even that often." She slid the onions off the cutting board into the pot with a long sigh.

"I'm proud of you for trying."

Becky grunted and brought the knife down on a clove of garlic. "Thanks."

She stopped chopping to take a sip of wine. She waved her glass towards the corner of the room. Red wine splattered into the pot of onions. "You running the country from our kitchen?"

I followed her gesture and my gaze settled on the wrought-iron plant stand now housing overflowing folders and binders, my laptop, and library books on how to start a business and garden design. A jar full of pens and pencils, a stapler, paper clips, and my cell phone lay strewn across the folders and books. Hot-pink sticky notes covered the iron shelves, and several dotted the large green foliage of the philodendron trailing down the right side.

"Sorry about the mess."

"No worries. I was just teasing."

"If only Mom wasn't moving, I could have moved my operation to one of the rooms at her place. I'll figure something out soon."

"You've changed a lot since I met you. A couple of months ago you would have had a heart attack leaving everything scattered about when someone came over."

"It's just Martha."

"Even so, it's about time you relaxed. And I love that you're out doing what you love."

"Thanks," I said, even though her positivity still couldn't curb the continuous loop of doubt plaguing my thoughts. Despite my worries, the venture was keeping me occupied and enthusiastic. I was busier than I ever thought possible with all the research, writing, and designing. I loved being the one making all the decisions, from business card design to marketing ideas and implementation, even which bank to start a business bank account with.

My free time was so limited now that I often turned down Alex's frequent date requests, which wasn't typical of my relationships-past. But I found the snail's pace of my relationship with Alex suited me. With Frank, the moment we met we were like conjoined twins. My relationships prior to him began that way too. And then there was Scott, who I didn't even date, but vaulted straight into bed with.

"So, how's Mr. Perfect?" Becky asked.

"Good," I replied with a tiny shake of my head to rid it of Scott.

"You done the deed yet?" she asked with a sly grin.

I felt my face heat up.

"Rosie! When? I want details." She tossed the knife aside, wiped her hands, and plopped down beside me at the table.

"Wait until Martha gets here," I mumbled, my face smoldering further at the thought of divulging the details not once, but twice. Would I ever get used to the depth of our sharing?

"Oh, come on. Out with it."

I groaned, knowing I wouldn't escape her inquisition. I reached over and snatched my emergency work chips from the top of my planning binder to delay hunger pains since Becky appeared to have abandoned her cooking duties. Her ADHD might hinder any *Top Chef* aspirations.

"It happened last weekend."

"And you didn't tell me! Bad girl. So, how was it?" she asked, flicking the bag around in her direction and shoving her hand inside.

"It was good. Great, really."

She frowned. "That didn't sound too convincing."

"No. No. It was nice, romantic. He even closed the curtains. It was great not to worry about my thighs."

"Whatever, you're skinny. Romantic, huh? That's good. Passionate, too?"

I stared out at the sheets of rain. Sex with Alex was incomparable to my experience with Scott, which was simply a release of all my built-up anger, frustration, and loneliness. This was different. I was different.

"Yes," I said. "It was wonderful."

She grinned and hopped up, heading back to her spaghetti sauce, one of two meals she had learned how to cook so far. "Fabulous. I'm so happy for you."

My phone dinged a text. I ignored Becky's arched brow and sneaked a quick peek.

"Miss u. Call me if u want 2 get 2gether later."

Did he want a booty call or did Alex genuinely want to see me? Or was he being needy like The Banker? *Like Jay,* I reprimanded myself. I still slipped from time to time and used the old nickname. I glanced at Becky, unsure about asking her when her phone dinged too. She hesitated and nibbled her lip before picking it up. She checked the message and dropped the phone back on the counter without fumbling out a response.

"He can wait," she said, shrugging and taking a slug of her wine.

"Mine too," I said with a grin. I silenced my phone and dropped it on the counter beside hers. I raised my glass in a toast. "To girls' night."

"To girls' night," she said, clinking my glass.

We both glanced down at our phones as we gulped.

*****

An issue with my blog the following week sparked a raging debate in my mind about whether I should call Scott. Our Friday night card games had disbanded, and a work emergency had prevented him from attending the last Garden Club meeting. He hadn't called or made any attempts at contact for several weeks. I hadn't seen him since he had given me the tutorial. I had no idea whether he even knew about Alex.

After struggling for hours, I finally gathered the courage to call.

"Could I pick your brain with a few website questions?" I asked, picking at a hangnail.

"Actually, I'm swamped. Could I get one of my guys to call you?"

"Oh, no no, no. It's fine. I'll figure it out. Sorry to bother you."

He sighed. "It's fine. Stop apologizing."

"What's wrong?" I blurted out, desperate to know, even though I didn't want to ask him over the phone, but in person, when I could gauge his reaction by his handsome face.

"Scott?" I said when he didn't respond.

"Singles Shack. Alex. I guess I had hoped…"

"I'm sorry."

"You're always apologizing, Rose. Please stop. You have to do what's right for you. I just…I really liked you."

Liked?

I paced down the hall. "I knew this wasn't a good idea from the start and now I've upset you. I'm…" I caught myself before apologizing again and wondered briefly whether he was right about that.

"Bad timing," he said.

"Bad everything. Well, maybe not bad everything…" I said, slumping down on the sofa.

Scott groaned. "Rose…"

"Shit. I'm sorry. I don't know what's wrong with me. That was completely uncalled for. Do you think we can be friends?" I asked quickly, hoping he would ignore my inappropriate flirtation like I was trying to ignore the implications of it, what it meant with Scott, Alex.

More silence.

"Maybe one day?" I prompted, tucking my knees to my nose and laying my forehead on the knobby bones. I didn't want to lose one of the few friends I had made in the last ten years. Although with that comment I couldn't blame him. I deserved it.

"Maybe."

"Okay," I said in a whisper, my voice further muffled in the gap at my legs.

"Rose?"

I lifted my head to speak so I wouldn't have to repeat myself. Desperate to keep my voice level and avoid sobbing or sniffling, I forced a professional, almost curt tone. "Thanks again for the website. And your encouragement. Especially for that."

"You're welcome. Good-bye, Rose," Scott said, before the line went dead.

"Good-bye, Scott," I replied, pulling the phone from my ear. I shoved my head back between my knees and wept.

CHAPTER TWENTY-TWO

I curled up on the outdoor sofa in a rare patch of sunshine and sipped a glass of Gram's favorite port. It was the anniversary of her passing and I had several hours to reminisce before our annual dinner in her honor. My thoughts kept turning back to Frank's behavior after her death, and even with the knowledge I'd gleaned in the last five months, I had difficulty believing he was the monster he turned out to be based on how he had reacted at the time. But if there was anything I'd learned in the last few months, it was that Frank always had an ulterior motive.

The day I heard Mom speak the unfathomable, I withdrew the cordless phone from my ear and stared at it, unable to comprehend her words. When they broke into my consciousness, I opened my hand and sent the phone skittering across the ceramic tiles of our kitchen. I stood motionless, paralyzed with my hand outstretched. I don't even think I blinked. Frank raced to scoop it up. He thrust the phone to his ear, listened, hung up, and enveloped me in a rib-cracking embrace. I emitted a guttural howl. He refused to let me go when I shoved him away. When I kicked and screamed and pounded my fists on his chest, he held me tighter. And when I slumped to the floor, he slumped down with me. He stroked my back as I sobbed into his lap and after I calmed down enough, he drove me to Mom's, where he brewed cup after cup of tea.

Frank's strong arms encircled us both at the funeral parlor and at the cemetery, where rare early snowflakes drifted down and dusted the ground before melting. He brought the turkey and vegetables Mom was planning to make for Thanksgiving dinner to the food bank and managed to scrounge up his own food for days when my appetite vanished. The house remained tidy and my supply of tea, fresh. He even shed tears at the funeral.

Why?

I bolted upright. The pale pink and chocolate brown afghan Gram had crocheted for me for my nineteenth birthday slipped off my lap.

In the weeks that followed the funeral, Mom and I found the strength to sort through her house, move items we cherished to our homes, and bundle up her belongings for charity while weeping into her lavender-scented clothing. Frank had helped with the heavy lifting, arranged the contents sale, and found the real estate agent. He had even offered to contact the lawyer, but Mom and I already had. At the time he appeared so concerned about us I never thought anything of it.

"It would be nice for you to have a bigger car," Frank had said several weeks after the funeral. We were cramming items from Gram's into my car to bring home. "An SUV maybe, so you can fit in more of your gardening stuff. You're always complaining your car is too small." I couldn't find fault with his logic at the time.

A couple of weeks later, he mentioned it again. "We could use some of the inheritance from your grandmother to buy it. Wouldn't that be a nice way to cherish her memory? You'll have a truck to cart home flowers and gardening supplies. Or we could consider looking at cottages. Or what about another trip to Europe, go back to the town she was born? Maybe take your mother?" He had wrapped his arms around me when I began weeping again at the thought of never puttering in the garden with Gram or fetching her glasses of ice water on a sweltering day. She was always too stubborn to listen to the heat advisories and would garden "if it needed doing" as she used to say.

I pulled the afghan up around my shoulders and shuddered at Frank's persuasiveness. His ability to spin what he wanted and make it look like I wanted it too or that it would be something good for me, was mind-boggling.

His inquiries about Gram's estate had barely even registered during my grief. It never occurred to me he was salivating over her money, but looking back now, I had no doubt.

Frank had wanted the inheritance.

"Bastard," I breathed, remembering the strut he'd developed to accompany the dreamy smile on his face when he thought I wasn't looking. Engulfed in grief, the observation hadn't registered. Until now. I sprung up and stalked to the kitchen, leaving the afghan where it fell on the patio. I slammed cupboard doors until I found dear old Jack. Two ice cubes and a tumbler full, I slumped back down outside and tucked the blanket around my waist.

I twirled my glass. The crackling and tinkling of the ice flashed memories of dinner parties Frank and I used to host. I gulped the cool liquid and welcomed the heat blossoming in my chest.

How could I not have known? Why didn't I see? They were two of my favorite questions in the last few months. And I still didn't have any answers.

I stared at the amber liquid. "Liquid courage" Gram used to call whiskey, always adding "But courage can give you troubles, dear, especially drunk ones."

Two glasses later, my brain sufficiently loosened with liquor, another memory surfaced, one I must have buried six feet under along with Gram. I leapt off the sofa and sent whiskey flying into the impatiens. I scrambled inside, seized my purse, and slammed the front door. It took three attempts to lock the door behind me.

*****

Gray clouds darted across the sky and swept away the patch of sunlight I'd curled up in. By the time I arrived and jabbed at the doorbell, my arms were raw and crimson. I cowered into the corner of the door frame to protect myself from the biting wind and fumbled in my purse for keys. Mom was faster though, and the door swung open as soon as my fingers made contact with cool metal in the depths of my bag.

"Rose," Mom said, her hand pressed over her heart. "You startled me. You only have to ring the doorbell once you know. I haven't lost my hearing."

"Mom," I wheezed as I stepped inside, struggling to breathe from my run. I kicked off my ballet flats. One was black and one was brown. One might even have been Becky's. I ignored them and turned to her, still panting.

"Rose, it's barely past noon," she said, waving away the fumes.

"You tried to tell me, didn't you? About Frank? You and Gram…" I beat my chest with a fist and dropped onto one of the kitchen chairs that would soon be moved to an unfamiliar location and reduced by two. "You knew. And you tried to tell me."

"Oh, Rose." She sank into the chair beside me, her eyes filling with tears.

"Why didn't you push more when you tried to tell me, when you told me about my inheritance?" I asked, still unable to believe I'd forgotten about the money Gram had left me—money that had her wishes attached. I could see why I'd shoved it into Pandora's Box, though. If I'd let it out, I would have had to examine what Mom and Gram really thought about my husband—and whether they were right.

"Even if I'd droned on and on, would you have believed me?" she asked, her voice barely audible.

I shook my head and tossed up my hands. I had no idea what I would have believed. My husband or the two women I trusted most in my life. It was the most terrifying thought I'd had since leaving Frank.

"I would have been angry," I said. "And Frank would have used that. You were right not to force the issue." I knew I was right, just as Mom was for not saying anything further, for not pushing me.

"It was all Gram," Mom said. "After you and Frank left one Sunday night, out of the blue she shook her head and said, "I just don't know about that Frank. I can't put my finger on it, but I don't trust him." Too charming, she'd said. Being as charmed as you, I dismissed it, but she'd opened my eyes and I began observing things, like you visiting less and his rare appearances. I started paying more attention and noticed how quiet and withdrawn you'd grown. I was frightened if I forced the issue I would lose you."

I knelt down at her side and reached up to brush away the tears sliding down her cheeks. I wrapped my arms around her waist and rested my head in her lap. She stroked my hair in the steady rhythm she used when I was a little girl.

We remained melded together, neither of us breaking the silence.

"I can't believe she figured him out," I said eventually, hoisting myself up. I rubbed my knees, aching from the ceramic tiles. "Why didn't she say anything? I might have listened to her." I leaned on the counter and stretched my legs after dropping two tea bags into the ceramic teapot.

"We were never one hundred percent sure. She worried you might not listen to her either. We had an in-depth conversation about it when we changed the executor on her will. When I suggested Frank, she balked and looked at me like I was crazy."

"Some intuition she had," I said, shaking my head.

"She lived long enough to develop it. You have too, now. You'll see." Mom smiled while I poured the tea.

"Here's hoping."

"It was then that she told me she was worried about Frank getting his "grubby hands" on your half of her estate. There was no way to prevent you from spending it on something he could access or enjoy or might gain from, but she made me promise to tell you her wishes, that your portion of her estate was for you and something you wanted and that Frank should have nothing to do with it," she said, shaking her head.

"You kept your promise," I said, recalling the devastating conversation we had in Gram's kitchen, surrounded by boxes.

"But at what cost? I shattered your faith, your trust in Gram and I the second I opened my mouth. You were so shocked, so crushed that we doubted your choices and worried about your husband's motives." She shook her head and more tears fell. "I will never forget the look on your face. I had never seen you so upset. It broke my heart. Both that you felt that hurt, and that I was the reason for it. And that there was nothing I could do to console you. A mother's nightmare. A lot of good it did too. You were so defensive of him, shouting you were married and made joint decisions. You barely spoke to me for months. And you still didn't leave him. Maybe you even stayed longer because of it."

"It's not your fault, Mom. You did the right thing. And maybe it did help. We're standing here now, aren't we?"

"I suppose," she said, raising her hand to her pearls. "What did you do with it? The money? I never asked, I didn't want to risk upsetting you all over again."

"I bought the truck and banked the rest," I said.

"You never spent it?"

"No. To be honest, I kind of forgot about it after I put it into the mutual fund account Gram set up for me to teach me about investing when I was fifteen. I don't think I could have thought about it without having to question everything." I pondered the situation for a moment with my separation hindsight. "A lot of time passed in between the time you sat me down and told me Gram's wishes and the day her will was finalized. During those months, something must have clicked. I told Frank I screwed up the dates and times of the appointment with the lawyer so he couldn't attend. And then I lied again about amount of my inheritance. I never told him I got half of her estate. Maybe I realized more than I knew at the time," I said, remembering how far Frank's face had fallen when I revealed my inheritance.

Something had held me back from confiding in him, both about the estate and their feelings about him.

"What a relief. I've wondered over the years what happened."

"I think I shoved it under the rug, desperate to forget about it. I guess Gram's plan worked." I said, shrugging.

"Could he have found out about it?" she whispered, her eyes darting back and forth like the room was bugged.

"Relax. I told you, I never told him."

She shut her eyes, tilted her head back, and released a heavy sigh. When she looked back at me and spoke, her tone was sharp. "Could he know now, Rose?"

My mouth dropped open like a trap door. "Oh my God. I don't know. I never said anything but what if he found out? What if he knows? I filed the statements away, but never opened them. I never needed to. I have to go home. I have to check the website, my account online. Or find the statements. Shit." I flung open the front door and sprinted down the street, the memories of the missing money that started this journey taunting me. I heard Mom huffing and puffing as she trailed behind me.

CHAPTER TWENTY-THREE

I dropped my head into my lap and forced a deep yoga breath to ward off hyperventilation. I also hoped it would help me remember my password. I couldn't wait until the bank reopened after the holiday to find out about my money.

The butternut squash I had intended to roast glared at me. We'd forgotten about dinner. There was no time to shove a turkey in the oven now.

"That's it," I said, whipping my head out of my lap and slicing my hand through the air. "From now on I'm banning Thanksgiving."

I began to cry.

"Shhh," Mom said, rubbing my back while sifting through a pile of papers with her free hand.

I had lugged the three bankers boxes crammed full of my files and all the photocopied papers from Frank's office into the kitchen.

"Don't even think of bringing that glass of wine anywhere near this table," I barked at Becky, who had bounced into the room after changing out of her workout clothes and filled the monster glass with Merlot. How the girl didn't sweat was beyond me. "I know this table looks like a photocopier puked on it, but I can't afford any accidents on this stuff."

"Come on," she pouted.

"Not the best idea," Mom said, backing me up. Her middle finger pushed up her glasses before returning to flip through the stack of papers in her lap.

Becky downed half the glass, set it on the counter, and made her way over to the table. "So, what are we looking for?"

"A recent LLMS Mutual Fund statement. A huge deposit in Frank's accounts." I moaned. March was the last statement we had managed to locate so far and even though I had exhaled sharply in relief at the balance it showed, seven months were still unaccounted for. A notice, an amendment, or some form of marketing could have reached Frank's hands before I got around to changing my address. What if someone made a mistake and it was never updated? I could have neglected to grab some pertinent mail on my way out. There were so many variables I couldn't think straight. I felt like a shaken bottle of champagne, my head set to fly off with the slightest agitation.

"He couldn't get my money, could he?" I jumped up and circled the tiny kitchen. "Could he transfer it without my authorization?"

I stalked up to the counter and snatched Jack back out of the cupboard. I reached for the tumbler I'd abandoned earlier on the counter.

Mom approached me, reached into the cupboard, and placed a tumbler next to mine. Becky appeared a second later and repeated the gesture. The bottle rattled on the rim as I poured. Mom placed a hand on mine to steady it before extracting the bottle from my clenched fingers and sending a steady stream of whiskey into the three glasses.

I tossed back the shot and yelped at the inferno blazing down my throat.

I resumed stalking the hall, my feet pounding a steady rhythm while they searched, my hands shaking too hard to sift through papers.

Mom snagged my hand on one loop back through the kitchen, anchoring me in place. "Rose, think. Could you have ever said something to Frank?"

"No way. If he found out, it wasn't from me." I flopped onto the only vacant chair and forced my eyes shut. The sound of papers rustling danced through my ears. I could barely remember the weeks following my departure, let alone that day. Did I remember to grab all the papers when I left? Papers... Papers...

"You've got to be fucking kidding me," I said, snapping my eyes open, bolting upright, and lunging for a pile of papers. I ignored Mom's reprimanding glance about my language. It was a fuck me kind of swearing day.

"Have either of you found any statements from the last five months? From anywhere?" I demanded.

Becky nibbled her bottom lip. Her head darted from side to side, and I heard the familiar twirl of Mom's pearls while she shook hers.

"What did you remember, dear?"

I shoved a hand in the air in a rude silencing gesture I knew my mother would hate, but couldn't help myself. I didn't want the memories to fade away. I slammed my eyes shut again and tried to remember.

I had been propping up the wall across from Becky's toilet, trying not to throw up while listening to a young, bubbly customer service representative blather on about the environment and email statements. I agreed just to get her off the phone. Rather than listen to them use the environment as an excuse to save postage, it turned out to be faster to ask for paperless statements when the conversation began.

Paperless.

I wasn't attached to paper and no longer had room to store it, so I had opted for paperless billing. On all of my accounts. I never even missed my statements after setting up all my bills and accounts on automatic monthly payments.

"Rose?" I heard my mother say. I opened my eyes. She had moved to the counter and sipped whiskey in tandem with Becky.

"I don't... How did I not know..."

"He was an asshole?" Becky said.

"He was a bastard?" my mother added.

They clinked their glasses together and sipped again.

"No. Well, yes, but no, that's not it. When I changed my address, I set up paperless billing and statements for all of my bills and accounts."

"That would certainly explain your lack of existence since you moved in with me according to these files," Becky said.

"God, I'm such an idiot," I said, dropping my head in my hands.

"Don't be daft, dear. You were panicked."

"It still doesn't mean anything. The money could still be missing," I said, sliding back to the dark side of worry and obsession.

"It means we have a lot less to worry about," Mom said with her never-ending voice of reason. "If you didn't tell Frank and stopped your statements, then the odds of any foul play are slim."

"I think your mom is right, Rose. You can call first thing in the morning."

The last statement lay open on the table. I picked it up. Several figures were displayed before the decimal point. It was a lot of money. Money that Gram knew I needed to shelter. Money I had conveniently forgotten since tucking it away. Money that was the only secret I had ever kept from my husband.

My stomach dropped down an abandoned well. "Shitty, shit, shit, shit. Does he... Will he... Is Frank entitled to half of this?"

"Oh fuck," Mom said, her hand flying to cover her mouth with the transgression. "Excuse me," she said under her breath.

Becky muttered obscenities as she snatched the bottle and began sloshing more whiskey into our glasses.

My heart thundered off my rib cage and a shudder wormed through me at the thought of Frank's sticky fingers getting hold of what Gram, Mom, and I, each in our own way, had worked so hard to protect.

Becky swiveled around, plucked the laptop off the counter, and plopped it down on the papers still littering the table. "That, my dear friend, is why they invented Google."

CHAPTER TWENTY FOUR

I was determined not to sit alone just over a month later on what would have been my seventh wedding anniversary. I decided to throw myself a party, an un-anniversary party.

Hors d'oeuvre platters lay scattered on the table, bottles of wine and beer chilled in the fridge, and glasses lined the counter–except the ones Becky, Martha, and I had already pilfered and filled with Cabernet. I popped the phyllo pastries I'd concocted in the morning–wild mushroom with onion and red pepper with goat cheese–into the oven. Wiping my hands, I noticed the office clutter in the corner. Instead of hurtling up and down the stairs to remove the offending items and entertain with a pristine kitchen, I chose to leave it. I knew better now. This kitchen looked lived in. It was lived in. My house with Frank had been a shell.

Martha and Becky were still upstairs primping, after helping in the kitchen all afternoon when Mom arrived. She removed the wrap draped across her shoulders and I realized how good the move had been for her. Her house sold the same day it went up on the market after we weeded through multiple offers. We both accepted that although the house would be bulldozed, our memories couldn't be destroyed. She bought her dream condo a day later and had secured thirty-day closings for both. She had only been in the condo for a month, and already she looked less fatigued and moved with more ease. Even her hair was styled differently. I wondered if there was something more to it, but let it slide for now.

"I'm so proud of you, darling," she said with a wide smile before squashing me in a hug.

"Thanks, Mom," I said, tucking my hair behind my ears. I had new hair too, a sleek bob with caramel highlights. It took much longer to perfect than my usual ponytail, or air dry with mousse, but I loved my new 'do and hadn't been able to stop running my fingers through it all week.

We wandered down the hall when the doorbell rang again. I cracked open the door to find Alex grinning at me. I leaned out, pressed my hands on his chest, and plastered a kiss over his grin. I pulled back and shivered. The late November air transported me back to both the day I met Frank and our wedding day. Frank had insisted it would be more romantic to get married on the anniversary of the day we met, while I preferred a warm, sunny day. Instead, I said my wedding vows on a gray, frigid, rainy November day. Pushing away the thoughts, I seized the edges of Alex's leather jacket and tugged him inside. I closed the door on the memories, the crisp air, and the smell of wood smoke, and pushed Alex against the wall and planted another kiss.

"Geez. What's gotten into you?" Alex asked, pushing me away. "Let me go. I want to make a good first impression."

He shrugged off his coat. I couldn't help the disappointment that settled low in my abdomen. Wasn't I worth kissing regardless of who noticed?

After making the introductions, Alex–knowing Becky also sported a new hairstyle–complimented her hair and then began charming Mom with tales of England while I grabbed him a bottle of Keith's. Becky had settled on the more fashionable Beckham bob and pulled it off where many couldn't. She looked fantastic, her green eyes popping from beneath her bangs. If only she could keep her outfit stain-free for ten minutes until everyone else arrived.

The doorbell chimed again and Becky rushed down the hall after insisting I stay with my guests.

I overheard her from the kitchen. "It's all Rose. She waters them and picks the dead thingies off. If it was left to me, they'd be long dead by now."

I wandered out and discovered Abby removing her coat. I planted a kiss on her cheek.

"They'll be gone with the frost tomorrow," Abby said.

"But we've had frost already. Haven't we?" Becky said, her wrinkled brow swiveling back and forth between us.

"With the pots so close to the house and under the awning they're protected, but it's supposed to be much colder tonight," Abby instructed. She caught my eye and I couldn't help my wide smile and wink. It had taken some convincing, but she had finally agreed to take over my classes next year when I left to concentrate on my business. From the way she beamed at me, I knew she'd love it.

"Come on, let's get you a glass of wine," I said, linking my arm through hers, only to have her discover my mother in the kitchen and wriggle away from me.

"Susie, you look fabulous. I can't believe we keep missing each other at club meetings."

"So do you, Abby," Mom said as they embraced.

"How did the move go? Do you think you'll miss working in the garden?"

"Terribly. Looking at them though, not tending to them. These old bones couldn't hack it anymore."

Abby laughed. "Lord knows what will happen to me when that day comes. Hopefully I'll drop dead while digging in the garden and die gazing up at my roses."

I handed Abby a glass of wine and diverted my attention away from their disturbing conversation. I turned to Alex, who had just made Becky laugh. She cocked her head and grinned up at him, her eyes wide and twinkly. She tugged at her hair and giggled again.

Alex leaned in. She was flirting with him. My stomach fluttered. I took a deep breath and reminded myself he wasn't Frank.

"Let's get together for lunch," I heard Mom say, after shrugging off my insecurity. "Surely you can take time off to eat now and then."

Abby nodded. "Definitely. With our regular coffee chats about her classes and garden design, Rose has taught me I need to start doing some living before I end up spending my entire life in the store."

Mom reached out and grabbed Abby's arm. "Are you considering giving it up?"

Abby sighed. "At some point I'll have to, I suppose. Hopefully I can sell it or let someone else take over the reins. I'd hate to have to close the doors and let it go. I'd always hoped it would be Rose."

I spluttered my wine.

"But she sorted herself out," Abby continued like I wasn't standing right there. "Garden planning and design is more appropriate for her than hiding behind the flats and trolleys of plants."

"I think it's the best thing she ever did. Besides leaving that good-for-nothing husband of hers."

"So proud of you, honey," they said in unison, beaming.

My eyelids fluttered and I fought back tears. They both reached over for a hug but I pushed them away, pointing to my face. "No, no, no. I'll ruin my makeup and this took me an hour to master."

"So nice to see her taking an interest in herself again," Abby noted.

"We need music," I said, an excuse to escape my character evaluation.

"I thought I'd never see her again," I heard my mother reply as I walked into the living room. "I thought I lost her. She took a long walk around the garden, got lost along the way, but found the right path. I have my daughter back. And she's..." Her voice cracked. "And she's new and improved."

"She's redesigned," Abby said.

"Rosie redesigned," Becky added, and their laughter floated down the hall to where I was standing.

I pushed play on Becky's iPod and "I Will Survive" drowned them out. Becky had insisted on creating the playlist for tonight, and I chuckled at her first song choice while I stood staring out the window, digesting the words I'd heard. I couldn't deny the truth of their statements and was surprised myself by how far I'd come in a few short—some long—months.

I was more confident, had more energy, more drive and desire than I'd ever had before. I smiled and laughed more. I teased and became disappointed if Alex didn't get my stupid jokes. I spoke up for myself more and didn't meld my life into Alex's. So many changes. And the biggest change was "The Happy." Becky had christened it a couple of weeks ago. "You've got 'The Happy,' don't you?" she'd said, bobbing her head one evening at my endless smile. I couldn't ever remember feeling this content. While Becky moaned about not having The Happy, I told her it would come. But I might have lied, because sometimes, when I couldn't sleep at night, I worried. Would it end? When would it end? I had difficulty believing anyone could stay this happy forever. What if my business went belly up? What if Alex's perfection was an illusion? What if he was like Frank and I couldn't see it?

A shadow outside on the path startled me. Peering through the curtains, I struggled to make out who it was before moving to open the door. Slumped against the frame, illuminated by the porch light, were two dimples. Behind him stood a mop of blond hair.

"Scott, Adam," I said, smiling. I took in Scott's unzipped leather jacket, faded Levi's, and the sprigs of dark hair protruding from his shirt. His eyes sparkled. I ignored the thumping in my chest and invited them in. When I had extended the invitation, I hoped any awkwardness would dissolve and that our easy banter would resume. I missed their presence and was grateful they came, despite the situation. Regardless that Scott and I didn't work out, I wanted these men in my life. I could only hope he felt the same way. I felt The Happy expand and engulf the two creatures on my doorstep. Now if only my heart would stop pounding when he was around.

"Nice haircut. It suits you," Scott said.

"Oh. Thanks," I said, running my hand through it. I gestured towards the kitchen.

We walked past the wall Scott had shoved me against, his hands and lips roaming. My face flared. Then I noticed Alex and it became a three-alarm blaze. What the hell was I doing? Stop it, Rose, I commanded. I dove into the fridge, finding it once again useful to hide my rosy cheeks. I retracted myself only after hearing Becky introduce Scott and Adam to Alex, knowing I never would have survived it, especially after that thought.

I handed bottles of beer to Scott and Adam. Alex draped his arm over my shoulders and grinned down at me. He dipped down and kissed my nose just as the doorbell rang for the last time. Martha's husband, Mark, arrived and a heated hockey debate broke out when Mark revealed he cheered for a rival team. He held his own with the gaggle of Toronto Maple Leaf fans and I liked him instantly.

I filled glasses, prepared trays of food, and gathered empties. I wondered when the right time would be, and when Mom and Abby eventually returned from the dining room and rejoined our chatter, I couldn't wait any longer.

I cleared my throat. "Hey, everyone. I uh, I have an announcement," I said, bouncing from foot to foot like I had twenty women ahead of me in line for the restroom after a super-sized soda.

"Rose?" Mom asked, eyes wide and glancing over at Alex only to discover he looked just as confused. I wondered if she thought I was pregnant or if Alex and I had gotten engaged. Scott's eyebrows furrowed. Becky looked perplexed.

Maybe I didn't go about that the right way.

"I bought a house!" I shrieked before any further confusion could ensue.

"Goodness," Mom said, fanning her face with her hand.

"You're leaving?" from Becky.

"Congratulations," Martha and Mark said simultaneously.

Alex remained silent.

"Where?" Scott piped up.

"That's the best part. It's two blocks away!"

"Within walking distance for stumbling home!" Becky squealed and engulfed me in a bear hug.

I wiggled away. "It's a fixer-upper, so it might be a while before I'm out of your hair."

I had begun searching the day after Google spit out the results. According to divorce laws in Ontario, an inheritance gained during a marriage was typically not split in a divorce, unless invested in the marital home. Frank had no access to Gram's money after all. And after confirming with my lawyer, I wasted no time finding a real estate agent and starting the grueling search.

Thrilled to downsize from the monster home I shared with Frank, the two-story, detached house I purchased was exactly what I envisioned living in. It needed work–hence the reasonable price– and I was somehow able to secure it without a contractor swooping in and outbidding me to tear it down and rebuild. The basement would require renovating from its 1960s wood paneling, but that could wait. The first priority would be remodeling the kitchen, and I couldn't wait to meet with the contractor and discuss knocking out walls for an open concept space for future gatherings.

Everyone started talking at once, discussing the demolition of the older homes in the neighborhood. Adam patted me on the back with congratulations, stating how thrilled he was not to see another home in the area subjected to the wrecking ball.

"You didn't tell me," Alex whispered, taking me aside. He sounded disappointed.

"Sorry. Everything happened so fast this week and with preparing for the party, I figured it would be easier to tell you and everyone in person. It made sense to announce it tonight." I smiled up at him.

"Okay," he mumbled.

I wrapped my arms around him and my eyes met Scott's. With a genuine smile on his face, he mouthed "Congrats," while raising his beer in my direction before lifting it to his lips.

"Thanks," I mouthed back.

I pulled away from Alex and looked up at him. "I'm really sorry," I repeated.

He shrugged and looked away.

It stung. Especially after Scott's heartfelt congratulations. Was Alex more than just disappointed because I didn't tell him first? Did he expect us to be buying a house together? So soon? My stomach lurched. I wasn't ready for that. We'd only been dating a couple of months, not nearly long enough to consider moving in together. I filed away the questions I had for him. It wasn't the right time.

"What's the garden like?" Mom asked.

"That's the best part," I said, waving my arms around. "It's a blank canvas."

The gardens sold me on the home, or rather the lack thereof. Where there were any, they were overgrown, or replaced with shrubs, and even with the cold weather withering what plants were still there, I could already picture how I was going to redesign it.

My own home. With no one to tell me what to do with it. It was exactly what Becky had said the first day I met her buying every shade of pink impatiens. I looked over and found her punching Adam playfully on the shoulder. Where would I have ended up without her that day? She had changed my life. I only hoped she could find The Happy. She deserved it.

Everyone cheered at my garden revelation, someone proposed a toast, and glasses clinked. I raced upstairs to retrieve the real estate listing. In my happy haze, I forgot about Alex's possible insecurity and stopped noticing the heat low in my abdomen each time I stood near Scott.

*****

I sipped my third cappuccino, still exhausted from party fatigue, and picked up my house listing from the kitchen table. "I can't believe this is mine."

"It took months for it to sink in after I bought this place. I knew I was home when I started slapping red paint on the front door."

Alex, who had been more subdued than usual as we tidied all morning, grunted from where he stood loading the dishwasher. "It's great, sweetie."

Becky arched her eyebrow. I wasn't the only one who noticed his voice didn't seem sincere.

"Thanks," I responded, ignoring it and pecking him on the cheek. "Why don't you take a break and have a shower?"

Minutes later, the pipes groaned and Becky grabbed me, jerking her thumb at the ceiling. "What's up with him?"

"No clue. Initially, I thought he was annoyed because I didn't tell him about the house first. But now I wonder if it's because he pictured us picking out china already."

"He does seem really into you. Maybe both?"

"God, I hope not. It's way too soon."

"Good for you, honey. You know what you want. Stick to it. Trust you're making the right decisions," she said, smacking my ass with the towel before she resumed wiping the counter. Becky's cooking, tidying up after herself, learning to scrub her sticky stains off the counter, and even asserting herself more with Jay continued to surprise me. Would she revert back when I left? Would I?

I looked around the near-tidy kitchen where a couple of hours ago empty platters and glasses littered the counters and table. I'd enjoyed the evening for a change instead of clearing up after everyone and perfecting the house for the next morning. Would I lose all the changes I'd made too? I shook my head. There was no way. I was enjoying my more relaxed self too much.

We continued cleaning in comfortable silence and I considered Becky's statement. Why wasn't I concerned about Alex's disgruntled behavior? Did I not care enough about what he thought? I never once questioned making the decision on my own, and now I wasn't particularly worried he might be upset. Maybe I had changed. Or maybe I didn't care enough about him in the first place. Maybe I wasn't willing to let him sway my decision. Or maybe I didn't trust he would be supportive. One good thought about me for every bad thought about Alex. Now I just had to sift through which was right.

Upon quick inspection, there were many things I now realized I trusted. My decision about the house, the gardening business, and allowing all the new wonderful people into my life were three enormous changes I was proud of. But did Alex factor into any of those things? He was doting, kind, sensitive, and caring. He could be moody at times, something I'd noticed in the last few weeks, and complained when I turned down his frequent requests to see each other. But I remained firm and never wavered. Had Becky noticed something? Something I couldn't see yet? Was Alex trying to change me? Had I not noticed?

"I have news," Becky said, interrupting my thoughts.

"What's going on?" I said, reaching out and grabbing the counter to brace myself. I dropped my gaze to find her ring finger. I hadn't noticed a ring last night, but why would I look? Oh God, was it a ring? I couldn't tell. She had a towel draped across her left hand. If not, were they moving in together or something?

"I didn't want to tell you yesterday. It was your night. We talked about the holidays Friday night. Jay asked me to meet his family." Her grin could have lit a Christmas tree.

I blew my breath out in a steady stream and smiled to hide my thoughts, both about her boyfriend's lack of interest in her family and friends—evidenced by his refusal to attend the party last night—and what Scott would do for Christmas without her.

"That's fantastic," I said instead, keeping the thoughts to myself.

"Come on. Be happy for me. Please?"

"I am. I guess I'm still reserving judgment. It would have been nice to see him last night."

She sagged against the counter. "I know. But he already had plans he couldn't get out of. It's been better lately. It really has."

"I know it has. You've been around more. But he still doesn't come here. I only know what he looks like because of that first night at the bar. He hasn't even met Scott."

"Creature comfort. He likes his own bed. And I don't blame him. It's a little slice of heaven. And we're taking it slow with family, but now, with talking about Christmas, we'll see."

Yes, but he initiated the conversation, not you, I thought. I knew Becky was eager for him to meet everyone, but she never would have brought it up. Jay had to make the first move because she didn't want to scare him away. I peered at her and restrained from voicing my opinion once again. She really was trying, and I didn't want to jeopardize her efforts and the progress she'd made. Since our argument Becky had spent more time at home, and even went out with Scott and Adam. I gleaned this information while we all huddled around and mumbled outside of her earshot and compared notes. But we all still had concerns. I could only hope one day she'd realize Jay wasn't for her and she could make it on her own.

CHAPTER TWENTY-FIVE

IKEA at noon on a Saturday could be used as a torture tool. Lining the labyrinth were streams of strollers; red-faced, screeching toddlers; optimistic college-aged kids looking for a cheap deal; and couples bickering over everything from sofas to candle purchases. If Alex hadn't been at my side, I would have fled. Actually, I wouldn't have gone on the weekend in the first place, but he had insisted on tagging along when I mentioned the potential shopping trip.

As we wound our way along the maze and among the throngs, my excitement dimmed not only with each elbow and cart nudge I received, but with Alex's ideas, comments, and suggestions. I found myself wishing I'd gone alone. Midweek.

"This is nice," Alex said, running his hand along a black rug with a beige swirl pattern.

I felt my nose turn up in a wrinkle.

"You don't like it," he said, his voice sounding close to a whine. And I had plenty of comparisons. We had just left the kids' section.

"It's not really my style. A bit too dark for my taste."

"They would be great for your bedroom. Or I could even picture them in front of the TV," he continued, as if he hadn't heard me.

"I'm not taking the TV."

"I thought it was yours?"

"It is. But I'm leaving it for Becky."

"Why the hell would you do that?"

Surprised, I whirled around to face him. "Because she's been a great friend and I wanted to leave her a going away present and a thank-you gift."

"But she's not leaving. You are. She should give you something. A housewarming gift," he said, nodding as if satisfied with his answer.

I wasn't.

"Then you know nothing about friendship," I said and walked away.

He chased after me. "Of course I do. And I can see when you're being taken advantage of, like you were with Frank, even if you can't. I'm only looking out for you," he said, smothering me into a hug and kissing my forehead.

I struggled to free myself. "But that was by my lying, scheming, bastard of a husband. Becky's nothing like him," I said, defending my friend and stomping on the spark of doubt he had ignited.

He arched an eyebrow.

"She never asked me for it. I decided to give it to her myself."

"Oh please, how many times has she moaned about it since you announced you were leaving? The time she threw her arms around it and kissed the top, telling it she'd miss it? Don't worry. I'm looking out for you," he said, grabbing my hand and leading me against the flow of people. "You should get shelving units to frame it on either side."

Alex's comments exploded in my mind like a grenade. Shrapnel sliced through my darkest thoughts and protruded from my worry.

Becky didn't expect me to leave the TV. I hadn't mentioned it to her, and I was positive the idea hadn't even flickered across her mind. And even if I did take the TV, I didn't need a new cabinet. I could apply that money elsewhere.

I stumbled and felt his grip tighten. Alex didn't think Becky was a good person. Who lets someone they don't know move into their home? A good person. And why was I, in light of all this new information, allowing Alex to continue dragging me against the heavy foot traffic? When had my mouth become sewn shut?

I swallowed hard.

"Oh. This is nice. You should definitely buy this," he said, pointing to a dark-stained bedroom set. Somehow he had forgotten to mention his preferences for this particular room of the house on our first round of the maze. "You don't want white, it will show the dirt too much, especially with all the gardening stuff you do, coming in covered in it."

While Alex had a point about the dirt and darker furniture, I had already decided I wouldn't be buying a bedroom set from Ikea. Kitchen cabinets, yes. A couch, maybe. Shelves, definitely. But my new bedroom set was to be a gift to myself, a treat. It would be something white, or an antique white and definitely not dark-stained wood from Ikea. There had been enough wood dominating my bedroom in the last few years to last a lifetime, thank you very much. And not in a good way.

"Actually, I'm going with my mom to look at bedroom furniture next week," I said, finally finding my voice.

"Why are you going with her? We're here now."

"Alex," I said with a heavy sigh, the shell-shock evaporating. "I'm not getting dark wood furniture. I want white. I'm not getting a TV accessories because the TV is staying at Becky's and I'm going to buy a smaller one. I can always go to her place if I want to watch something on the big screen."

"What are you going to do without a TV? What if I come over and we want to watch a movie? Or if I want to watch the game? You're making a mistake. She's taking advantage of you. She's leeched off you for months. You'll see…"

"Stop slagging Becky," I said, my voice firm, with a side of angry.

His jaw locked and crimson flushed up his neck. I'd seen that look before. Oh God. How had I let this happen to me again?

"We're done, Alex."

"But we didn't have time to look at…"

"No, Alex." I interrupted, my hand flicking back and forth between us. "We're done, through."

"What?" he said, spittle flying. "You need me. You can't dump me. Where will you be, stuck with those losers leeching off you?"

"Alex, lower your voice, people are starting to stare."

"Of course they are. You're dumping me in IKEA for God's sake. Stupid bitch," he hissed, his blue eyes turning to ice.

I gasped.

"Everything okay here?"

A man with a receding hairline, tufts of gray over his ears, and bifocals perched off the end of his nose, came into focus.

I shook my head, spilling the tears that had pooled. "Just leave, Alex."

"You'll be sorry, Rose. You'll see how they're all using you and realize I was right."

"Maybe the problem is with you, Alex." I shuddered like I was witnessing a plane crash. But it was my life coming crashing down.

He stalked away and didn't look back.

"Thank you," I mumbled to my rescuer. At least this time I wouldn't fall for him.

"No problem," he said, smiling so gently I wished I'd had a father like him, all soft and huggable, sensitive and protective.

"Really, thank you," I said, repeating my first, shocked effort more earnestly.

He shrugged. "Retired police officer. You get used to predicting a domestic. And he seemed like one waiting to happen."

A domestic.

A woman standing nearby with short salt and pepper hair touched his arm. "Herman?"

Desperate to avoid their concerned gazes, I mumbled another thank you, whipped around, and began bumping and pushing through the crowd. I ignored the impulse to crumble into tears and flop onto one of the pre-made beds I stumbled past.

A domestic.

Eventually, I turned in the right direction and slapped the door to the ladies' room with the heel of my hand before hurling myself into a stall and sobbing.

A domestic.

I couldn't shake the words. How could I have gotten involved with another asshole? This one someone a police officer said might even be abusive? *Abusive.* Frank was horrid, but he never would have laid a finger on me, although I supposed he did abuse my brain, manipulate my mind.

When I finally opened my eyes, I studied the industrial tile floor for a while. It looked inviting. I wanted to lie down and curl up, not caring about germs or whether anyone would see me or if I'd get locked in the store like the girl years ago in Walmart. But a stubborn refusal to crumble washed over me. It only took a couple of months to uncover Alex's overbearing tendencies. Next time it would be even faster. I took one deep breath and then another. My tears subsided.

I opened the stall and splashed cold water on my face.

"Shit," I said to my blotchy reflection as I patted it dry.

I was stranded. Alex had driven us there.

I abandoned the bright yellow bag containing a few small shelves, two decorative pillows, and a bag of tea-lights where I had dropped it beside the restroom door. I buttoned my coat and strode out into the crisp December air.

*****

"But at least you caught it early," Becky said, after I filled her in on the IKEA insanity.

"I suppose."

"Honestly, Rose, you can't tell anything in the first few weeks of a new relationship. You're so submerged in lust you can't see clearly."

"I guess."

"In the end, you figured it out."

I shrugged.

"Come on. Give yourself some credit."

"I guess."

"More words, please. And you did. You figured it out. And now you have the rebound over and done with."

I cocked my head. "I do, don't I?"

"Do you want me to stay home tonight?"

"No way. You've been looking forward to this for weeks. I'll be fine," I said, attempting to ooze confidence I didn't feel.

"You sure?" she said, looking skeptical.

"Yes and besides, you can't let that hair go to waste." I pointed at her bob, pinned back in a semi-updo. Becky had arrived home from the hairdresser moments after I'd slammed the door shut. I couldn't let her to miss the gala charity event. It had something to do with Jay's company and she'd been yapping on about it ever since he asked her.

"Do you want me to call your Mom?"

I shook my head.

"Scott? Martha?"

"Just go get ready," I said, pushing her toward the stairs.

She looked back at me, brows furrowed.

"I'll call them if I need to," I said.

"Promise?"

"Promise. Now go. I'll pour you a glass of wine."

She nibbled her bottom lip. "Maybe I shouldn't drink anything. I was kind of hoping you'd say you wanted me to stay home. I'm so nervous. I've never been to anything this fancy. I'm going to fall flat on my face."

"You'll be fabulous. You strut like a runway model in three-inch heels, so I think you've got it covered."

"What if the hem of my dress catches?"

"It'll be fine."

"I should have gone for something shorter."

Becky had selected a form-fitting gold dress and when she modeled it for me, I regretted not tagging along with her on the shopping trip. I couldn't even remember where Alex had dragged me that day, but if I'd resisted, I could have convinced her to go with black. Her choice was stunning, but I worried about her spill factor and stains. Not that I would have flung that on her already fraying nerves, either then or now.

"You'll be gorgeous and perfect. Now go. Oh, and thanks," I said as she began climbing the stairs. "And thanks to Frank in a roundabout way."

"For what?" Becky said, turning around.

"That TV," I said, pointing into the living room. "It's what I very publicly dumped my boyfriend in IKEA over."

I started to giggle.

"What are you talking about?" Becky said.

Her worried face spurred me on and I began laughing even harder.

"I dumped my boyfriend in IKEA," I said, unable to help my snort. "Who does that?"

"A woman who knows what she wants. What section were you in?" Becky said, beginning to laugh along with me once I proved I wasn't going to collapse in despair.

"Bedroom," I said through my giggles.

In a heap of laugher, we dropped onto the bottom step, sitting side by side among the sea of shoes we both now contributed to.

"What the hell are you talking about?" Becky asked, wiping tears from her eyes.

"When I leave, the TV is yours. A thank-you for being the bestest friend a girl could ask for."

Her eyes went saucer wide.

"Cat got your tongue?" I teased.

"Seriously?"

"Yep. It's my gift to you." I smiled at her through tears, these ones happy, grateful globes that replaced the giddy ones I had just wiped away.

My throat strained at the effort to speak. "I don't know what I would have done without you."

Becky shook her head, regarding me for a moment before lunging over for a hug. I had to push her away to avoid ruining her hair.

"You've been awesome too," Becky squeaked. "But seriously? The TV?"

We sat in silence, each of us lost in thought. I smiled, thrilled at the joy I was able to bring her.

"Man, I'm glad I didn't do my makeup yet," Becky said with a short laugh. A few tears trickled down her cheeks.

I reached over and swiped them away. "Enough already. Let's go get you ready."

CHAPTER TWENTY-SIX

I cracked one eye open. 4:05a.m. I groaned and yanked the covers over my head, hoping Becky's drunken wandering would stop so I wouldn't fully wake up. I'd only fallen asleep an hour ago after spending the evening dissecting my relationship blunder with Alex. I didn't want thoughts about the situation to break consciousness and send my mind roaring and reeling for another few hours.

Another thump. I rolled over and faced the wall.

My thoughts of slumber shifted, and Alex barreled back into my brain. Hours earlier, I had grasped how his opinions had grown larger and more profuse, like fertilized weeds, as our time together progressed. His criticism leeched into every area of my life to the point where I'd started doubting myself and my decisions. It mirrored my relationship with Frank. Frank's modus operandi had been different and carried out with a much smoother edge, but the desired outcome was the same: control.

But at least I'd figured it out earlier, I thought, flipping over. I stared at the moonlight dancing across the walls. I hadn't thought about my rebound being over until Becky mentioned it. Maybe it had all been too soon. Maybe I hadn't even been ready for a rebound.

I flung the comforter back and sat up. Becky wasn't usually this noisy. I strained to listen further and heard muffled sobs. I rushed to her room, my bare feet slapping the hardwood. Why was Becky even here? Was Jay? Were they fighting? I paused outside her door to ensure I hadn't mistaken sex groans for sobbing moans.

I hadn't. I pushed the door open while calling out to her. "Becky, what's going on? Are you alone?"

The sobbing increased in pitch and frequency while I stumbled over items scattered across her room. I tripped on something and grappled with the edge of the bed before my knees made contact with the hard wood floor. Ignoring the throbbing, I reached out and patted my hands around on the bed, eventually landing on her hip. After my hands roved some more, I discovered she was curled up in a tight ball. She still hadn't said a word.

"Becky. What's wrong?"

She whimpered and curled inward even further.

"What's going on?" I asked, reaching for the box of tissue she kept on her bedside table. I hesitated, unsure what my hand might glide over. Thoughts of condom wrappers, battery operated devices, or snotty tissues stopped me. I stretched higher and flipped the switch on her lamp. My eyes stung as they adjusted to the light.

Becky yanked the pillow in front of her face and started shrieking. "Don't look at me! Wanna be alone. So stooopid. Go…"

"Becky, we've been over this. We can tell each other anything," I said, prying the pillow away.

I gasped.

Her hair was matted to her head in clumps. Leaves and twigs clung to her now defunct up-do. Makeup streaked her face, but it wasn't enough to cover it. No amount of makeup would have.

"Who did this to you?" I demanded, pulling back the fingers that had flown up to cover her face. Her French manicure was chipped and one nail had been torn off, leaving a jagged edge.

"Who?" I roared, clutching her hands while trying to meet her gaze.

Her eyes darted back and forth like a caged animal.

I dropped her hands and shut up. Screaming and pinning her down probably wasn't the right tactic. Becky shoved me away. I caught her weak, flailing arms and crushed her to me. Her breath, erratic and hot, warmed my skin through the thin T-shirt I wore to bed.

I leaned back after a few moments and pushed a chunk of hair off her face. I tried to make her look at me, but she grunted and swatted at my hands.

"Becky. How did this happen? Was it Jay? Did he..." I said, switching to a hushed tone.

"No," she screamed, her eyes finally locking onto mine.

Thank God.

"He hit you though, didn't he?" I whispered.

Becky squeezed her eyes shut and moaned before crumpling back down onto the bed. She curled her knees to her chest, tucked her head down, and began whimpering. Her shoulders bounced around like the Mexican jumping beans I had when I was a kid.

I inched up to lean against the headboard and gently tugged Becky toward me. She curled around my legs with her head in my lap. Progress. I rubbed circles on her back and ran my fingers through her hair with one hand. The other clenched open and closed at my side. I counted the number of leaves and twigs in her hair. I counted the number of polka dots sprinkled on Becky's pink and white sheets. I clamped down on the desire to clean her room. I was desperate to do something, but Becky wouldn't budge and until she unlocked her cemented mouth, there was nothing I could do. I'd never felt so utterly helpless.

My thoughts whipped from rage to willing myself to calm down. I had to remind myself to breathe. It took strength I'd never known before. No wonder Scott looked so angry whenever he spoke about her past. He wasn't controlling like I'd thought, but concerned and worried. Scott! I had to call him. Now.

I wiggled to extract myself, but Becky clutched my legs.

"I'll be right back," I whispered, sliding a pillow under her head. "I'm going to make some tea and get some ice."

I dashed to my room, snatched my cell, and scrolled for Scott's number while tearing downstairs to brew a cup of chamomile tea, find some ointment for the cut on her lip, and ice for the yellowing lump forming around her left eye.

Scott's phone rang and rang.

"Please don't his let phone be on silent. Please don't let his phone be on silent," I repeated over and over. I had no other way to reach him.

He picked up after six rings.

"Scott. It's Rose," I whispered, unable to keep the panic from my voice.

"Huh?" His tongue was thick with sleep. "Rose? What…"

"It's Becky."

"What happened? Where is she?" he asked, his tone now clipped and concerned. Rustling sounds echoed through the line.

"Not over the phone. She's here," I said, popping four ice cubes from the tray onto a tea towel.

"I'll be right over."

I heard a muffled "Shit" before the line went dead. Whether he stumbled over something, stubbed his toe, or whether he cursed about the situation, I couldn't tell.

*****

"Hello?"

A tremor shuddered through Becky's body at the deep male voice. Her fingers clawed at my leg and she bolted upright, immediately clutching her head and groaning in pain.

I gagged at her fragility and fear.

"It's just Scott," I told her and called down. "We're up here."

I swallowed hard at her attempt to glare at me. Although the lamp couldn't have been stronger than a ten-watt bulb, Becky's mangled face was clear despite the shadows. One of her gorgeous green eyes had almost swollen shut. Her nostrils flared above the gash in her lip. At least I'd been able to clean off most of the blood.

I traced a finger along her forehead. "You'll forgive me for calling him eventually," I said.

She slumped back against me where we had remained since I cleaned her face, applied ointment to her lip, and ice to her eye. Nothing had eased her tears.

"Hey…" Scott said in a hushed tone, entering the room.

Becky buried her face in my lap, her shoulders heaving with each sob.

I bit down on my lip to keep it from wobbling.

"Oh, Becks. Shh, It's okay, it's okay," Scott said, dropping down next to her on the opposite side of the bed.

"Adam's coming," he mouthed to me.

I nodded in acknowledgment. "I'll be right back, honey. We need more ice cubes." I eased myself out of Becky's embrace, which sent her sobs soaring in pitch and frequency. I shut my eyes, wishing I could shut my ears, each sob shattering my heart.

I forced myself to move. I needed to unlock the door for Adam. When I pulled the bedroom door closed behind me, I couldn't help but glance back. Scott had pulled Becky's limp body into his arms and was rocking back and forth, running his hand over her hair and murmuring soothing sounds and assurances.

I bolted. I flew down the stairs, flung open the front door, and gulped the frigid December air. The rumble of Adam's car filled the silence before two beams of light appeared, and the car jerked to a stop at an awkward angle.

Adam flew up the path. "How is she?"

I put my hand on his arm. "She'll be okay. It's serious, but nothing some makeup won't cover." He winced. "No need for stitches. Or the hospital."

"She wasn't…" he asked, his hushed voice cracking.

"No," I said, squeezing his arm. "She's a very lucky girl to have you care so much about her," I said, as understanding bloomed. I'm not sure why I never realized it before. "You're in love with her, aren't you?"

He looked away, shook his head and sighed.

"Well, your secret is safe with me," I continued after his silent admission. "But maybe it shouldn't be. Maybe it's time we all…"

"Scott," he said simply.

I bobbed my head in a nod like I understood. But I didn't. If Scott had let Adam be with Becky, none of this would have happened. From the look on Adam's face, he knew it too.

I pulled him into a hug. He smelt like fabric softener and peppermint toothpaste and had such a strong, yet comforting hug. I sunk into him as much as he clung to me. Becky was one lucky woman.

If Scott would ever approve.

*****

I steered Scott downstairs to the kitchen after Adam slumped down on the bed next to Becky. I poured two mugs of steaming hazelnut coffee. The smell I had grown accustomed to over the months now made me gag, but emotional exhaustion called for cutting corners.

Scott snagged my shuddering hand, swung me around, and almost crushed me in his embrace. It didn't take long for my strength to evaporate. Fat, hot tears coursed down my cheeks and soaked his T-shirt.

"I'm so sorry, Scott," I moaned into his chest. "I should have made her stay home with me."

He grunted. "No 'if onlys' or 'what ifs.' It would have happened anyway. Somehow it always does."

I pushed away and looked up at him. "This has happened before? Like this?"

I didn't get an answer and barely had time to register his face was wet with tears before Scott's mouth crushed down on mine. With his stubble scraping my chin and his hands stroking my hair, my face, my back, the disconnect with Alex became immediately apparent.

I pulled away panting, ashamed when I remembered Becky.

Scott's heavy breathing matched my own. He took two steps back and ran both hands through his hair before resting them on the back of his neck. "Shit, Rose, I'm sorry. I… I wasn't thinking."

I shrugged, unsure about his regret. "I was just as responsible."

"It's just, I hate…cheating," he said, averting his gaze.

"Cheating? You're seeing someone?" Becky hadn't mentioned anything, but why would she since I was so ensconced in Alex?

"No. Alex."

I shook my head. "Surreal doesn't even begin to describe the last twenty-four hours. I broke up with Alex yesterday. In IKEA of all places." It felt like decades ago.

Scott exhaled. A slow smile spread across his face. He took two steps forward, cupped my cheeks, and touched his lips to mine so tenderly I couldn't help the little sigh that escaped. A creak forced us to pull apart. We looked up at the ceiling and then back to each other with worry. Scott weaved his strong arms around my waist and pulled me close. We waited.

"She's sleeping," Adam said, walking into the kitchen. He stopped and looked back and forth between us.

I smiled, eyes wide, and with a look I hoped seemed encouraging, I bobbed my head toward Scott. Adam swung his head back and forth like a dog shaking off water. Subtlety was not one of his strengths.

Scott picked up on it right away. "What's going on?"

"Don't…" Adam said.

"Adam's in love with Becky," I said, shrugging out from under Scott's arm. "I'm going to sit with her now. You two probably have a lot to talk about." I ignored the shocked look on Scott's face and stood on my tip-toes to kiss him. I bolted past Adam and his death stare.

It needed to come out. Although noticing Scott's flared nostrils and hearing their failed attempt at a hushed conversation, I couldn't help but worry. Maybe it wasn't quite the right time to divulge the information. Scott's sister had just been beaten. He might project his anger onto Adam. I climbed the stairs and prayed

I made the right decision, that they wouldn't raise their voices and cause Becky more fear, and that Scott would get over his shock and brotherly protectiveness to see how perfect Adam and Becky would be together.

CHAPTER TWENTY-SEVEN

I felt Becky shift beside me. "Hey, honey. How are you feeling?" I croaked, struggling to sit up.

"Head hurts," she moaned, holding her hand over her eyes. "Thirsty."

"I'll go find you something." I ran my hand along her back before sliding out of the bed I had only managed to sleep an hour in.

I wiped sleep from my eyes and crept downstairs. Scott was curled up on the couch with his head resting on one arm and Adam sat upright in the armchair with his head bobbed forward like he had to sleep with one eye open in fear of Scott's wrath. Neither was bruised and no blood was visible, so at least they hadn't fought after I revealed Adam's feelings.

I tiptoed down the hall and into the kitchen. My nose caught our blunder first before I noticed the scorched tar at the bottom of the coffee pot. I snatched the handle and refrained from hurling it against the wall. I flipped on the tap and began scrubbing, rinsing and repeating.

Someone needed to invent an espresso machine that whispered and not gurgled and hissed like a century-old boiler, I thought. I heard thumping behind me and whipped around, wielding the coffee pot above my head like a weapon. Bubbling burnt hazelnut goop dribbled down onto my head. Scott and Adam lumbered into the room, eyes wide.

"Put that thing down," Scott said, approaching me with a sympathetic smile. "I guess we're all a bit jumpy. We came running at all the clatter."

I must have looked confused because he continued. "You were probably banging the coffee pot on the sink. Here, let me finish it."

"I've got this," I said, nudging him away while inspecting them both further for signs of a struggle. Still no blood.

"How is she?" Adam asked, his voice hoarse.

"All she's said so far was headache and thirsty." I grabbed a glass out of the cupboard, filled it with cold water, and set it on the counter next to the ibuprofen. "Here, bring her this while I make some fresh coffee."

Neither one of them moved.

"Uh, I'll go," Scott said to Adam. "And then you go up after."

"You guys have any Bailey's for the coffee?" Adam asked once Scott left the room.

"Have a look," I said, wrinkling my nose.

"What happened?" I whispered after we sipped in silence for a few minutes, his grimaces lessening with each sip. There was a reason the hazelnut and Irish cream flavor combo hadn't caught on yet.

He shrugged. "It went. We're guys. We don't talk about feelings. Maybe we never had a reason to before."

"You can go up now." We both jumped at Scott's gruff voice. He slouched against the door and my heart splintered to see the sorrow in his eyes.

Adam leaped from his chair and rushed past Scott. His pace then slowed like he was trying to make it less obvious he was sprinting to get to his best friend's sister.

I couldn't help my grin at Adam's enthusiasm. I reached into the cupboard for another mug. "I wish I had a brother like you to look out for me."

"Sit down," Scott said, placing two hands on my shoulders and guiding me to a chair. He kissed the top of my head before heading back to the mug I'd lifted out.

"You just have to find the right man instead," he said, pouring the coffee.

"Maybe I finally have," I said, getting up and walking over to him.

"I'm so grateful for all you've done for Becky."

"She did the same for me. We're family now."

"Married us off in your mind already, have you?"

"No, I..." Flustered, I felt myself turn Rosie Red with the fridge too far away to hide in.

"I get it. Relax, Rosie." Scott laughed and held his hand against my flaming cheek. I leaned into his palm.

"I worry..."

"Stop worrying so much. And I'll try to stop too. About her," Scott said, gesturing towards the ceiling with his free hand. "Maybe if I hadn't been so hard on her about dating my friends, this wouldn't have happened. I know Adam would never lay a hand on her. I can't believe I didn't see it."

I turned my head and began trailing kisses down his fingers and palm. "You said last night, no 'if onlys,' remember? Maybe there's a reason in all of this madness somewhere. If this hadn't happened, the two of us wouldn't be standing here right now. And Adam wouldn't be upstairs with Becky."

I felt Scott flinch. It would take some time for him to get used to them together.

"Come on," I said, squeezing his hand before getting up. "Let's go upstairs. I think we could both use a little sleep."

"Sleep. Is that all you have in mind?" A grin broke through and banished the worry lines.

"I don't... I'm not sure now is..."

"Shhh. Stop thinking," Scott said, tugging me down the hall. "I know. It's not the right time."

*****

I opened my eyes to discover it was well past noon. I inched out of Scott's arms and pulled on the same outfit I wore last night. After staring for a moment at the gorgeous man I had just unwrapped myself from, I pulled the door shut with a quiet click. I couldn't help but smile and wonder how I'd gotten so lucky.

"Becky," I called out when I saw her standing at the sink gulping from a glass.

Water shot out of her lips, spraying the window and her glass slipped from her fingers. It shattered in the sink. Becky clutched at the counter before inching around, wiping the spittle at her lips with the back of her hand.

I gasped.

My hand slapped my mouth in horror at both my reaction and the sight of Becky's mangled face. Her lower lip now protruded far beyond what any lip plumping service could provide, the cut had scabbed over, and a yellowish bruise appeared. Her left eye had swollen shut and was approaching the same shade of black as the mascara she had applied the night before.

"Sorry," I groaned, mortified at my response.

"I haven't even looked in a mirror yet. Maybe I should wait," she said, attempting a grin while gently prodding her eye and lip with trembling fingers.

"It's not that bad," I said, unsure of what to say.

"I know the drill. 'It could be worse,'" she mimicked.

"Scott told me about your ex-husband," I blurted out, grateful she cracked open the door to her past.

Silence stretched into an eternity and I regretted my words, worried she would retreat further into herself.

Becky turned with a sigh and shuffled away. I thought I'd lost her until she slumped onto one of the kitchen chairs and began speaking. "Scott probably made it seem worse than it actually was. Sometimes I wish I never had to tell him, but I needed help. I had no one else to talk to."

"You have me to talk to now. You have all of us. I wish you had told me," I said, unable to keep the hurt and concern from my voice.

"I probably should have, but I wanted you to take me seriously. You needed someone strong when we met and I didn't want you to think you'd moved in with some crazy lady and go running back to Frank."

"Are you kidding me? You saved my life. And you're not crazy."

"Stupid, maybe."

"What happened?"

She sighed. "It was near the end of our relationship. Like usual, we were always fighting. After one particularly nasty fight, I threatened to leave. He slapped me. It was the end of the argument. I was dazed and confused and he was horrified. I let him gather me in his arms and apologize. He changed after, became more attentive, more loving. He agreed to whatever I said. It lasted a month. Then it happened all over again. The third repeat I told Scott. I was stupid. I should have left after the first time."

Her shoulders curled in before they began twitching, and I realized I had never seen Becky cry before last night.

"It's all right to cry, Becky," I said. "God knows I've shed enough tears in your house to give it a thorough cleaning."

She continued, her eyes glistening. "I just wanted to be past it all. I didn't want to remember. It's like a bad dream or movie. You see it happen to someone else and think 'why doesn't she just leave?' That's probably what you're thinking. But it's not that easy. I don't know why, but it's not. It should be. Husband hits. Wife walks. But it's not. It's really not."

Sobs wracked her body, but I sensed she wasn't ready for another hug. I passed her the box of tissues from my makeshift office desk instead.

"You must have been terrified," I said.

"I was numb. Probably in shock. I didn't know what to do. I didn't know what he was capable of, what else he might do? You hear so many horror stories. That's when I called Scott. He threatened Justin. He got me out."

"You're so lucky to have him."

"Just like you're lucky to have such an amazing mother," Becky said, somehow smiling through her tears. "Scott's a pretty wonderful big brother. I don't tell him enough."

"He knows. Loved ones always do. And my mom loves you, by the way. You're like the second daughter she never had. You can talk to her too. Anytime." I squeezed her hand before getting up to refill her glass of water.

Becky seemed lost in thought when I placed it in front of her, so I let her gather her thoughts. To avoid all the questions I wanted to toss at her, I gathered the glass pieces from the sink and wrapped them in newspaper. I loaded the dishwasher with our mugs and then turned my attention to the counters. Running the sponge over them wasn't satisfying enough, so I reached for the cleaning powder under the sink, intent on scouring them instead.

I heard rustling above. I looked at Becky. She winced.

I dropped the rubber gloves on the counter before sitting down across from her. I grabbed her hand. "You don't have to talk about it now if you don't want to. You can wait," I whispered, even though I hoped she would spill it now for her own sanity.

She nodded, tears streaming from her good eye. "I might as well get it over with. I don't want you all tiptoeing around me forever. Wait until they come down. I'll tell you all at once so I don't have to repeat it."

I nodded and squeezed her hand, wondering whether confiding in us would be the end of it, or if she would be telling the story over and over again. To the authorities, to lawyers, in a courtroom in front of a judge and jury. I prayed she would be strong enough.

Scott had been adamant about police involvement. We lay entwined under my duvet and discussed the situation in hushed, urgent tones. Certain we couldn't force Becky one way or the other, I remained firm about it being her decision and that she'd have our support whatever course she decided. I ran my hands along Scott's back and shoulders, kneading the knots and wiping the worry away. His stiff shoulders finally dropped and his eyelids fluttered before he drifted to sleep.

I remained awake, staring at the wall and wondering what Becky would do, what I would do. The fight with Alex replayed, rewound, and replayed again in my mind. I couldn't shake his icy glare or the retired officer's words. I agonized over Frank's finger marks etched in my skin. Scott tightened his grip around me in his sleep whenever I shuddered.

Scott wandered into the kitchen and knocked the thoughts away. My heart jolted at the sight of him, something I'd never felt with Alex and sadly, not even Frank. He flashed two dimples and I smiled back, but immediately nodded in Becky's direction to alert him to her presence. In our early morning tangle, we decided to delay springing our status change on her, and I didn't want him to out us. I bit my lip, hoping he wouldn't repeat my reaction when he saw her face.

Scott didn't gasp like I had when Becky flew into his arms and wept into his shoulder. Instead, he held her like a fragile china doll and stroked her hair. His jaw was solid and his eyes distant when they finally met mine. I swallowed hard and slid my hand into his behind her back. I couldn't fathom how angry he must be, but it was clear how much he cared.

Seeing Scott with Becky, I could picture him comforting me, kissing the scraped knees of our children, and wrapping his strong arms around me forever. He wouldn't try to change me or refuse to let me grow. Instead, Scott would encourage me just as he had been for months and allow me to flourish. He wouldn't ever lie to me. He would never berate me or make fun of me. He would talk and listen to me. He would never demand his shirts be ironed or expect me to cook his dinner. He would help instead. He would kiss me passionately for the rest of my life. He would cradle my head in his lap and stroke my hair. He would cuddle up to me every night. He would never, ever hurt me. He would love me the way I deserved to be loved.

Breathless at the revelations, I squeezed his hand before returning to my coffee duties. It was an odd situation in which to realize you loved someone, but nothing from the last twenty-four hours had been ordinary.

I heard the creak of the stairs and grabbed another mug. Becky pulled away from Scott, shuffled backwards, and dropped into a chair. She stared down at the floor and held a hand over her mouth while Adam stumbled into the kitchen, rubbing his eyes. Her ragged breathing shattered the silence of the room.

Adam moved to the table and fell at Becky's feet, where he traced his finger along the edge of her swollen, bruised eye and swiped away the tears that continued to fall. He didn't even flinch. It was like he knew it would never happen again.

CHAPTER TWENTY-EIGHT

"I'm so sorry," Becky squeaked once we were caffeinated.

"Don't..." Scott and Adam said simultaneously. Awkward glances darted around the table Becky had yet to look up from.

"Don't apologize, Becks," Scott said.

I slid my hand under the table and clutched Scott's fingers in a vice grip.

When Becky finally looked up, she glanced from Scott over to me and then down at my arm extended towards his lap.

I dropped his hand and leaned away.

She tried to arch her swollen eye and smile. Her face contorted in pain. "So, you two?"

I shrugged at Scott, and with the same magnetic effect I had ignored for so long my hand reached out and clasped his again.

"Shit, Becks, we didn't want to tell you yet," Scott said.

"So what, all of a sudden because you're interested in my friend, now it's okay for me to be interested in yours? Whatever. It's about freaking time you two got your shit together."

I smiled, pleased she was teasing even if her grin was more grimace.

"If my head wasn't pounding, I'd jump up and do a little dance. What a bunch of self-denial idiots we are," Becky said, shaking her head and turning silent again.

Although we all realized how much we had gained last night, we were painfully aware of how much was lost. I stared out the window and watched snowflakes dance down on the patio, silently willing Becky to speak.

Suddenly, she drew in a sharp breath and it tumbled out of her along with the story. "Jay was drunk. He held it well and I had no idea until we left the gala. I wasn't. I refused to make a bad impression by getting hammered. He didn't tell me he'd booked a hotel until we were leaving and when I 'whined' about not having an overnight bag, he berated me for complaining after he did something nice for me. When I joked about the walk of shame, he grew more agitated so I shut up. I wondered about asking the cabbie to stop so I could get out. But I didn't.

"He has this vein in his neck here," she said, jabbing at her throat before continuing in a monotone, detached voice. "That throbs when he's angry. It wouldn't stop pulsing, not even when I complimented and praised him about the gorgeous room. When I realized that wouldn't pacify him, I suggested he sleep it off and strode to the door. But I was shaking too much and wobbled in my heels. The last thing I wanted to do was fall. I moved as fast as I could, but it wasn't fast enough. He snatched my arm and whipped me around. He twisted my arm behind me and barked that we were going to get our money's worth out of the room. He shoved me backwards and was on top of me the second I fell onto the bed. I faced the wall and lay still. He didn't like that. He vaulted off the bed, panting. I saw his hands pumping in fists beside him. That's when I knew I was really in trouble, that between the fist pumps and that vein, I needed to get the hell out of there. But I had no idea how…"

Scott released my hand and rubbed his jaw several times before clamping back down and crushing my fingers in his large palm. Adam stared at her, unable to hide the anguish on his face.

"We're all here for you, Becky," I said.

She looked down at the table and continued. "I knew I had to turn on the charm. It was the only way. Slowly the pulsing vein slowed and he softened. Until he really softened and couldn't get it up. Then he started screaming. It was my fault. I was a frigid bitch. I couldn't turn him on. I refused to be baited and told him to go find someone else to fuck then if I repulsed him that much. He stalked to the bathroom and slammed the door. I snatched my dress, purse, shoes, and ran. I didn't want to risk waiting for an elevator, so I bolted into the stairwell, which luckily was right next to our room. I yanked the dress over my head and ran down all twenty-two flights holding it up around my waist until the main floor where I tugged it down, shoved my feet in my heels, and ran out."

Scott, Adam, and I exchanged confused glances.

"How did he find you?" I asked.

"So, so, stupid," she said, her voice catching with each sob.

"Becky?" I said, my heart hammering in my chest. "Did Jay do this?" If he hadn't, the situation was much worse than we had all imagined and discussed last night. At least we had known who had assaulted her. If he wasn't the perpetrator, it could be anyone.

She shook her head. A negative. Wide eyes flew around the table.

"What happened?" I asked again. Both boys had been rendered mute, apparently.

"I was so upset. I thought he was different. I thought he was 'the one.' Sorry," she said turning to Adam, her voice barely audible. "Are you sure you want to hear all this?"

"How long have we been friends now? I already know almost everything about you. And there's nothing I don't want to know. No secrets." He reached over to swipe away her tears. She leaned into his palm and sighed before continuing.

"I stumbled down the street. I couldn't get over how stupid I was, how I fell for the same shit again. He would have hit me just like Justin had. It was only a matter of time. I couldn't understand how I was always getting into these situations. I couldn't handle it. I walked and walked. I probably could have walked all the way home. But I didn't. I wanted to process. I wanted to sit. There was a nice park." She shuddered.

"Oh, Becky," I said before I could stop myself.

Scott and Adam both inhaled sharply.

"I told you. Stupid."

"You're not stupid," I said, swallowing my rage, unable to fathom how she believed she was to blame. From her startled expression, I hadn't hidden my anger as well as I thought. I softened my tone before continuing. "You probably had more to drink than you realized. You were upset. You weren't thinking straight. Even so, this is not your fault."

Becky shivered but remained silent. Scott and Adam's faces mirrored how I felt. Completely and utterly helpless. I extracted my hand from Scott's and stalked to the living room. Returning with a blanket, I knelt down and draped it around Becky's shoulders and tucked it around her legs. We all knew how to try and handle the situation last night when we thought it was Jay. But it wasn't.

I reached up and tipped her chin to face me. I stared into her good eye. "You need to tell us what happened, Becky. I know you're terrified, but we need to know so we can help you. We're not going to let anyone hurt you ever again," I said, channeling the firm voice of my mother.

Adam's arm circled around her and Becky softened into his shoulder. I couldn't tell if she would continue or remain mute. So far she hadn't divulged anything other than to let us know Jay wasn't responsible.

I squeezed her knee as I shifted myself off the floor. Becky jerked her leg away at my touch and buried her head into Adam's chest. With a sharp glance back at her, my concern grew. Was she avoiding the entire story because of something even more horrific?

Adam lifted Becky's head up with his finger and kissed the tip of her nose before laying his forehead against hers.

I gagged.

I dry heaved again as I fumbled to get off my knees. Stumbling, I ripped open the patio door, bolted out, and dropped into the fluffy snow at the edge of the garden where I began retching harder and longer than I ever thought possible.

I had no idea how much time had passed when Scott pulled me up and wrapped me in the blanket I'd just tucked around Becky.

"I don't know what to do," I cried.

"I don't either, Rosie."

"Maybe Adam can get her to talk?" I said, looking up at him, yearning to see those dimples again instead of the sadness that hid them.

"Maybe she needs more time."

"I don't know how much time we have. With this snow. Evidence…" I trailed off, kicking the fluffy snow with my slippers.

"I know. But we can't push her. She'll turtle even more. You were the one who made me see that last night."

"Maybe we should all get some more sleep?"

"As long as you wrap your arms around me and never let me go," Scott murmured in my ear.

"Deal," I said, smiling up at him before clamping my hand over my mouth and turning my face away. "Shit. Sorry."

"Doesn't matter. I still want to kiss you."

I scrunched up my nose. "You're insane. Let me brush my teeth a few hundred times and then you can kiss me forever."

"That sounds perfect," he said, running his thumb over my lips.

We turned around at the sound of the patio door sliding open.

"Police station. Now," Adam commanded.

*****

We dashed down the hall and found the wall propping Becky upright. Her coat drooped over her slumped shoulders. I wrapped my arms around her and led her to the stairs, worrying she might not be able to stand while we put our coats and boots on. Who knew what bruises and injuries were hidden beneath her clothes?

Becky collapsed onto the step where just the day before we'd laughed at my break-up and her good fortune about the TV. Life was so fragile. It could shatter in seconds.

Becky's breath hitched once and then again before the story spewed out of her. "I heard them coming. They were very loud, drunk and stumbling. I knew it was too late to run when they saw me. One of them sat down next to me. He smelt like cigars and cologne. The other two shuffled from side to side while they watched. He told me I was pretty. I snorted. I'd been crying for hours. I looked like shit. When I moved to get up his hand clenched my wrist and pulled me back down. I told him not to touch me. He laughed. Cackled. Like a hyena. He…"

Scott and Adam remained statue-still. I slid down beside Becky and hugged her to me.

"I fought. I scratched. The other two stood watch. Fucking cowards. How could they just stand there? How could they not stop him?"

"I don't know, honey. I don't know."

"Fucking cowards," she shouted, her voice reverberating in the tiny hallway.

We all jumped.

"There's the feisty Becky we know," I said, squeezing her shoulders.

"I'm still here," she squeaked.

"We'll get them, honey. We need to make sure they never do this to anyone else."

"I was lucky, so fucking lucky," she said, dropping her head.

"I know," I whispered, stroking her hair. "How…"

"He was holding me down," she interrupted, her chin still in her chest. "I didn't feel the snow, the cold. I was numb from sitting on that stupid bench. I struggled to get loose. I clawed. He slapped me across the face. My frozen cheek shattered into a million pieces. I tasted blood, but had no idea where it was coming from. He clamped his hand down on my mouth, his fingers sliding bloody streaks across my face. My purse had fallen a few feet away. But they didn't want it. They wanted me. I didn't want to die, another statistic, another stupid girl like some dumb TV show. Struggling didn't work, so I played dead. Somehow I thought it would stop them." Her voice cracked. "But that's for bears. Not men."

"Then I heard voices. Under his slippery grip, I managed to crane my neck to see where they were coming from. The two cowards glanced over their shoulders and shoved their heads together, whispering. When I realized it wasn't their voices, that someone else was close by, I began kicking and clawing again. I screamed the second he yanked his hand back from my mouth. Until his clenched fist connected with my face. Hard. My screaming stopped. So did the voices. Stars floated through the darkness. He stopped covering my mouth. He probably thought I wouldn't struggle anymore after he'd used his fists. More shouting pierced the ringing in my ears and I could tell they were closer than before. I felt him fumbling at my waist. I screamed again until he clamped back down, his fingers sliding over my face. I tried to bite his hand, but he knew exactly how I needed to be restrained."

Becky stopped and took three rapid breaths before continuing.

"When the voices resumed, closer again, one of the cowards yanked him off. I spit at him, sending blood splattering in the snow. He cocked his leg. I tried to scoot away, but I was still dizzy and wasn't fast enough. His kick shot through my frozen thigh like a bullet. I screamed again and the two douchebags dragged him away. I waited, unsure if they would come back, but unable to run because of my leg. Suddenly, the other voices sounded like they were beside me. Petrified they might be worse than the first three, I scrambled to my knees. I used the bench to hoist myself up, and hobbled in the opposite direction to the street. Thank God a vacant cab was passing by."

"Oh Becky," I said, pulling her head to lean on my shoulder.

"I was so stupid. I should have called one of you." She sat up straight and looked at me. "Thanks for calling Scott," she said, before turning her attention to her brother. "And thank you for always being there for me. And for calling Adam. And for breaking your rules." She attempted a smile before addressing Adam. "And you… well…" She shrugged and smiled.

"We'll always be here for you, Becky," I said. "I can't believe you let us think it was Jay last night."

"I didn't, not on purpose. I wasn't thinking. I was probably in shock. I think I still am."

"Can you manage leaving now?" Scott asked, his fists clenched and pumping by his side. "The police really need to be informed."

A fierce compulsion to eradicate his worry coursed through me. I longed to unfurl his fists, finger by finger, bringing each one to my lips.

"I'll go, but I'm not sure anything will come of it. I don't remember what he looked like, what any of them looked like. It was dark. Even if I scratched him, I've washed my hands many times since and with this crazy weather, I doubt there's any evidence at the park."

"They can still warn others who use the park," I said.

Eventually she nodded.

When the boys left to warm the car and clear it of snow, I thought maybe she might confide in me with their absence. "You weren't raped, were you?" I whispered.

She looked me in the eye. "No. And the ridiculous part is that if I had been, I was with Jay before. Well, at least until his passive pecker. And he wasn't exactly gentle while I played along. Who knows what bruise or scrape would have belonged to whom. I've seen enough *Law and Order* to know the situation would have been a disaster. The defense and prosecution lawyers would each argue it was the other party who caused the injuries, never mind how I would have been judged for the whole situation. I should have stayed with him. Then this would never have happened."

"No," I said, the vehemence in my voice startling me as much as her. "You could have been sitting here just the same. You need someone who will love you and cherish you and protect you. You deserve it more than anyone I know."

"Ready?" Adam asked, poking his head in the door.

I smiled and nudged Becky towards him. He wrapped his arm around her and ushered her down the path to the car. Scott stood shivering in his leather jacket, waiting to open the door for his sister. We locked eyes when he looked up, and like two magnets pulled apart, I slid beside him and snapped into place.

EPILOGUE

5 Months Later

I stood at the patio door and observed the beehive of activity in my backyard before stepping outside with another tray loaded with beer, iced tea, and water. The Victoria Day weekend was predicted to break records for blazing heat again this May.

I dodged the dogs running in circles around me and placed the tray on the cast-iron table I'd purchased last week. My housewarming and "divorcée-rette" party had turned into a gardening party after Scott and Becky conjured up the idea that the collective housewarming gift should be a day of labor to assist me with my backyard redesign.

"Hurry up already with that beer," Becky hollered, while whacking a slab of grass against the ground to knock off excess dirt. She pitched it aside into the pile that would be moved to compost in the corner. Martha knelt next to her, duplicating the actions. They were clearing a rectangular area that would soon see vegetables sprouting. Mom and Abby stood nearby at the back fence clipping and bundling the branches of shrubs and trees Scott had already trimmed or completely removed. The yard looked completely different within hours. They couldn't have picked a more perfect gift.

The dogs scampered over to Becky at the sound of her voice. "I didn't call you, girls," she said, giggling when Buddy lunged to lick her face.

"Buddy, Roxie. Come," I commanded, and crouched down to gather them into cuddles they were far too hyper to receive. Since I brought home the baby beagle four weeks ago, Roxie was proving more work than I had ever imagined possible, but the rewards were priceless.

They tore off when Becky came over and gathered a beer and two waters.

"Beer for me," shouted Abby after noticing Becky's choice for her.

"Me too," Mom said.

"We're going to run out of beer if you two keep drinking," I teased.

"What's this about running out of beer?" Adam said, rounding the corner carting a wheelbarrow full of top soil. "What have you ladies been doing every time we go out front? I'll go on a beer run." He dropped the wheelbarrow where he stood.

"Get back to work, you lazy ass," Becky said, swatting his arm and passing him a bottle.

"She's such a slave driver," Adam said, the bottle he chugged unable to hide his wide grin.

"Who is?" Scott said, wheeling another full load. He almost crashed into Adam's heels.

"Your sister."

"At least you had a choice. I couldn't give her back as much as I tried to when she was born."

"Hello? I'm standing right here. I can hear you guys, you know," Becky said, handing out the remaining bottles.

Everyone laughed. Scott's adjustment to Adam and Becky together took only a few weeks, and even he couldn't help commenting on how happy Becky seemed once the memories of that night began fading. Her assailants were never caught, but Becky never regretted her attempts at preventing another girl from suffering the same fate by going to the police, regardless of the interrogations about her private life and the events surrounding why she was in the park in the first place. Public warnings were issued for the area and we never heard of another assault.

Becky had confided in a hushed whisper one evening over a bottle of wine that she and Adam were taking things slow. They had waited weeks to have sex and she said for the first time she didn't mind, she knew they had loads of time. She didn't worry about what it meant or feel any sense of urgency. She said it was how she knew it was right.

It was the total opposite of my relationship with Scott. There was nothing slow and steady about us. We weren't inseparable, though, and spent much more time apart compared to any of my previous relationships. Yet I didn't feel anxious about it and Scott never complained like Alex had. We were both so busy building on our dreams and goals. We converged whenever possible, including working together on a project for one of the multiple women's shelters he now devotes much of his free time designing websites for. The Garden Club was going to begin building a sustainable rooftop vegetable garden for them in the next few weeks.

"Mark?" Martha called when her husband approached with yet another wheelbarrow. "Go on a beer run."

"Sure," he said, stripping off his gloves and dropping them on the ground next to the house.

"Now that's putting the whip to good use," Adam said.

"A happy wife is a happy life, my friend. Besides, it's going to buy beer she's droning on about, not taking out the garbage."

Roxie snatched one of the gloves and bolted off with it, tossing it in the air and shaking it dead.

"Ignore her," Scott said when I moved to chase her. "She'll get bored with it eventually."

I scooped up the remaining glove to remove the temptation and watched Scott take a swig. He was so much more laid back than

Frank ever was. So much more helpful. Frank would have grumbled the entire time, where Scott simply swiped his brow with his T-shirt and kept moving without complaint. He was even interested in learning about gardening, especially growing vegetables. They were at opposite ends of every spectrum and the differences caused surprise, laughter, and even thoughtful musings when I wondered how I had stayed with Frank for so long. But the last time this thought traveled through my mind, I realized I wouldn't have Scott in my life if I hadn't married Frank and then left him to end up on Becky's stoop. Maybe everything does happen for a reason, I'd mused.

"We'll put on the barbecue in an about an hour," I said to Scott. He planted a kiss on my lips. Yet another difference. Frank was never keen on public affection. Scott held my hand for hours and even kissed me on the street—not in the get-a-room kind of way—but a peck here and there. It might have been my favorite difference, or at least ranked in the top five.

Scott and Buddy were becoming a permanent presence since I moved in two months ago. When they weren't here, Roxie wandered around searching for Buddy and I found myself reaching for Scott next to me on the couch or in bed, only to find it vacant and cold.

Although this was my house, we often made decisions together, both of us aware he would be moving in soon. We were fortunate enough to have the same taste in many aspects and rarely disagreed. I worried sometimes that we were on our best behavior because it was still so early in our relationship, but I suspected it was different. Frank and I disagreed on many things from the beginning. I just hadn't seen how much I deferred to his opinion. But that Rose was gone now. A new and improved version had taken over and she was sometimes a little too much, veering stubbornly in the opposite direction when Scott suggested something or was firm in his opinion. Learning to compromise was the most challenging aspect of our relationship.

"Rose, what are you planning to plant here?" Mom asked.

"Dahlias," I said. "Loads of them." I twisted around to find Scott smiling at me from where we stood side by side watching the scurrying. I suddenly wanted everyone to go home so I could wrestle him to the ground and have my way with him. I blushed and looked away, but not before he noticed and cocked an eyebrow. We would never lose that spark.

The night before Scott had spooned up behind me after I tucked the dogs under two fleece blankets on their over-sized cushion beds and slipped under the covers. "You're going to be such a great mom," he whispered.

I gasped and flipped over to face him, my lips seeking his in the darkness. "A puppy and a baby are a little bit different. And then there's the difference about how they come to be. Buy a puppy, make a baby. It's a…"

"Shhhh," he said, putting a finger over my mouth, in my mouth and dragging my lips to his.

"Maybe we could practise though," I mumbled, barely able to get the words out.

"Practice makes perfect," he said, kissing his way to my ear. "But I'd rather make perfect now." He strung kisses along my forehead, across my eyes, and on the tip of my nose.

I stopped breathing, wondering if I had heard him correctly.

"Dahlias would be lovely here," Mom said, jolting me back to my garden. My thoughts swung to making her a grandmother faster than I ever imagined possible a year ago.

"Dahlia," Scott whispered, clasping my face with his dirty hands and showering me with kisses. When he pulled back, his eyes held mine as he reached down. His thumb skimmed across my belly.

I sucked in my breath at his touch.

He dusted his fingers across my abdomen once more before seeking my hands. "Dahlia," he repeated, unwavering in his gaze, dimples flaring. "I like that."

The Happy almost swallowed me whole.

We definitely weren't talking about gardening anymore.

HOW TO GROW POTATOES IN A BARREL

1. Obtain a large container like a barrel, a huge recycle bin, or an old garbage can. It must be cleaned well and have holes in the bottom for drainage.
2. Fill the bottom with soil, compost, and peat moss. You can even have the barrel cut into quarters and add top sections as they continue to grow.
3. Cut and quarter one or two sprouted potatoes depending on the size of the barrel and plant them two inches apart.
4. Water regularly but don't over water. Do not keep it soggy.
5. When the shoots grow six inches, add more soil, compost, and peat moss to cover half the stem. Never cover the leaves.
6. Repeat this every time the plants grow another six inches until they're just shy of the top of the barrel.
7. After they flower, dig up the potatoes and find them hiding all the way from the top to the bottom of the barrel.
8. Donate to your local food bank

ACKNOWLEDGEMENTS

I have been blessed to join a profession of wonderful people, and am eternally grateful for all the new friends I've made along this journey. I'm also incredibly fortunate for all of the friends and family that have supported and encouraged me over the decades I've wanted to write "My Book."

A massive thank you to Samantha Robey, Samantha Stroh-Bailey, and Francine LaSala for editing, insights, feedback, friendship, and endless patience with my punctuation issues. Kathryn Laceby, Ilse Laceby, Cathleen Holst, Lucie Simone, Jennifer Poole, and Monika Prosetakis, I can't thank you enough for being my early readers and awesome feedback providers. Without you all, Redesigning Rose would still be a stack of jumbled papers on my desk.

Thank you to the lovely Jane Speed and Carte Blanche Creative for my gorgeous cover design.

Thank you Sue White for your tremendous support, Monty and Cathy Ship for the Friday night novel chats, Bob and Anne Sproule for the use of your pool when my outdoor office became unbearable, Jennifer Johntson for the potato barrel knowledge, and my book blogging gals, Kaley Stewart, Sabrina-Kate Eryou, Jen Herron, and Kathryn Laceby for your encouragement and support.

To my two Grannies: Your strength and history has always astounded and amazed me. You continue to be a source of inspiration, even with one of you lost to us. I have been so blessed and honored to be able to know you and learn from you. Rose's Gram doesn't even begin to do you both justice.

Dearest Rodney White, my finishing this novel was a direct result of your untimely passing. Your unfinished manuscripts redirected me back to my book when I had strayed, spurred me on through the home stretch, and had tremendous influence over the completion of this novel. Your support and our writing conversations will be forever missed.

Tim and Patrick Laceby, you are the best two little brothers a girl could ask for. Thank you for all your love and support over the years.

Kathryn Laceby, you have the title of sister in law as my brother's wife, but the 'in-law' add-on is irrelevant. You are my sister. Thank you for introducing me to Marian Keyes and chick lit umpteen years ago and for all the bookish love ever since. I truly appreciate you reading every scrap of writing I have produced in the last fifteen years. Without you, this novel would never have been written. And rewritten. And rewritten.

Mom & Dad, you brought me into this world, you've supported my decisions, and provided a roof over my head for more years than I care to admit, first while I floundered, and then while I flourished and followed a dream. Thank you doesn't even come close. Mom, reading multiple drafts without complaint is just one of the reasons you're super mom; all of your comments and suggestions that made this book stronger is another. Yet one more is all the cups of coffee, the snacks, and the lunches you provided while I wrote under the canopy of cedars in your yard.

Reno, our story is a thousand times better than any book could ever be. Thank you for your endless patience when I babble about books and writing, for your delectable weekend meals to give me extra time to write–or pretend to be writing so you'll make something yummy–and for encouraging me to follow my dreams.

Thank you for being my happy ending and showing me fairy tales really do come true.

www.ingramcontent.com/pod-product-compliance
Lightning Source LLC
Chambersburg PA
CBHW031300170626
46807CB00001B/242